AVENUES BY TRAIN

Farai Mudzingwa

CASSAVA REPUBLIC

FEEDING THE AFRICAN IMAGINATION

Abuja – London

First published in 2023 by Cassava Republic Press

Abuja – London

A CIP catalogue record for this book is available from the National Library of Nigeria and the British Library.

ISBN: 978-1-913175-50-4

eISBN: 978-1-913175-51-1

Cover design: Jamie Keenan

Book design: Deepak Sharma (Prepress Plus)

Printed and bound in Czech Republic by Akcent Media Limited

Distributed in Nigeria by Yellow Danfo

Worldwide distribution by Ingram Publisher Services International

Dedication

To Annastasia and Alexio Noah whose presence is stronger with the passage of time.

Akuruma nzeve ndewako

1

1974

Listen, when the ancestors bite your ears. Natsai and her friends raced across the foot bridge on their way from the early morning Roman Catholic Church mass and teased whoever came last.

"Whoever is left behind is left behind," the same voice blurts out again.

"Onyo marks!"
"Seti, seti ..."
"Go!"

Theresa was the slowest kid. She wheezed all the way down the foot path. Their little heads disappeared into the reeds along the stream and only their shrieks and squeals sounded until they popped up on the home side.

On this April school holiday Sunday, on which they stopped by the shops on their way back from church and each bought a loaf of white bread for morning tea, six kids emerged panting and giggling on the other side of the stream. Theresa did not.

She dances,
Come see,

In her watery den,
She dances...

As the kids reported the incident to their parents, Natsai rubbed her ankle where the njuzu had grasped at her, before she had slipped through and it had reached for Theresa instead.

A watery viscous hand slides up out of the water and webbed fingers run up her foot. The prehensile grip around her ankle tightens.

Fingers so cold they register as a burning sensation. A jolt, an electric shock of feeling, shoots up her leg.

The elders sighed and word spread from mouth to ear around Miner's Drift, that another one had been taken.[1]

After this taking, as with the others before it, parents forbade their children from walking across the wetland or wandering near the stream and the deep pool near the narrow footbridge. "Take the longer route over the vehicle bridge," they cautioned. "That family, those ones, they don't pray properly; that's why these things happen to them," said others.

Theresa's family gathered and performed a bira renjuzu at the pool to appease the water being. During the bira, the spirit of the taken child whispered from the watery depths, and through vigorous dance, the family elders learned what they needed to sacrifice before the njuzu would release the child. It took the better part of a week to source a goat, and in more costly fashion, the requisite mature black bull. "She is of VaDziva," they chanted in unison to the water entity. "We are kin," they pled, while clapping in sombre rhythm. Not a single tear was shed, for shedding tears would seal her fate.

---

1   Miner's Drift was named after Henry Miner, the biggest and worst poacher in all history. Killed 1 200 elephants "on horseback". Died instantly when a rhino he was trying to shoot sat on his face.

And so it was, that after days of carrying out these and other rituals, she was returned to the surface unharmed, poised for life as a healer.

As the gathered petitioners wipe the water from their eyes and wring out their garments, they catch sight of a little girl crawling up the bank on her hands and knees. She has emerged at the edge of the pool, water streaming and dripping from her, her thin dress clinging to her drenched body. The child is gasping as she tries to adjust to breathing the thin air above the surface.

Theresa's mother rushes to embrace her. The faraway gaze in the child's unblinking eyes does not alter.

Back home, Natsai sat rubbing her ankle, "Mai, they are saying that if it touches you then you are now a bad person."

"Those are witchcraft things my child. Let them touch each other there where they do those things at night."

"Asi Mai..."

"Ah you Natsai, what is it with you today?"

Natsai started to raise her foot up to show her mother the mark on her ankle. "The thing, it was crying. I think it was trying to say something."

"Do not talk about those heathen things in this house, do you hear me Natsai? We pray in this house. People who believe in those njuzu things do the works of darkness. If you were another person you would bring me my rosary so we can pray right now."

2

Tracks Of My Fears, 1984

Ride with me. I'm about seven years old with a shiny bald head courtesy of a weekend visit to Miner's Drift by my grandma Mbuya Maswiti and her razor blade.[2]

Everyone calls me Gerry.

I have a squad. Dalitso, Takunda and me. Takunda's parents own the Continental Supermarket and he is forever telling us how busy his father is "bal-an-cing the books". Dalitso's parents run Chinopisa Bakery which bakes shiny sugar buns for the whole town. My parents are both civil servants at The Ministry and also devout members of the Roman Catholic Church. Father sings in the choir (between me and you, he does this to get Mother off his back) and Mother prepares the girls for marriage. My older sister Natsai is cool.

---

2   The fall of Portuguese East Africa in 1974 brought a wave of exiles across the border. Some dropped off the caravan here in Miner's Drift and others carried on to Harare and some over the other border into South Africa. The salty colonial Portuguese who couldn't lord it over there, as independence became inevitable, settled here and opened little businesses and created absurd little micro-fiefdoms. The mindfuck is how, when MNR/RENAMO started shooting up the new Frelimo-led Mozambican state, newly independent Mozambicans streamed back across the border and next thing you know they are now interpreters under their former colonisers yet again, in these little fiefdoms. Comrade Samora Machel must have let out a big, "What the actual fuck?" up there in Maputo. It is what it is, I guess.

Walking in town with Father is such a gas. I lead the way and he is right behind me with a steady clippity-clop of his leather shoes and his *Farmer's Weekly* tucked under his arm. Every so often he will clear his throat and I will adjust my pace accordingly. All too often, he will come to a complete stop as he chats to people. They will make way for me and then greet him. He will enquire, "Ah, Mr So-and So, how is the family? Ah, Comrade So-and-So, how was such-and-such meeting?" And then he will say, "Ah, work is work. But there is always more to be done." And then he will tap his magazine and comment on how the rains are late this year or how the country needs a winter crop. Or, in a lowered voice, and only to a select few, how certain things in the country are not how they should be, given what we have been through. When he is done, he will clear his throat and we take off down the pavement.

After weeks of pleading and promises to be good, he agrees to buy me a bicycle from Zambesia Cycles next to the Post Office. The owner of the shop is this hunched man with windblown grey hair who lives above his shop and sits behind the counter during the day. He puffs away at a pipe in his mouth which he only pulls out to bark at his assistant. His shop assistant, who does all the talking for him, is forever chasing our squad away from the shop front when all we're trying to do is catch a glimpse of the new bikes in the window. That guy deserves what's coming his way, if you know what I mean.

On the day that we come in to buy my bike, I strut into the shop with my shorts pulled high and my chest full of air. The assistant glances down at me, purses his lips, then greets Father. Father says, "Ah Comrade, how are things in your establishment? Are things going well?" The assistant wipes his brow, then looks over at the man behind the till, then back at Father. Father puts a hand in his pocket and starts whistling while looking around the shop. The assistant stiffens and creaks over to the old man. The pipe comes out of the owner's mouth while the assistant explains with the help of his hands. The pipe hovers outside the downturned mouth and the assistant's hands keep gesturing. In the end, the pipe is placed on the counter and the owner drags his feet over to Father.

Father gets straight to the point. "My son wants a bike. What do you have for someone his age?"

The owner rattles off words I don't understand. Here and there, I pick up a word in English. He uses a lot of hand gestures as if his upturned hands could speak for him. Father seems to understand him but replies mostly in English. Here and there, the owner glances over at the shop assistant and Father stares down the owner who mumbles something under his breath before carrying on. The shop assistant keeps shifting from one foot to the other like a gum tree swaying in the wind. Father taps his magazine when the old man speaks, and other times, lets out a drawn-out whistle, all the while with his other hand in his pocket. This man's style is something else, I tell you.

There are only two options: either the Choppers or the regular Twenties. I run my fingers along the long Chopper handlebars and Father clears his throat. I slide over to the Twenties. I seat myself on a red bike and it feels just right. The seat is a bit stiff but it will do. When flicked, the bell chimes and echoes around the shop. That seals the deal. Father does what Father does and I wheel my new red bike out of the shop, he tucks his *Farmer's Weekly* back under his arm, and the pipe goes back into the owner's mouth.

Walking down the street, I ask Father about the old man and Father says that he's from far down the highway, from a town called Tete along the Zambezi River in Mozambique, and that he only speaks ChiPutukezi.[3] "He is one of those who

---

3   The little town has long been a place of migrants. Mostly, the Chewa, Nyanja and Vemba from the north, seeking refuge. A tough home for those who never leave. But also a home for those who leave the small town itself to seek fortune in the cities and lands abroad, become exiles

refuses to accept that times have changed," Father adds. I ring my bell twice.

***

My squad and I are in our final year at Little Mermaids Nursery School. Our teachers can't wait for us to leave. My role in the squad is one of charm and persuasion, if you know what I mean. I get us in and out of trouble. Dalitso could whip Takunda and I with two fingers of his left hand while taking gulps of milk in the other hand and bal-an-cing a football on his right foot, but he humours us and lets us get away with all kinds of nonsense. Takunda's family is rich. He's the bank, I'm the sweet talk and Dalitso is the muscle. So this is my crew when we set off on our cycles, on a journey across town to Pfumojena township, venturing into territory far from what is familiar to us, so I can show them the stream where the njuzu lives.[4]

Dalitso is taller and broader than all the other boys but he never fights or argues with anyone. He has this calm, steady manner that I copy and aim to improve each time we hang out. He doesn't punch Takunda at times when Takunda should be punched, which tends to annoy me. Dalitso sometimes comes to school wearing his showy clothes. He wears a small cloth cap on his head, a jacket with long sleeves, and long pants all made of the same shiny fabric. His dad wears similar clothes, his mom wears full black. On these days the other kids at Little Mermaids tease him. Takunda used to lead the taunts. That's one of the times Dalitso should have punched his teeth out, but he didn't. I

---

themselves, only to come back where their souls never left. My younger self couldn't wait to get going.

4   Pfumojena, Mashayamombe and Nehanda townships, created as war-time confinement camps referred to officially as "Protected Villages" and more appropriately as "Keeps" by the people who were forced into them during the time when "this country was beautiful," were named after vanquished African spiritual mediums, military heroes and legends.

think Dalitso's clothes are cool. That's also why we became friends. Takunda stopped laughing at Dalitso's clothes when he realised that I had started hanging out with him and then we all started hanging out together.

***

Sisi Natsai told me about the njuzu that lives in the stream near our old house in Pfumojena township. She also showed me the strange marks on her ankle where she says it touched her when she was little. Three tiny dark lines that never fade: she says those are the njuzu's fingertips. She has been marked and it must mean something, she says. She made me promise not to speak to Mother or Father about the marks. Of course, I did tell the kids at Little Mermaids Nursery School the following day, as one does. The atmosphere at breaktime was highly charged. Most of them didn't believe me though. The kids who did believe me were scared senseless of the njuzu. They too had heard the stories about young girls being taken underwater. A current hummed through their minds and little sparks of fear kept them on edge.

***

Electricity. That energy that bridges the divide between what is scientific and technological and magic. That's the reason the colonisers challenged the gods of nature when they built Kariba dam to create hydro-electric energy. Electricity to power industry, commerce, indeed technological modernity, and electric trains to more efficiently shunt resources to the ports and up to the metropole. Trains that weren't there to carry people but made for raw materials and munitions, routes from mines to factories to towns. The first trains were those beast-drawn wagons that circled and laagered and fired seven-pounder cannons right up to Fort Salisbury. Unlike those Batonga living on the Zambezi who resisted the damming of the great river, who would oppose and want nothing to do with this brand of modernity, the local people along the wagon routes embraced or succumbed to the invaders and sought work on the railways, the most ambitious attaining the station of the wagon driver. At the time, the wagon driver was the envy of other men and the heart's desire of women. The one who rode in on the beast of modernity and whose wife, it is said, cooked only with the poshest of oils, *grease*, as they called it then.

***

Takunda's father has just bought a brand-new white Peugeot 504 sedan and he's now getting all the attention at Little Mermaids when his dad drops him off.[5] I could be chatting away with little Tari Makanda, showing her what I have in my lunch box, when guess-who swings by asking her if she wants to ride in his father's car at pick-up time? Such a show off, I tell you. Takunda also has a new skateboard and the girls do not notice me anymore. It is under these pressing circumstances that I announce that I have passed by the njuzu's stream, seen the water spirit on many occasions and will take the squad there if they aren't afraid.

Gasps and squeaks ring out across the playground; swings hang mid-air with frozen kids suspended in them; Mandy Wilson's ponytail shoots up straight above her head in fear; Taka Moyo tries to clench his little bum but the frightened farts shoot out of his tiny Adidas shorts in rapid bursts; Mrs Dube steps out onto the verandah, swinging the bell to end breaktime but no one moves; a gust of wind blows up little Tari Makanda's yellow skirt but none of the boys giggle. Takunda clears his throat. I look across at him.

"Let's go see it," he stammers bravely.

---

5   Between 1965-1980 the UDI Rhodesian Front regime of Ian Smith was under international sanctions which the French decided to ignore. And so at the turn of independence, Peugeot, Renault and Citroen vehicles were ubiquitous on Zimbabwean roads.

"Let's," I say.

***

Where the gods may anger then forgive, nature tends towards patience and measured wrath. Hubris brings catastrophe, the world spins off-balance. Take for instance the series of gas explosions ripping up from deep in the bowels of the earth at Wankie No. 2 Colliery in June of 1972. Resulting in 424 miners' bodies forever sealed in a carbon tomb. It is almost as if some deity held a grudge carried over from the floods on the Zambezi of 1957 and 1958, and feeling slighted, decided to thwart whichever energy source these humans need to power their brand of civilisation or drive their locomotives. It is almost as if the earth does not approve of its belly being excavated or its riverine lifelines being choked and harnessed.

And so, on this specific morning in 1984, despite all the warnings that the spirits have given to the unhearing, an electric train departs from Harare. The wagon driver, posh as his earlier incarnations may have been, is posher still as the driver of an electric locomotive of the National Railways of Zimbabwe. This lively chap has awoken in a sweaty bout of coughing, then left his dwelling in Chenga Ose, an aspirational residential development on the outskirts of the city already showing signs of decline, to jog, splutter and gasp through the early morning crowds striding towards the bus stop, stale beer still on his breath, the pungent smell of a greasy perm stuck in his nostrils, as is the cheap perfume of last night's special friend, someone he cannot wait to get back to in a couple of days' time. His trotting gait gets shorter as his chest gets tighter and his breathing raspier. At one point, he bends over on the side of the road and grasps his knees while dry heaving and forcing out wheezes that culminate in a high-pitched whine. *Too many smokers in the bar last night,* he tells himself. *The air is too dry and cold today,* he mumbles to a passerby who shakes her head and steers clear of him. *Four months just coughing*, he grimaces, while standing up straight again and taking off towards the bus that awaits him.

***

Back in Miner's Drift, I'm the first to get going on this bright morning. Dalitso is dressed in his white tunic and wheeling around in his driveway when I roll up to his gate. I punch him in the shoulder and he laughs, then punches me back. He has held back on the punch but I still wince and blink. "Are you okay, Gerry? Sorry, shaa."

"Haa, it's not sore. Don't worry." I blink away tears.

"Do you want to see my grandpa? He's sitting in the sun outside the cottage."

"Not now, Dali. We need to go. Remember we are on a mission today?"

Dalitso starts wringing his hands.

"Okay, but I promised Sekuru Jairos I would sit with him today."

"He will be here when we get back. Are you afraid now? Should I tell everyone at school that Dali is afraid?"

He shuts his eyes and works out his thoughts on his fingers. I know not to interrupt him because that will just make him start all over again. I shuffle my feet and look around the garden. There is some movement in one window but I can't quite make out who or what it might be. Little birds dart and dive between shrubs. A gecko bobs its head up on a rockery. "*Gum-kum, bang your head on the rock, Gum-kum, bang your head on the rock,*" I chant to myself a few times. Stubborn little fellow refuses to oblige me. I saunter across the driveway and peek behind the house to the cottage and sure enough, Dalitso's grandpa is slumped in an armchair with his head tilted at an angle to catch the sun rays on his stubbly chin. A newspaper has slid off his lap and lies at his feet, pages threatening to flip open in the breeze. Dalitso releases a long breath. "Let's wrestle."

"What?"

"Let's wrestle. If you win, we leave straight away. But if I win, then we go and sit with my grandpa."

"No, I don't want to wrestle you. You're too big." He's a mountain of a chap, I tell you.

"What if we go another day? Like, why do we have to go anyway?"

"Dalitso?"

"Okay, what should we do then?"

"I'll lift you."

"What?"

"If I can lift you then we have to go."

Dalitso starts to ponder again but I can't take another round of his thoughts. "Dali, we need to go. Come, let's finish this now." He yields.

I step behind him and lock my arms around his belly. He starts laughing the instant I squeeze. It takes a couple of attempts with me grunting and him roaring and elbowing me in protest. Dali's mother shouts above the commotion, "Hey, Jayi! What's going on there? No fighting, you hear me? Is that you, Gerry?" We untangle and straighten our clothes.

"What are you doing here anyway? Go and play somewhere."

I look at Dalitso in victory. He accepts defeat. We pull up our bikes and head out towards the gate.

"Who is Jayi?"

"Heh?"

"Your mother called you "Jayi"."

He smiles and glances at the back garden.

"She calls me that sometimes. It's my grandpa's name. He's called vaJairos. That's why I call him Sekuru Jairos"

"Oh, okay. So, it's like your second name?"

"Yeah, that's why I must sit with him in the afternoon. He tells me stories about lots of things."

"Like fairy tales?"

"Not really. Well, sometimes. But mostly stories about where he grew up and stuff. He said that he walked all the way from Malawi for days and days and he just followed the railway line all the way here."

"Where is Malawi?"

"It's a country far from here."

"Oh, okay."

"And then he tells me all this stuff about being nice to other people and respecting other people and saying 'please' and 'thank you' and that I must 'remember where I'm from'."

"Is that why you wanted us to go and sit with him? To hear stories?"

"Don't be mean, Gerry."

"Fine, fine. I'm sorry, big guy."

"Yeah, but it's okay I guess. Grandpa is funny. You should see how weird he starts sounding when he talks about the train. He talks about it like it's a scary monster or something. Mom says it's because he saw too many things on that long journey as he walked down here."

"Wait, are you afraid of the railway line? Is that why you're acting weird?"

"Me? No, of course I'm not afraid of anything."

Dalitso fumbles with the latch, finally closes the gate behind us and we take off towards the shops.

***

Harare. The train driver makes it to the station in the city just in time to clock in but he needn't have bothered. The departure has been delayed and the signal technicians are standing around perplexed.

"This has never happened before. It's just not working. We are not sure what's going on. We have tried everything, even shutting down the whole system and then switching it back on again."

The driver finds a bench in a corner to snooze while they figure it out. His chest has a burning spot that he tries to soothe by taking slow careful breaths but every minute or so he lets out a volley of whinnying coughs.[6] When he tries to lie prostrate on the bench, his insides at first rebel against the motion then impale him into the wood. A boozy highlight reel from the previous night flashes in and out of his mind. What was her name? Peggy? Patience? Petronella?

***

We pass by Takunda's dad's bakery to pick him up. He launches into us. "You guys should have been here ages ago. Where were you? I've been waiting and waiting." Dalitso and I just exchange glances. We know he will calm down as soon as he is done acting like a little power-drunk bully. I ring my bell and look to the side but keep Takunda in the corner of my eye so I can see his reaction. He mumbles something about his bell not working and how his dad can fix it but he's getting him a new one instead. Takunda is so easy to work up, if you know how. He's in a new red Spiderman T-Shirt, same as mine. I got mine first, naturally. Our cycles are the same colour, red, because everyone knows red bikes go faster than blue ones. I have a Raleigh that you can fold in the centre, which is cool. Takunda has a Raleigh too but his bike is a Chopper with the long handlebars and a 3-speed gear. It's not that I don't like Choppers but that long seat is just weird. Also, who puts a small front wheel and big back wheel on the same bike? When we eventually set off, after Takunda is done being angry, we pass a couple of kids from our school and he changes down his gears for no reason. Such a show-off. He thinks his bike is faster because of the little gear thing but we'll see. Mine has a louder bell and it works.

---

6   "Long Illness" is what they said in the papers and in the news, back in the days when AIDS-related deaths were newsworthy and still a devilish phenomenon mentioned in hush-hush tones. Euphemisms that mask our fears. The tuberculosis, cholera and typhoid, malnutrition, kidney failure from the backbreaking work in the mines and fields, all naughty descendants of the ancestral poxes that drifted in on those colonial wagons.

***

Back at Harare station, the switchboard lights up and the signals are working again. The driver rouses from his dreamless sleep feeling as if a steam train is charging around in his head. When he gets up, his insides stay behind on the bench while he staggers onto his feet, and when they then come up into his belly, they swim up into his throat. He heaves painfully, then wipes his mouth with his sleeves. He has had rough mornings before but this one is laced with trepidation. He could still get this day off as sick leave but he also knows that he is walking a tightrope with all his drunken missed days. He shrugs and heads to the platform boards. He needs no prompting from the station manager, knowing he has to make up for lost time. He pulls out of the yard and accelerates out of the city, sliding out with well-practiced mechanical motions. He has done this routine so many times that the responses are automatic: he flips switches, turns knobs and pulls levers in a daze. He usually blows the horn when passing Chenga Ose. It is his good-luck ritual. A part of him wishes his neighbours knew it was him driving the engine. Indeed, he has told people often about his important position, bragged while drunk.

This morning a fog hangs over Chenga Ose. A fog unlike any he has seen at this time of the year. The white orb appears as an opaque wall across the tracks and extends into nothingness in each direction. The engine ploughs into it. A chill passes through him and brings on another volley of coughs and sneezes. The locomotive is going at full tilt and blows through the white blanket, the wagons rattling at pace. A sense of dread washes over him as he takes measured breaths to calm himself down.

The train emerges from the fog and a pastoral landscape opens out with the city behind him. The train's contact to the electric line above the train sings out and the contact of the wheels on the rails responds. The trucks rattle on as the train sweeps into wide curves and down through gently sloping valleys. It cuts through the hillside along a dyke and the red banks of earth zip by in a blur. On the other side, a cluster of shops, a crossing, fields and fields of some crops too young and low-growing to recognise, another cluster of shops, and beyond the fields, a weir that strains to contain a river whose pent-up waters are eager for a signal to erupt.

If the driver were to observe these hills that he has passed mindlessly on numerous trips, he would count seven. Seven hills that the ancients may have considered sacred. If he were to hear the voices echoing around the granite boulders, what would he hear? Pleas from those who came before, not to blast away the hillsides? Not to alter the configuration of this granite amphitheatre which lends an elegiac acoustic quality to the rainmaking ululations of old women who brew millet beer? Are these not the hills of Bangidza, the first hills of the first people? Would the voices of the ancients ask the driver what is a road or a railway, and what mighty gods do they serve who demand that they shift mountains and dry rivers? They would certainly insist that he look more closely at the fields and see the morning sun gleaming on the sweaty backs of farm workers whose fathers and mothers followed these same tracks to break their backs in these fields. They would ask the driver, "Who dares to *own* land?" The ancients would want to know if those who cleared this land knew that they were cutting down rain-making trees. It is as if they knew that tobacco would take and take from the soil, depleting it of nutrients. As if the interlopers and forgetful youth did not care to know that the people of the soil embedded the fertile umbilical cords of generations before and generations to come, in the same earth. The ancestors would warn that to leach goodness from the earth is to starve the people of the soil. They would advise them not to take as if this land never had those who lived upon it and with it, those whom they exiled from it and who now live it in their dreams. Those who came before would demand that these hills be protected from quarry excavators and mining shafts in which cages and pulleys are worn and strained to the limit. If only the train driver would prise open his heavy eyelids and see these bal-an-cing granite boulders used by the ancestors as granaries, burial sites and worship sites. They would show him these forgotten battlefields, sites of ambush and the desecration and betrayal of a people. Then, he would feel the ground shake, ever so slightly, as the train thundered across rivers that had been cut off and around valleys that had been flooded. If only he would see that our people now fish and hunt under cover of darkness. If he were to listen, allowing the ancestors to bite his ear, he would feel each sideways shake of the carriages as the spirits in the hills leaned into the train.

Alas, the train attains top speed and locks in. The driver sounds his horn and conquest reverberates through the hills. The train swerves again and thunders on, fortissimo, unstoppable.

***

Miner's Drift. On our bicycles we speed along a wide footpath until we join the road heading into the township. Takunda and I pedal ourselves ragged trying to get ahead of one another to maintain front position. We get to the slight incline that leads up to the railway crossing, riding abreast and pumping furiously. Dalitso keeps up effortlessly, uninterested in our competition.

"Stop, the boom is coming down." Takunda focuses ahead while riding on.

"You first."

"Look Takunda, the lights are flashing!"

"I don't care. You must stop."

"No, you. I said it first," I counter.

"Doesn't matter. I'm in front."

"No, I am."

"No, I am."

"No, I am."

***

The train begins the long sweeping arc over a ridge and into Miner's Drift. Dotted along the ridge are the verticals of mining scaffolding and pulleys. The town itself is not visible yet, save for grain silos and a couple of communication towers. The train driver looks at his watch and sees that he has made up for the lost time. He takes a deep breath and swallows to ease his throat. His tongue catches on the roof of his mouth. He looks around for the bottle of water he knows is somewhere in the cab. The headache is now at full steam and he feels hot, feverish, his insides begin their revolt again. The sideways rocking and jolting of the train has had him fighting off nausea for a while. He looks ahead and sees that he has turned into the final straight entering the town. Ahead, he can see flashing lights at the crossing and the booms coming down. He sounds the horn, then turns back and resumes his search for the fallen water bottle.

***

The train horn blasts into my ears.

I start pumping my brakes while keeping my eyes on the train. Takunda's foot misses a pedal; he cuts across me and jams our front wheels. We both land in the red dust. Dalitso comes crashing into us. I push him off me, but I push too hard and my shove lands him in the path of the train.

***

The driver sees the water bottle rolling under his seat and reaches for it, crouching low. Shakes his head and struggles back onto his feet. He unscrews the cap and takes a few painful swallows. The hot reflux remains lodged in his tract. A mouthful of water only nudges it down a notch.

The tracks in front of him, at the crossing point.

Something there that shouldn't be. White blanket. No, not déjà vu. Small this time. He sees a little kid in white garments scrambling up onto his feet, right there on the rails.

Not possible. But yes, there is someone, there is this fucking kid. The ball of acid stops in his tract. He just stares as it happens. The acid burns. Paralyzed to the spot. Why does he not move? The corrosive burn radiates outwards into his chest and belly, rises back up his throat. What is he doing on the tracks? *Why this, why now?* His stomach lurches and caustic bile shoots back out of his mouth. *No*, he thinks, *no, not this.* Shaken, unsteady, light dimming, he lunges for the brakes.

***

Trains blew past him, Sekuru Jairos, at intervals as he walked. He travelled alone but knew he was part of a long human chain seeking their fortune southwards. There was evidence of those who were travelling ahead of him. Remnants of a fire here. Tall grasses flattened out as a temporary bed. Empty cigarette packets, matchboxes, corned beef tins, rotting flesh picked at by crows and vultures, a mound of earth the length of a grown man, with stones laid over it and stuck in at the head a crude cross made from branches and tree bark. Sometimes he passed groups of men working shirtless to repair the rails, shivering with fever and sweating with exhaustion, replacing timber on the tracks, laying new lines at a mile each day for trains they would never ride.

Sekuru Jairos swore at each train as it blew past. A great beast snorting clouds of black dust and sparks of fire, with red eyes, a shrill bellow, a charging animal with insatiable hunger, gasping and heaving forward, grinding its jaws. He spat on the railway tracks and cursed them as he set off each morning. Swore he never wanted to see another train ever in his life, if he only made it to Salisbury, and if anyone ever made him look at one again, he would never let them rest.

***

High in the skies, a line of storks breaks formation and scatters. One spirals downwards in broken flight.

A small thud of noise, insignificant, no louder than the odd calf struck down on the tracks.

Somewhere near the boy sprawled in the dust, another boy is screaming, hands covering his eyes. What cannot be unseen.

The bird impacts the ground in a soundless burst of white feathers.

***

Up on the ridge, the earth is trembling: shaft cables snap in quick succession, sending loose cages crashing down into the depths.

Streams in surrounding farms break through weirs and cascade downstream in cathartic waves of release.

Below Pfumojena township, at the pool in the stream, bubbles rise from the depths and sigh into the surface air. Reeds tremble in waves radiating outwards from the pool, sending weaver birds into upward surges of panicked flight.

***

I lie in the dust looking around me. The top of the rail is smooth and shiny. The sides are caked in dull soot blending in with the dirty quarry stones and wooden sleepers. The smell of the hot tarred road at midday, oil, steel and red clay soil fills my nostrils. I sit up and stare. At the tracks, at the pair of feet and white garment. The train blows past with a sound like a rounders bat swinging into a small bean bag. Like a bag of flour landing on the floor in a puff of white.

Then train brakes start screeching and the horn blasts long and hard. The trucks speed past and mesmerise me. The horn trails off and a high-pitched whine rises louder and louder. I have energy rising within me, singing in my veins and making my limbs tingle. All I can see is what is directly in front of me. Inside my head blankness, that is all I know. Time slows down and then stops. The whining recedes. It's all too quiet now. The sky closes in on me. All around me the world darkens.

The figure in white reappears but it is now Sekuru Jairos sitting on the tracks in his armchair, staring at me. I squeeze my eyes shut. When I peek through them again, it is now Dalitso. My heart leaps into my throat and thumps at my epiglottis. I squeeze my eyes shut again. I do not know for how long. I want to keep them shut forever.

Slowly, I reopen them. It is Sekuru Jairos again, and he stands up, eyes boring into me and points at me. Silently, he mouths,

"You. You. You."

His voice loops in my head, over and over. Then he fades away.

The sky rifts apart and light filters back in, widening my field of vision. A heavy molten light that leans on me. The surge of energy abates and seeps out of me. My limbs weaken under the weight of the sky.

The train has come to a standstill further down the track. A man, bent double, vomits beside the engine. Running feet come closer. Distant scream after distant scream floats in from above and across the tracks. Silence again.

The world has cracked open.

Then someone places a hand on my shoulder and shakes me, hard. I can see what they are doing even though I cannot feel it. My teeth are grinding back and forth, molar on molar, bone on bone, and I can't hear what they are saying. The whining sound pierces my hearing again but not as loud as before. Overhead, the noon sun blinds me like the township tower lights in the evenings, sunspots floating black and giddy.

I squeeze my eyes tight closed and scream into the dust. I feel the raw strain in my throat but I do not hear my voice.

***

Dalitso is gone.

3

Fight or Flight? 1988

Listen, this isn't the worst day this week. I'm standing-standing at the gate and waiting to see if Sisi Natsai has brought me anything from town. I'm always the one she talks to as soon as she gets home, calls me to sit down on her bed. She sits across from me massaging her ankle with those three thin lines still visible.

"Sisi Natsai, am I also touched by the njuzu?"

"Why do you ask that?"

"Because I'm always doing bad things and Mai is always angry at me."

"What bad things are you talking about, kid?"

"Like that bad thing that happened at the railway. Maybe that's why Mai is always hitting me?"

"You must forget about that, Gerry, you hear me?"

"But what if everything happens to me because I'm also touched and I don't know it?"

"Gerry, look at me."

She sighs.

"You've done nothing wrong, okay? No-one, nothing touched you. Don't worry about all that for now."

"But I don't understand why…"

"Shhh kid. You'll understand when you're older. Trust me."

"When, Sisi Natsai, when will I be older?"

"Soon. Then I'll explain everything to you, I promise."

"Should I also pray about it like Mai does? Mai says prayers answer everything. Even when she's hitting me."

"You can pray if you want to, little brother."

"Do you pray, Sisi Natsai? How come I've never seen you praying."

"Oh Gerry, add that to the list of things I'll explain to you when you're older."

***

Stay with me, time is passing. Today I'm in the lounge, sitting in Father's chair while watching *The Mukadota Family* on TV. Mai Rwizi is chasing Baba Rwizi, aka Mukadota, around the sofa in their one-room house because she has caught him entertaining his mistress, Machipisa.[7] In real life, Mother comes back home from another day of work in the Girl Child Department of The Ministry and is instantly on me like dust on Vaselined legs.

She is forever threatening to sell me to the Gule dancers from Pfumojena township if she ever returns home and finds her vegetable garden unwatered. On this day, even though I haven't sprayed a single drop of water on her garden, she has a hunch that I have been selling some of her tomatoes in the neighbourhood, and therefore she is in a temper. She can't prove her hunch and I deny it vehemently so she mumbles, "You will not see heaven if you carry on like this," and then walks past me into her bedroom.

At some point though she has a stroke of genius, decides she's being too soft and sweeps back into the lounge with a slim black belt in her hand. It has occurred to her that the dusty kid sitting on her sofa watching TV, with the crocheted sofa covers scrunched up and swallowed by the cushions,

---

7   Over the last couple of decades The Ministry has taken over the role of national jokers, clowns and fools par excellence. Safirio Madzikatire aka Mukadota, though, was the real deal.

deserves some correction. She slides some rhythm into the belt strokes.

"I-told-you-not-to-watch-TV-until-you-have-bathed."

The strokes ring out sharp and land with a sting that feels like a surface pinch at first, but then slowly the sharp strokes pierce into flesh and flick pins into my bones.

At whipping time Mother grows an extra arm. There is always one arm coming down as another cranks up. She has me pinned. Braving it, I squirm headfirst between her legs and briefly get my face caught in pleated waves of georgette. Trapped and squirming. She lands a few quality strokes.

To escape these assaults on my person, I usually run into my bedroom and wedge myself against the door but on this day, I turn left out of the lounge and head out the front door.

The taste of freedom.

I carry on into the dimly lit driveway. Somewhere between the front door and the gate I decide I've had enough of this home life and look around for my dog Spider.[8] At some point in a ten-year-old boy's life, he comes to a fork in the road. Life is a series of decisions and mine have escalated. Left or right? If I'm going to run away, then I need a companion. No point in running away if you can't do it properly and if you don't have a Mudhara Bonnie to your Mukadota.

It's now dark outside and I can't see the branches of the guava and mango trees in the front yard. For a few moments I pause to catch my breath in the shadow of the trees. Trees are a shelter for me, a safe place to hide out. In my haste to get away from my mother and the belt, I rushed out of the house empty-handed. Now I've decided to run away from home and haven't packed anything to take with me into exile. Shirtless, panting, unshod and face still wet, hot and salty, I stand at the gate waiting for Spider. He will be at the rear of

---

8   While Zimbabwean names are a recognised institution – Energy, Psychology, Knowledge, Forget, and so forth – our dog names do not receive the "Spot-light" they deserve. Animal names are a perennial favourite – Shumba, Tiger, Spider.

the house at this time – hanging outside the kitchen door listening to the clatter of pots and waiting for an edible scrap to fly out the door. There is no discipline to Spider's begging. No decorum. Depending on how rough his day at the office has been, evidence of which would be holes dug all around the garden, he will either be staring animatedly at the door or scratching furiously at it. Waiting at the gate, I start to realize that my journey into the great unknown might have to be a solo effort.

The warm darkness within the yard is comforting for me. I don't need light. I would know my way around every ridge, rockery, tree and flower bed with my eyes closed and walking on my hands.

There is a faint glow of moonlight but the clouds hold steady and it stays hidden. The darkness outside the gate though is a whole different proposition. Peggy, the town ghost, tends to lurk on the highway, a kilometre or so away, and there are streets and houses and the shops in between but I'm not taking any chances. The sounds of rainwater dripping from leaves overhead and the smell of hot soaked earth mingle in the evening air. Everything is quieter, only the muffled noise from a neighbour's TV and distant traffic reach my ears. My whistle doesn't get past the lump in my throat. In between sobs, receding heaves and anger, my mouth is not whistling. That whistle can get my hound here in an instant. I developed it to sound like his name; a feat which makes me proud. My pride in this though has been dented because Spider also responds to any old whistle from any old mouth. His is a politics of the stomach. His loyalties lie with whoever fills his bowl.

I hear the scurrying of Spider's paws in the darkness. He is on me before I can raise my arms against him. Face licked, chest wildly scratched and deep breaths taken, I unlatch the gate and he races out past me. It's a significant moment, I tell myself: I take one last look back at the house I have grown up in. I have had so many happy moments here. My first words and my first baby steps towards Natsai, both of which I'm certain were spectacular triumphs. So many birthday parties, learning how to ride a bike and receiving Spider from Father on my eighth birthday – but now it's time to go.

Spider is a shaggy, fawn-coloured, gangly contraption with sparkling grey marbles for eyes and two rows of magnificent teeth which he employs on all occasions. He bites to greet, tease, eat and play. Good old Spider – my brother from another species – with a name from yet another species.

I turn away with a heavy heart, latch the gate and set off down the road. A cool damp breeze blows to remind me of my inadequate clothing. Various enticing odours – meat stew, tripe, fried eggs – from cooked suppers are drifting across the street, clashing in my nostrils, and threatening to jeopardise my expedition. To miss out on supper is a challenge.

Street lights have come on. They always come on in the same sequence. Pop, pop, pop. There is a curve in the street out to the right and they shoot round that bend and up to our house in rapid succession. I always pretend I can outrun them. As things stand, I will never see these lights come on again. Never again shall I stand outside by the gate with Spider panting by my side, eager to be let out, ignoring Mother's shouts and threats of violence, contemplating how many eggs and pints of milk I would need to eat daily to get fast enough to outrun the Despondency Avenue street lights.

Spider comes to a halt and waits in the road a few metres from me in the amber glow. He has enough empathy to allow his travelling companion to wrest free of his attachment to his former home. I continue down the road and he capers a few steps ahead of me. We walk two houses down to the corner of the street and I feel this is far enough. We shall set up our living arrangements here under the corner streetlight, far from the woman in that house and the haunting memories that hopefully will fade over time.

And so, I stand under the streetlight surveying my new lodgings and trying to mark out a boundary fence with a fallen twig. This is going to be good fun. The sensation of freedom and adventure is throbbing in my scrawny chest, drying my face and making my fingers itch. The latter may be a bout of hives. All my Boy Scout skills are going to come in handy: I can now knot a bowline-on-the-bight and am working my way towards my first compound knot. I have also been for two hikes and two overnight camps.

It is dark though. I peer around the corner and Alarm Street is lit in most parts but also has tree branches and foliage blocking out the streetlights in some parts and throwing down holes of darkness. No fear here. Spider is having a good time prancing around the corner, disappearing into the dark spots and then jumping back into the light with his mouth ajar and tongue flapping around. Being outside the gate is a rare treat. The only time he gets to play outside is when my old man comes back and he bolts out the gate soon as it is opened. He streaks one way down the road barking at the neighbours' dogs and then streaks back down the other way fleeing from his shadow.

Another wave of cooked supper drifts in, this time from the neighbours across the road who always cook nice food. I almost befriended their son Forget a few months ago and tried to visit him at mealtimes but their maid kept telling me he wasn't in even when I could see him opening and closing his mouth through the lace curtains in their dining room. Grilled sausage comes riding in on this new wave of cooking odours: my stomach rumbles a bit and nudges my face in the direction of my former home. I take the quickest glance backwards and then focus on my new residence.

Spider starts barking wildly and leaping into the air and snapping at something. It's a flying termite. The mutt is insane. The first insects of the rainy season are coming out of the termite hill across the road and flying towards the streetlight.

Spider goes delirious. He leaps into the air and clamps his jaws over one, promptly spits it out when it flutters on his tongue. These are the larger flying termites. A flurry of them drift into the light and start circling around the lamp post and up towards the bulb. A squadron comes in and the fluttering sounds turn into white noise. Spider stiffens and looks at me; I stiffen and look at Spider. All it takes is one giant winged monster to brush against my ear and we both bolt off back to the evil house of punishment, Spider three leaps ahead, and me scrambling hot on his cowardly heels. These flying termites fill me with dread: sometimes in my bed at night I feel as though clouds of buzzing insects are swarming overhead to torment me and drive sleep away.

We crash into the gate with Spider leaping and bashing into it and my hands fumbling at the latch. Inside the house, Mother has positioned her sofa to ensure I will be within striking range should I attempt to walk through the lounge, and so I stand just inside the doorway, with a hand on the handle. What to do? The minutes go by with the stalemate maintaining a steady intensity until Sisi Natsai walks in again from work.

She reads the situation instantly.

"Every day you're hitting the child, Mai, why?"

Mother straightens up and then starts rolling her belt in a tight coil. "He doesn't listen, this one," she responds. Then she sucks her teeth and reclines back on the sofa. "Proverbs 13: verse 24 tells us that a child must be corrected," she declares. "If you were another person, you would take him out of my sight right now."

Mother believes that the world would be a better place if people everywhere received beatings regularly. I am people. Her house is everywhere. She exclaims "Kusarohwa!" whenever she sees anyone acting in a manner she doesn't approve – and then swiftly throws a glance in my direction.

Sisi Natsai rubs my head and I feel warm inside. She looks across at Mother and shakes her head. I cling to her skirt and steer clear of Mother as we go to my sister's bedroom, our refuge.

***

My school is two turns away from my house. If I walk out at the right time, then I join the large group of kids already on their way. The school kids trickle in from the roads around the school and by the time we get to the school there is a swollen river of green hats surging in through the main gate. I'm late today, as usual. I slow down when I get to the first corner. My hastily abandoned lodgings from the previous night are in a sad state. The streetlamp has long gone off and there is a clump of dead termites and scorched wings stuck between the plastic casing of the bulb and the protective wire gauze. At the bottom of the lamp pole, where I had started to draft my house design, the ground is covered in a thick carpet of silvery termite wings. The morning dew has them clinging together and adds a sheen as the sun rays glance off. The corner bears the scent of wet earth and abandoned flight. I trudge past with a heavy heart. Then I realise I'm late so I start running and weaving through the uniforms. The gang of older kids is turning at the second corner up ahead. I can make out Nevertheless ("Never" for short), Challenge (Chale), Petunia (Petu), Agenest and Choose (the last two are brothers) and a whole bunch of other kids coming in from the other direction. The boys are in their khaki shirts and shorts, green hats and ties, with grey socks and brown shoes. The girls are in their green-and-white pinafores, green hats, white socks and brown shoes. There is an unfamiliar pinafore with a loose green ribbon dangling out from under the hat. She laughs and I catch a glimpse of her face.

A blue Renault sedan reverses out from a house on the left side. Dalitso's house. There are no dogs at that house and the kids turning at the corner do not break into a sprint as the gate opens. As happens whenever I pass Dalitso's house, my inner ears start ringing and I feel unsteady on my feet. The ground feels shaky all around me. The blood rushes up in my face and ears, loud and thudding. I think of Natsai's voice telling me not to worry and the tremors subside. The faint whistle of a train shrills somewhere in the distance. The blue car turns towards town and I jog on. The group has turned the corner and is now out of sight.

I dislike the new girl Loveness from the precise moment
she turns to face the class. At the same time, I have to get her
attention. She stands in front of the class and Mr. Gumbo
instructs her to tell us her name, which school she's coming
from and where she lives. When she starts speaking, she looks
straight at me. She could stare at the wall, or at her shoes like
most kids do, but she doesn't. She's definitely trying to get at
me. She turns to look at Mr. Gumbo when she's done and the
green ribbon brushes her shoulder. She sits two seats away
and I start composing a letter to her.

"Dear Loveness, you are so very much pretty. I want to be
your boyfriend."

I practise writing it out in my exercise book and then
spend the rest of the morning summoning up the courage to
slip it to her.

She stays behind when the whole class rushes out for
breaktime, just looking at the walls and back of the classroom.
I mumble a few words.

"I can show you these pictures if you like. So what do you
think?"

"Who are all these people?"

Her gaze pans around the classroom.

"It's some students who used to learn here long ago."

"So where are they now?"

Our classroom walls are lined with framed black-and-
white team and class photographs. Some of them are faded
and go back to the 1960s. They are in chronological order
and the latest, near the door, is from 1983. She gets up and
steps round the classroom commenting on the length of the
boys' shorts and at some of the girls' hairstyles.

"How come there are no pictures after 1983, yet we are
now in 1988?"

"They took their cameras with them when they left.

She just looks at me and goes back to her seat.

"Why don't you go outside for breaktime? Don't you have
friends?" she asks.

"I have friends," I say. It stings.

She smiles.

"Why don't *you* go outside for break?" I ask in turn.

"Well I don't know anyone here yet and my half-brother said he would come to my class. He's in Grade 7 too."

The bell rings to end breaktime and the other kids rush back into the class before I can move away from Loveness's desk. The boys start jeering at me and when Mr. Gumbo storms in he makes all the boys put their heads on our desks and he whips us twice each on our backs with the flexible cane he calls Bazooka. No one knows Mr. Gumbo's real name. We know it is not "Gumbo" because he told us that was his war name. When I unwittingly asked him what a war name was, he made me march up and down the front of the classroom for the whole afternoon. Mr. Gumbo also has a limp. His left leg is shorter and somewhat stiff; it seems not to bend at the knee and so he dips and drags it as he walks. The story going around among the kids is that he got shot in the leg during the liberation war and they put metal pins in it and that's how he got his name. The story he told us is that he was hit by a grenade and his leg was flung up into a tree. He climbed up the tree, got his leg and then pinned it back to his thigh using the pointy end of his AK-47. He then carried on fighting and killing all the mabhunu they were fighting.[9] He told us this story one morning when we were supposed to be learning long division. I preferred the grenade story.

He tells so many war stories in class that the parents of some kids have asked the headmaster to move them to a different teacher. He doesn't stop. The stories aren't so much for us as they are for himself. He will break in the middle of some sentence and start barking out a story. He keeps addressing some unseen "maComrade" as he narrates, his

9   Possibly deduced from "maBoer", which Uncle Kenneth Kaunda, ancestors bless his revolutionary soul, kept referring to by that spicy phrase at Nelson Mandela's funeral service, or from mabuno, in reference to the interesting shape of, and the nasal intonations emanating from, the pointy noses.

voice getting louder and louder. I am scared sometimes but never cover my ears. Miss Clarke was my teacher before she left in the middle of the term to go to the newly-built Rhodes Farm School. Takunda also went to that fancy private school at the same time along with a whole bunch of other kids. In fact, every morning, we see the Rhodes School kids being driven past us while we walk to our council school. When we still had her, Miss Clarke didn't tell us any war stories. Just stories about her grandparents, who she called pioneers, and about them building a lot of stuff in the town. She was mostly concerned with telling us to speak proper English and sit up straight and have good manners.

Mr. Gumbo brings down his cane on the last kid and then starts crying, the cane still in his hand. I look up slowly from my desk and a couple of the boys peek up as well. He is hunched over, staring at the floor and convulsing. He weeps and sobs aloud the way Mukadota sounds on TV when he is pleading with his mistress Machipisa not to leave him. It is funny when Mukadota does it, but Mr. Gumbo is not a comedian and my back is stinging.

The wailing starts to sound rhythmical. He raises the pitch of his voice and then drops it before trailing off. It sounds like a familiar song, the wailing lament that The Ministry has been playing over and over again on radio and TV over the National War Heroes holiday weekend.

The other kids still have their heads face-down on their desks, glancing sideways at each other. Mr. Gumbo's heavy sobs continue. I slowly raise my head to look at Loveness. She is sitting upright. Her arms are crossed over her chest and she is staring at the teacher. The dry smell of chalk hangs in the air. None of us are sure what is going on and our tears are held back by fear and confusion. Loveness scans the room and then meets my gaze. She considers me briefly and then turns up an eyebrow and gestures at the man with the heaving shoulders. I shrug mine. She sighs loudly, then turns to the front again.

"Attention!"

"Atten-tion!"
"About turn!"
"About turn!"

The weeping man now jerks upright, shoulders back, barking out and responding to his own commands. All the kids are staring now. He has stopped crying; his face has gone full comrade and his left hand is held against his brow in salute. He furrows his brow and then switches hands. Petu is seated closest to the teacher's desk. She has had a front-row seat to the tears and the heaving. Between the sobs and the salute, she starts screaming. Mr. Gumbo ignores her. He shouts, "Forward march!" and strides across in front of the blackboard and out of the classroom. "Left, right, left, right," he yells. He dips and drags, dips and drags his way out of the door and past the windows and out of sight. We hear him break into song:

"We have defeated you, colonisers,
Losers,
You colonisers,
Losers, Coming to Zimbabwe,
Losers,
All the way from Biriteni,
Losers, All the way from America,
Losers, All the way from Furanzi,
Losers!"

Petu is still screaming and a couple of boys start laughing hysterically. The marching song rings down the corridor; the silence in the classroom has been broken. I lean forward towards Loveness.

"I heard Never say that he has a bullet from the war still stuck in his head. That's why he acts crazy like this sometimes."

"Which Never?" Loveness asks.

"Never, the one in the other Grade 7 class."

"Don't believe everything my brother tells you," she says.

"Ah *that* guy is your brother? He's a bully. But don't tell him I said that."

"Why do you say he is a bully? What has he done to you?"

"He gave me a nickname without even asking me."

"Isn't that how it happens? People just get nicknames and sometimes they don't know they have one."

"Well, he could have given me a better nickname. He just came up to me and said, 'Hey, little Jedza,' and I told him, 'My name is Gerry.' Never laughed at me and said, 'There he is, *Jedza wema Stedza* because you're just sitting in your chair there like a cool, steady guy.' Your brother is a bully."

"Well, maybe you should stand up for yourself, Gerry." And then she laughs.

***

From the day Loveness joins my class I manage to leave for school on time. I'm early, in fact. I can see the suspicion in Mother's eyes. She knows there might be an opportunity to deliver strokes of the belt but she's not too sure how to go about it, what is to blame. Much as she enjoys this whipping pastime, she enjoys it better when she feels fully justified and can recite her reasons for the caning as she goes about it.[10]

I'm up and ready to bathe before her now and she gets up mighty early. Mother comes from the crack-of-dawn generation. "The sun must find you sweeping in the yard" school of thought. This whole week, she leaves the bathroom with one mean eye cast in my direction as I wait to go in. I see the twitch in her left arm: that "I'll-figure-it-out-soon-enough" twitch. She has nothing on me, so she tries to take it out on Sisi Natsai. Mother shouts from her bedroom, "Iwe Natsai, do you want to spend the whole morning in the bathtub?" When she gets no response she attacks again with, "Do not finish all the hot water in there, do you hear

---

10 Mothers in the '80s could BEAT. Guys! Putting hands on the precious little children is now frowned upon; I'm all for this.

me?" At some point, with the water still running, Sisi Natsai responds that she is bathing in cold water. Mother falls back on the reliable, "Now, keep spending so long in the bathroom and your husband will return you," which Sisi Natsai ignores before coming out of the bathroom dripping. The mark on her ankle shimmers on her wet skin.

For the first half of the walk to school, Loveness and Never walk in from the opposite direction to mine. Halfway down the long street towards town, they turn into Despondency Crescent and join the widening flow of school kids shuffling to school. This week, they find me, on each day, waiting at that corner, pretending to tie my shoelaces. Bent down on one knee, hands fumbling about my shoes. Looking up now and again to see if the love of my ten-year-old life has appeared yet. And of course, when she does, I don't talk to her. I can't let the other kids see me talking to a girl. I can't meet her gaze without feeling like I'm on a swaying tightrope. The most I can do is move vaguely in her direction and avoid eye contact. I also don't want to talk to her on the walk to school because her brother, besides being a nicknaming bully, is a short-armed monster. Never is in our grade but four years older than me, three times bigger and he has the temper of a big black biting ant. That's why I call him Shingi-shingi.[11]But not to his face.

The story is that Never had to do the arm-over-head primary school entrance test. His arms are shorter than the candy stick in a packet of Red Lips Sherbet and so he started school when he was ten years old. Then the administrator at the Pfumojena Township Welfare Centre realized the little old man would turn fifty-seven before his arm could reach around his head and so they bundled him off to school with my age group.

---

11 *Hagensia peringueyi,* for the entomologists among us. These angry fuckers seemed huge when I was a kid. They also had a big ass sting that could cause you more pain than the pretty girl who would say 'Nah, let's just be friends' later in life.

The kids in our gang pick on Never daily. On the way back from school the river of uniforms splits and thins into small pools and streams. Our group taunts Never and scatters when he flies into a rage. He shakes and rants like the wrestler Moondog Max and the kids flail out their arms and yell out while scrambling backwards. The kids yell out,

"He's about to cry,
But no one has hit him,
He's about to cry,
As if he's been hit,
A cry baby cries,
When no one has touched him!"

He never catches anyone.

***

So, it's been a week since Loveness stood in front of the class on her first day at our school and dangled my heart on the end of the green ribbon in her hair. A week which has been whizzing past and Mother has been wondering what shavi has possessed her son's body. I still have the letter. I thumb it in my pocket while we're chatting in the classroom at breaktime, but I don't have the courage to take it out. Time always runs out. I tell myself "Just now Jedza," and then the bell rings and I go back to my desk.

It's evening and Mother is drifting around the house loudly humming Church yeRoma hymns so I seek refuge in Sisi Natsai's bedroom. She's hunched over her table, index finger hovering over the cassette player's Record button so she can record Michael Jackson's *Liberian Girl* when it starts to play on Radio 3.

"What's her name?" She asks me without turning away from her task.

"Whose name?"

"Gerry?"

"Yes, Sisi Natsai?"

"You know I fed you formula and changed your nappies?"

"Yes, Sisi Natsai."

"You know no one knows you better than I do, right?"

"Ehe kani, Sisi."

"So, what's her name?"

Before I respond she says, "Shhhh!" She hits the "Pause" button and then rewinds and resets the tape to record the next song without the DJ's voice cutting in.

"So, what were you saying?"

I tell her all about the girl in the green ribbon and she stays composed and rubs my head and tells me she'll make a good boyfriend out of me by the time she's done with me. She takes the letter, rewrites it to correct my spelling and grammar while giving me one of her much nicer letter pads and a clean envelope.[12] It is now settled; the letter must be delivered tomorrow. I am meeting Sisi Natsai and Mother in town tomorrow afternoon and I shall deliver the letter either on my way out or on the way back home.

***

Loveness and Never live on my route to town and the day has arrived. I want to go past her house and maybe catch a glimpse of her. But I'm also afraid. Never might be there with her and then I'll have to speak to him instead and then maybe he'll see that I like his sister. My knees start to weaken as I get closer to Loveness's house. The road to town stretches before me with the shops in the distance and yet they also feel one stride away. Loveness's house feels even closer. I feel like each step stretches to cover one house and that I'll be at her gate in three giant paces. My heart sinks into my stomach and beats

---

12 Kids these days don't know romance I tell you. I didn't do it this particular time but later, when I was a teenager, I would 'pfft pfft' some cologne on that letter and print "S.W.A.L.K" on the envelope so the pretty girl would know it was Sealed With A Loving Kiss.

fifteen times with each heel strike. I walk past Dalitso's house and the blood rushes hot through my ears in a churning that blocks out my thoughts and all the street sounds. The rumble is drowned out by a long bellow from a train horn. I feel this rumble every time I walk past Dalitso's house. It has become a part of the experience of walking this section of the road, of walking past his house, just like the sequence of little dogs and big dogs barking each time I walk past the white people's houses. White homeowners have been leaving the neighbourhood and now there are gaps between the volleys of yappy barks. There are fewer houses with nice gardens tended by gardeners in green over-alls, glimpses of maids in gingham and small dogs barking. Miner's Drift is changing.

I make it past Dalitso's house and the sound of the train fades away. The giddiness from passing Dalitso's house holds hands with my romantic anxiety and I fail to drop the letter in Loveness's mailbox. I keep walking.

I catch up with Mother and Sisi Natsai in the Bata Shoe Shop. They have already picked out a pair of Toughees and another of North Stars for me, but Mother makes me try them on first because, as she says, "This one just keeps growing as if he is eating fertiliser." Sisi Natsai is chatting with and smiling at the shop assistant who's helping us and Mother keeps throwing disapproving glances at them. She mumbles, "If you were another person you would be married already," at the back of Sisi Natsai's head as we make our way out of the shop. We have to part ways. Mother is going on to her church meeting and Sisi Natsai is going back to work. She is on lunch break from her job as secretary in a lawyer's office. She looks quite neat in her white blouse, pencil skirt and black heels. I tell her that she should model because she looks like the models in the magazines but she laughs at me and says she'll do it when I finish school and become her agent. A man with a Bible in his hand walks up to us, greets Mother, Sisi Natsai and then me, referring to me as his "brother-in-law" in the process. I scowl at nobody in particular. He is wearing a long-sleeved shirt and tie despite the summer heat. He is also wearing baggy pleated trousers and has a blue Eversharp pen sticking out of his shirt pocket. Mother chats excitedly with the pleated guy while Sisi Natsai secretly rolls her eyes at me. Their conversation ends and he says goodbye to Sisi Natsai and me. As the man walks away, Mother looks at no one in particular and sighs, "A temporary teacher. Now these are proper men, can't you see." She sets off towards her church and I grab my shopping bags. Sisi Natsai turns to me and winks, "Don't forget to post the letter, little man," she says, and then walks away.

I start feeling hot and bothered the moment I turn to walk back home. Loveness's front garden has brilliant green and white bushes that attract nasty green milkweed or stinkweed locusts, another menace that reminds me of winged tormentors hovering and torturing me late at night. The bushes are in flower right now and swarming with stinkweed locusts, but the insects are not why my heart right now is beating like the drums at the Church yeRoma, my treacherous heart bouncing around in my scrawny chest to the rhythm of the mbende drum beat on the ZBC News. My heart beating to the drums, my stomach to the rattles. A green winged locust with an armoured thorax and red-hinged legs could have fluttered up right before my face and I would have casually waved it away. Three of the monsters could have landed on my chest, dug their hooked legs into the fabric of my T-shirt and I would only have squealed a little.

"Fata mu-rungu! Fata mu-rungu! Fata mu-rungu!"

The church drums resound to summon the faithful in subdued metronome, reminding the congregation that the priest is white.

"Ku-dung ku-dung! Ku-dung ku-dung!"

The Jerusarema news beat responds.[13] My stomach is a riot. I get to Loveness's gate and draw the folded letter out of my shorts pocket.

---

13   Colonisers were not keen on natives getting excitable while playing their drums so they policed the drumming. Clever natives gave the drumming a biblical name and that placated the colonisers.

I get the job done in a nervous flash.

At first, I feel good. Well, more relieved than good. I'm sure nobody has seen me make my quick detour even though I'm hoping desperately that Loveness will be the one to check the mailbox. I carry on home with a lighter step, now free to be afraid of the green devils zipping back and forth across the road.

Later that evening when everyone is back in the house, I am chatty with everyone including Mother, who's convinced I've completely lost my mind. She feels my forehead with her palm and then flips her hand and feels it again with the back for a more accurate reading. She mumbles something about the thermometer that her great-grand-aunt borrowed during the year in which no female goats were born and then she walks away to check on her garden.

My relief is gone by morning. The next two days of waiting are agony. Each day is about a year long. I have calculated one day for Loveness to receive and read the letter. And another to write and post her reply. On both days, it rains incessantly from morning to evening. The weather report had stated that it would be "fine at first and cool later, with no chance of rain." Sisi Natsai laughed at the TV and predicted, as she always did, that the rain would pour down. Sisi Natsai walks back home in the rain, soaked to the bone, drenched and enjoying every cloudburst of heavy downpour. I sit by the window with an eye out for the postman, counting down the seconds. A jolt of panic shoots from my chest to my gut and down my pant leg each time I remember how I had bared my feelings in those two lines. Sisi Natsai arrives home and slides her bag into the open front door, calls to me to join her and cool down in the rain, then continues to ask me how my quest for love is going while standing in the rain as I maintain my dryness on the other side of the window. I have a strained relationship with bath water and all water by extension, so I resist her invitation to get soaked. "Come out, you coward. It's nice!" she calls. But I'm no fool. I catch sight of the mark on her ankle glistening as she twirls around.

Reluctantly she wrings out her sodden jacket, takes off her shoes and dashes in, heading for the bathroom to change and dry herself.

***

On the third day, on the advice of my self-appointed dating coach, I stay inside the classroom when the breaktime bell rings and drag my feet to Loveness's desk.

"Are you still waiting for your brother to show you around the school?" I ask.

"Maybe he's just busy somewhere."

"Did you tell him which class you're in?"

"He knows which class I'm in," She replies.

"What's going on with you and my brother?"

"I don't know. Nothing. What do you mean?"

"I'm not stupid, you know."

"Why? What has he said?"

"He doesn't need to say anything. I can see it."

"There's nothing. He's just a bully."

"It's okay if you don't want to tell me. It's no big deal."

We are both quiet for a while. I feel as though I need to keep talking but I don't know what to say. I don't want to say something stupid. Loveness disinterestedly watches the kids hanging around the school yard.

"How come you and Never are brother and sister? Why were you not living here before?" I ask.

She turns towards me. She hasn't really been paying attention to me until now. Not ignoring me as such but more like splitting her attention between longing to be outside and this boy that is so keen on being friends with her.

"When I came to live here my mom said I mustn't talk to people who ask me too many questions." She pauses.

"But you're cool, Jedza wemaStedza," she says and then she smiles. "Never and I have the same dad but different mothers. I have been living with my mother in Bulawayo, until now."

This is the first time she smiles at me. A full beam, not her vague smirk. It's also the first time she calls me by my "short" name – and the first time I feel it's *my* name.

"Oh and Jedza?"

"Huh?"

"Yes."

"Yes, what?"

"Yes, you can be my boyfriend."

***

There are no sports today and so the whole gang stomps through the school gates after the last lesson. Never doesn't wait for the kids to provoke him. He just starts charging at the kids and shouting, "Why are you looking at me?" Word has travelled fast. The other kids have figured out that something is going on between Loveness and me and have been teasing him about it.

He comes after me.

He goes for my ribs.

I stare at him. He twists the skin under my arms. He pinches harder. I won't let the tears come out.

He hisses, "We all know what you did at the railway line." And then he stomps off.

"I don't know what you're talking about and I'm not afraid of you," I yell at him.

He charges back, grabs my satchel and swings me round. My feet trot sideways, barely keeping me up and my arms flail about. It all slows down. Time. My breathing. My pulse. Everyone around me. First is the sensation of being yanked backwards and then a sinking feeling. Like falling but going sideways. Like when Father drives fast into a wide bend or corner without slowing down and I lean over to one side. I start turning and the events all come rushing back to me as jumbled memories. The butterflies in my stomach as I slipped the letter into Loveness's letter box. The plastic and rubber smell of new shoes in the Bata shop. Mother rambling on about her lost thermometer. I can't make out all the faces spinning by, all I see is a blur of bodies in uniform. I feel the tugs as he keeps reeling me back in like a stubborn fish. I'm trying to pick out Loveness's face from the bodies spinning before me. I'm vaguely aware of Never's shouting and at some point, I think I hear him say my name and Loveness's. Swiftly, the satchel slides off my shoulders and my arms slip through.

I fly. There is a moment of weightlessness. No force against my body, my feet off the ground and my vision a flurry of colours. Into the ground. It's a soft landing on the verge, off the tarred road. The landing knocks my head clear of all thoughts and I look up and around. Never looms above me. He is waving my letter in his hand while shouting something about the train and bad spirits and my family. He flicks the letter away. He raises my satchel high in both arms and then swings it down towards me.

**

When I open my eyes, I am lying on my bed. Sisi Natsai is talking to Loveness and then she says, "He's awake" and both of them sit down next to me. "How are you feeling? Does it hurt here? Does it hurt here? What about here? And now?" They take turns to fuss over me while I'm just lying there trying to answer all their questions.

"There's someone here to see you," Sisi Natsai says, and then she pauses for a response. I kinda shrug and she gestures to Loveness. Loveness leaves the bedroom and then returns with Never trailing behind her.

"He has something he wants to say to you," Sisi Natsai says, and then she makes way for the guy.

Nevertheless stands there sheepish, wringing his hands and rocking back and forth on his toes. Loveness prompts him, "Never, are you sorry for hitting him?"

"Uhuh." Nevertheless grunts.

"So, say it to him."

"Sorry."

"What are you sorry for, Never?" Loveness glares at him.

"Sorry that I hit you."

There is a silence. I'm not sure what to make of it all. I don't really feel anything. I'm just tired and still sleepy.

"Do you accept his apology, Gerry?" Sisi Natsai looks at me.

"Yeah, I guess."

"Alright, so both of you shake hands then. I have to go and pack," she says smiling.

"Where are you going Sisi Natsai?"

"I'll tell you later. Shake hands first, so these two can go home before it gets dark."

Nevertheless offers me his hand and we shake awkwardly while our sisters beam at one another and us. Mother's humming resonates down the corridor and then she swings the door open, "Ah, there he is. Lazarus himself. Back from the dead! Right, you two go home now before your parents start wondering where you are. You two, come, let's pray."

Never turns around quickly and Loveness glances at me before following him out of the room. Sisi Natsai sighs and kneels by my side while Mother flips through her Bible for a suitable verse. "If you were other people, you would both learn from this unfortunate incident. The devil almost walked through this house."

And then she swiftly launches into a sermon.

The prayer session is surprisingly short and includes references to the many superstitions in the town. The many people from the villages and their many backward beliefs. Those people from across the border and their heathen beliefs. She mentions that there are too many dark things in the town; "We can't even walk freely because wherever you leave your footprints in this town, someone can pick up your foot and use it for their witchcraft against you." She then concludes by saying that "the bad airs in this town are bent on following my children everywhere, but the Lamb of God shall triumph."

After Mother goes out, Sisi Natsai tells me that she will be leaving for the city. The lawyer she works for has taken a liking to her and her written reports, and brokered a deal for her to join a newspaper in Harare. She hadn't really given it much thought but now it was happening, the offer definite. "This little town isn't that bad, but I could do with some time away," she says. "Mai believes it will be hard for me to find a man to marry me because, according to her, all the decent men know city girls are fast," she says. I'm not sure what all this means but if she brings me stuff from the city and allows me to visit her then I'm okay with it.

"It's funny that Mai would say all that stuff she was saying," Sisi Natsai says, "because I've been having weird dreams." She says this half to me and half to herself, almost absentmindedly, but I can see she is slightly shaken. "I dreamt I was dragged to the bottom of a river or something, by something or someone I couldn't see."

"Are you not just thinking about what happened to you when you were a kid?" I ask.

"I don't know, perhaps. Maybe I shouldn't have told you about that. I didn't want to scare you."

"I'm not scared, Sisi Natsai, but sometimes I think maybe I have the same thing that you have."

"What thing, little brother?"

"You know I have told you that sometimes I'll just be walking down the street and then I start hearing a train, then I feel like I'm being chased or something."

Natsai takes a deep breath.

"I thought you would forget about that incident at the railway line. You seemed to have gotten over it."

"I don't think about it all the time. It just happens sometimes when I'm sleeping or when I walk past Dalitso's house. Am I cursed, Sisi Natsai?"

"What? No, Gerry. Don't ever think like that."

"All these things Mai is always praying about make me think that there is something wrong with me and you."

"There is nothing wrong with you or with me, Gerry. Mai is just one of those people who keep running away from themselves. Her work and the church are the only things that matter and anything else is wrong."

"But what if bad spirits chase me and bad things just keep happening to me?"

"Don't ever let those thoughts get into your little head. These are just silly dreams," she says. "Now go back to sleep, kid."

4

Ndave Kuenda, 2016

Pray with me. My landlady tells me about this one muporofita. She has heard, from the word in these housing lines, that he is brilliant. She sends word to him and he comes to the house and says that indeed, he can help me, and it is a good thing that he has come prepared for this exact misfortune, but he needs US Dollars to cast out this particularly bad ngozi I have embedded within me. He leans his staff against the wall and, in order for our eyes to be level, bends his thin frame all the way down to me.

"You do not say, have you not eaten a chicken that has been cast away?" he asks. "Because if that is the case then the work will be small, we will only need somewhere else to cast this thing."

After a while he asks again, "The meat you eat from time to time, is it all from the shops? Is it not from wandering animals?"

The truth is I hardly ever get to eat meat. Financially, circumstances are pressing. I have been living rough ever since my parents retired and moved out to the sticks. The house I grew up in, sold for peanuts and gone, like their pensions, swallowed up by whatever this country has become. And this thing, the muporofita just needs to take it out. Where it came from has nothing to do with him.

"It is going to overcome you and make you poor and have you roaming through the streets in dirty clothes," he says.

If he is as good as my landlady says he is, then he should know that my life has already been walking in circles. Everyone in this town knows this. If he had asked anyone on his way here, even the maBrasso boys selling fake gold to cross-border magonyeti on the highway, they would have told him, "Ah Jedza, Jedza is just everywhere, that one."

"How much are your services, Muporofita?" I ask.

"How much did you want to pay?" He responds.

"This is your service, so I don't know what you charge."

"Horaiti, so how much do you have?"

"I'm not a rich man, Muporofita. You can see me here just struggling like all of us."

"You can see for yourself that this is a big job here. We'll see what we can do if you can just take out the money that goes with this big job."

"Horaiti Muporofita, I have 80. Will it do?"

"It is not much but it will have to do since you have cried-cried."

I tell him I have no US dollars and he agrees to accept Bond notes, he will negotiate with the ngozi, he says. He calls it chinhu ichi, "this thing". Which I find odd because if he is not afraid of it, and if he is certain of his craft, then he will call it what it is and be done with it. If he is afraid to name it, then he may be unsure of himself, maybe scared to call forth what he cannot cast away.

First, I need a chicken.

He could have told me this ahead of time. Alas. He needs a new host for the ngozi. Some vessel to cast it into after he persuades it to come out of me. And so, my landlady (who is hanging around, the eager follower of events that she is) seeks a chicken from our neighbour and after a short haggle brings it into my room, which is where we are conducting these proceedings. Muporofita then tells me to kneel on the floor with my head bowed down and he also kneels before me with the agitated fowl pinned to the ground under his hands. A lively hardy chicken-of-the-people would have given this chap a hard time. Our neighbour rears the docile white day-old-chicks that go from crate to plate in six weeks so there is no drama from this bird. He starts chanting and addressing the ngozi while freeing a hand, once in a while, to grip the top of my head and shake it out of me.

"Rabiraradadadabibibi!"

"Ririririririrabadadabanororororoni!"

"Rabiraradadadabibibi!"

"Place money here, under the wings."

And so, I place a few notes (one-Bond bills) under the wings of the chicken which finally agitates it and it tries to flap its wings but Muporofita has a steady grip. "Rabiraradadadabibibi!"

"Ririririririrabadadabanororororoni!"

"Rabiraradadadabibibi!"

"This one is a stubborn one. Put in more money."

I tell Muporofita that I have placed all the money I have under the chicken's wings and he asks if I have Ecocash. He gives me his number and I punch it into my Ecocash app. "30 Bond," he says. I punch it in and 30 Bond goes through instantly. Ping ping ping.

"Rabiraradadadabibibi!"

"Ririririririrabadadabanororororoni!"

"Rabiraradadadabibibi!"

With a loud cluck, the fowl goes silent. By my estimation it is quite dead.

"It is done. Let us go."

We leave the room with Muporofita and his now-ngozi-bearing bird under one arm, its head flopping to one side, me trailing my landlady and our curious neighbour following behind me. Down the street to the last line of houses, along a path leading to the next block of stands, and then we stop beside an anthill conveniently at a spot hidden from the view of either row of houses.

"Is it properly out?" I ask.

"Yaa, it was an old one, this thing. Old, old. But it is out now."

"How far back in the past does it come from?"

"Very old. You called me just in time. It comes from the father who bore the father who bore your father's father. A great hunter, that one. He left his tools behind an anthill deep deep in the forests that are far away. This thing was just about to use you to go and fetch those tools. The ancestor wanted you to carry on his trade. But you are safe now."

A sinking feeling comes over me. I have been here before. But I have already committed to this ceremony and if the ancestors are good, what heals the tooth may well heal the leg, this time.

"Tell this ngozi that you are casting it away," Muporofita cries.

"I am casting you away," I mumble.

"Ah you, say it loudly like someone who wants to be rid of this thing!"

"I cast you away! There! Far far away!"

"Don't you hear now!" Muporofita says with satisfaction.

"Tell it to leave you and never seek you again."

"Go! Do not come back for me ever again!"

"Tell this thing that you are protected."

"I am protected!"

"Now let us walk back, you in front, and do not look back until we are safely within your walls, otherwise this thing will leap back into you."

That evening, when I am hanging around at the tuck shop at the end of my street, trying to score a loaf of bread from the owner Mudhara Mhene, the kids from my housing lines are taunting me about having been closed by the fake muporofita.

"He eats chicken every day, that one," they say.

While the people around the tuck shop are having their fun, the elderly owner asks me, "Why are you young ones so eager to believe these charlatans? Can't you just work hard like everyone else? Do you forget that the ancestors only give when you are tired?"

"Things are hard for me, Mudhara. I work hard. But it doesn't matter. I cannot save any money. I cannot start building even on a little stand somewhere. I'm leaving this town and its shadows. It is time I do something about my life before my head grows white and I have nothing in my name."

"But why leave your hometown for the city? The city swallows its young. You know this."

I look hard at him, thinking that surely he knows that this is a hurtful statement to make to me. He was here in this town when my sister left and eventually disappeared.

"Old Man, there is nothing for young people in this town. Your own children have also left. You think they are better than me just because they went outside the country?"

He stares at me.

"You are all my children, Jedza. You too. If you have to go, then it is right that you seek proper cleansing before you leave. Please hear me, an old man, when I bite your ears."

"That is all I'm trying to do, Old Man. Next time I come back to this town you won't recognize me. I will have a ..."

"Do not rush young man. Everything has its time. The flowers of the world are never-ending. If this is what you have decided, then come and see me before you leave. I will conduct a proper cleansing for your spirit." He adds: "Before these jumpy-jumpy chicken-eating charlatans finish taking all your money."

"No, Mudhara. I'm done with his town and all its superstitions."

***

Drink with me.

I scan my surrounds, up and down the pavement and across the street. A couple of girls are standing around. One seems a familiar face, too young to be loitering outside a bar.

She looks me up and down and I resist the urge to warn them about bunking school to hang around town.

I peer into the main bar of the Continental Bar & Restaurant. Call it Contaz. Contaz is right in the centre of town. You see, Miner's Drift clings briefly on either side of the Nyamapanda Highway which connects Harare to the northern Mozambican border post. Blink,and you miss it. Don't blink and you might still miss it. Contaz sits opposite the post office, next to a branch of Barclays Bank and across the road from a Shell service station.

The Contaz windows are painted out. When they renovated it from Continental Bakery and Superette, the new owners decided that it wouldn't do for drinkers to be seen drinking during the day. Not by those passing by and familiar faces to them in any case.

In addition, sometimes the lights are off because of load shedding and then it is just a dark hole in the wall. As I stare inside, my eyes take a while to adjust; it takes longer during the day when the brightness outside contrasts with the stale lager gloom inside. And so Pretty and Dorothy, sitting on high stools by the counter in that half-turned manner that allows them to catch any movement at the door or in their periphery, see me well before I see them.

"Ah, Jedza, little Jedza, today we are drinking with you in here," Dorothy pats the empty barstool on her left.

"I see the whole line is here today," Pretty laughs.

"What time did you both start drinking? Have you been home yet?" I enquire with mock earnestness.

"If we are not here then who will drink on our behalf, eh Jedza?" Dorothy reaches out for a hug and I lean in.

I drag the bar stool and position it closer to her but also turn it, so I too have a good view of the door and those approaching it from all directions. I slide my backpack under the stool.

Yes, we all live in the same street. Dorothy and Pretty rent a whole house down the road from my landlady's place. They send me to buy lager quarts some mornings. They will see me leaning into the morning sun and call out, "Ah, Jedza, why don't you walk down to the shops and get us a few bottles to remove the hangover, young one?" I will gather a few empties, stretch my legs to the shops, then sit with them for a bit. They are forever giving me tips on how to get a woman and how to keep one after I get one. They will ask me why they never see a girl leaving my room in the morning or me walking one home late on any afternoon, and then console me with hugs, warm cooked food and more beer.

"You look a bit more out of it than usual, young one. Is everything okay with you?"

"Ah, Sisi Dee, you know how it is. This life has its owners, you know."

Dorothy appeared about a couple years ago. Which is to say that is when she moved into my street, doing hair in her tiny front garden during the day, and then unwinding in the bars around town and, on occasion, selling bhaud for $5 or $15 depending on whether you wanted a quickie in the car or a nightclub backroom or you wanted to take her home at the end of the night. She was a bit late catching the wave of commerce that came in after the Bulkington Mine had started operations over the ridge and brought in hundreds of well-paid mine employees, contractors and their families. When I first saw her, she felt familiar and kind. Dorothy has a big heart.

Pretty, on the other hand, is an acquired taste. "Jedza, can you hear what Pretty is saying? She's saying that my bum is getting too big. Is there anything such as a bum being too big, eh?"

"Don't listen to this one, Sisi Dee. Her problem is that she thinks that just because she's a slender babe, she can get any man she wants now."

"The problem with both of you is that you don't know hotness when you see it. That is the problem with people who have never been to Harare."

The belt around Pretty's jeans is buckled to the first buttonhole. She has been around town for longer than Dorothy but I wasn't really acquainted with her. As she will point out to anyone at any time, she lived in the city at some point in her life, before fate sent her out here. I would see her going around with men in the bars, mostly from the big mine, and she would tease me and say when I got older, she would make me her boyfriend. She would laugh and her friends would laugh and the men she was with would send me to buy their round of beers and they would throw in a beer for me. Sometimes I knew the men, these would be the men from the farms and smaller mines, workers who had moved to Miner's Drift in the 1960s and '70s. Other times I would know the men and they would be uncomfortable and brush me off.

"But Pretty, if you're such a hot slender babe, why do you have all these colours all over your face, eh? Bright like a Christmas tree and it's not even September yet?"

"This is what the men want, my girl. Do not act like you don't see them all over me like little children who want ice cream."

Almost on cue, a man darkens the doorway while squinting into the bar. He walks in.

"Hey girls?"

"Hi." Dorothy responds.

He turns towards Pretty but she is stony-faced.

"What are you drinking? Let me get you a round?"

Pretty turns to Dorothy, "Do you hear something, my friend?"

"All I can hear are the cars driving past outside, my friend."

"Mxm, prostitutes. Stupid." Pretty flinches.

Dorothy changes the grip on her bottle and retracts her arm into striking position.

"Prostitutes who are dirty, mxm. That's why you gave me an STD."

The man turns away and walks out of the bar.

"See what happens when you deal with men without money?"

"Who is that guy, Pretty?" Dorothy asks while relaxing her shoulders and placing the bottle back on the counter.

"Urgh, some guy who did me then refused to pay me."

"Mxm."

"He's a son of a bitch."

"See, the problem with you slender babes, you just attract anything?"

"Pfutsek, I will hit you with this fist!"

They both laugh. Pretty, nervously so.

"Yah, but my friend, I'm just losing weight, hey."

She seems to be on the bus, as they now say of someone whose funeral is expected soon. I clear my throat. "Has either one of you seen Never?"

"That little Never has my money," Dorothy whines.

"What are you doing with little boys like that, Dorothy? He doesn't even buy beer, that little one," Pretty throws in.

"Hey, these things happen. It was a slow night."

"How about someone tries to answer me?" There is no sense of urgency in this bar on a hot afternoon.

"How about you buy us a round, instead of just asking questions?"

"I'll do that a bit later. I'm in a rush at the moment, I need to see Never."

"You talk such shit." Pretty says, shaking her head.

They both laugh.

"Brother Wilson, please give this young one a beer," Dorothy asks the barman.

"You know, if Dorothy can eat your friend, then maybe I can also eat you, Jedza. You look hungry. The only problem is that you have no money. But you can hook us up with free electricity in return."

"Besides not wanting any part of this arrangement, I'm afraid that he is going to get arrested before either of you can climb each other or give each other any electricity."

I'm not offended. Pretty flutters her lashes my way, in jest, but I have other things on my mind.

Wilson is behind the bar today and he slides my beer over to me. *Ndave Kuenda* is playing. He usually lets the whole *Zimbabwe Mozambique* album play out. Cool guy. The other barman is okay, but he tends to be a bit impatient with the customers. People say it's because he is related to the wife of the owner.

I greet Wilson: "Mukoma," and he says "Youngaz" back to me as he closes the doors of the fridge. I ask him if he has seen Never at all today and he shakes his head and replies, "Mayaz."

He takes a closer look at me and asks me, "Is it that you've just had a fall?"

He gestures towards my head and I brush the grass from my hair with my hands.

"You have gotten yourself into what, again? Do you not get tired, youngaz?"

"There is nothing here, Mukoma. Sometimes people just don't respect you even when they owe you money. Just tell me if you see Never passing by outside, okay?"

I ask Wilson if he is happy with the electrical connections at his house. If he doesn't feel that he's paying too much. If he wants to save some money in these hard times. He shakes his head and mumbles "Some people…" as he walks to his seat.

I swallow my beer straight from the bottle and start scanning the street through the open doorway. Dorothy leans towards Pretty, "Hey, but I have learned lessons that I didn't think I would still be learning at my age."

"What has happened now?"

"Ah, you, you know what you did last night when you let me take Mudhara Muza. Knowing full well that he is like that."

"Like what, Dorothy? You saw that I was already with that truck driver. I couldn't take Mudhara Muza."

"Ah, but you could at least have told me kuti he doesn't stop the whole night. My back today, my thighs, ah, you dropped me into a well."

"But at least he paid you, ka? He's not stingy, that one."

"Ah, money is money, but hey. Sometimes it's better to have these fast ones who don't pay than these ones who just carry on forever."

"But you knew all this when you pushed him to me, Pretty."

"Ah, me I knew nothing, my friend."

"Pretty, you know he is like this?" Dorothy opens her arms out wide to explain how hefty his mblambi is."

"Eh, my friend, me I know nothing." Pretty takes a long sip while avoiding Dorothy's glare.

"Mxm." Dorothy sucks her teeth then sighs.

"Did you not agree with him kuti if he takes it out then the round is finished?"

"He never took it out."

"Okay, but he should have stopped when he released his things ka?"

"He didn't release anything."

Silence.

"Two hours, my friend."

"Ah my friend, sometimes these are the lessons we learn. You know how the saying goes, learning never ends. Me, personally, I have only climbed that man for a short time, but I have heard some girls who swear by his long-play record. They call it dambarefu."

I scan the doorway. No Never in sight. I check my phone. Nothing there either.

A short while later, after the conversation has gone round from extended fucking sessions to the two greatest football teams in the world, Miner's Drift Pirates and Java FC, to the stingy guys who work at the railway siding, a blur with short arms swerves into the Contaz.[14]

Never walks up to the bar and banters with the girls and they try to shake a couple of drinks off him. He exchanges words with Wilson then pulls up a bar stool next to me.

---

14   The soccer talent was minimal and yet citizens trudged into Pfumojena Stadium religiously chorusing obscene war cries with no hope of either team ever making it into the national premier league. The only people whom I can say with any certainty profited from soccer in this town were the two sorcerers of each team.

"What's up Jedza?" Never enquires as if he has not read my "Please Call Me" text messages begging him to meet me urgently.

"Ah iwe, don't make me wait here and then you just arrive without buying beer," I say. He complies, by ordering a round of drinks.

"My friend, I was delayed by these young girls outside." He says. "I thought I could do something with them until I realised they were actually very young. One of them said that she knows you. *Maidei.* She said, 'Tell Jedza he must stop showing off and talk to us next time.' Young girls these days, ah."

I instruct him to extend a round to Dorothy and Pretty and he nods to Wilson. We grab our beers and move from the bar to a table in the corner, out of earshot of the two women.

The Bulkington Mine money is too hot to keep in these mine boys' pockets. It is easy to see why Never chose to go and work there straight after school. And why I was stupid to trudge behind an electrician, pulling his heavy toolbox for years, in a futile apprenticeship in a doomed country. Now I'm running around this mud hole wiring dodgy installations and Never, a general hand at the mine, is spreading joy in bars around town every weekend. I must now endure his silly banter so he can give me my ticket out of town.

"So, you've also decided to leave town like everyone who leaves and then comes back to show off and steal our girlfriends, eh?" Never taunts.

"Never, you, more than anyone in this town, should know that there is nothing for me here. It is only a matter of time before I end up digging around for gold."

"There is nothing for anyone here, Jedza, but you make the most of it."

"The words of someone who is holding nice money. You know very well that for the last few years my life has been walking around in circles. There is this thing my family has, this dark thing that follows us."

Never appears to ponder over my words.

"You know what," he says, "you have a point. There have been many times where, if it hadn't been for grace, we would have been sitting on logs at your funeral. You are one of those men Oliver Mtukudzi says survive by pure luck."

"Never, are you going to help me or not? This is not the time for your jokes or long stories. I am in a tight position, my friend."

"Ah horaiti. My Jesus. I'm just playing with you. I have told Loveness that you'll be in Chenga Ose this evening. She'll give you a call and meet you there. Did I tell you that she helped me get the place? Anyway she keeps a set of keys with her. The place is just a couple rooms and they haven't connected electricity, but you won't have a problem with that." Never laughs.

I ignore him, though I can't hide the relief.

He goes on, "I'll give you two clips, that's all I have. After that you'll have to make a plan."

"I promise to pay you back as soon as I'm settled that side," I say. "In the city there is money, unlike this village."

Never smiles.

"I'll also put it together with the other bits of cash I owe you," I add.

"You? Jedza?" He breaks into a laugh.

"Have you finished your beer?" he mocks, seeing clearly that I'm too anxious to drink. I laugh gingerly, not wanting to upset my benefactor, but the sun is setting fast and I need to get a lift out of town.

"When you go, make sure you come back. The city you are going to swallows our people, you make sure to be careful, Jedza wemaStedza."

"Let us also drink to Natsai," Never adds, and we both raise our glasses. We cannot pour liquor into the earth for Natsai as her soul is still drifting. She has not joined the ancestors. We hardly ever talk about her. But she is always this presence, binding, yet casting a shadow, that hangs over our friendship. And my departure to seek my fortune, kuenda kumarimuka, open-ended as it is, is much like hers, so many years ago.

"Jedza?"

"Jedza?"

"Heh?" I respond with a start.

"Are we drinking or are we playing a game of statue? No throat airlock is allowed when we're on duty."

I shrug the memories off and look around me. There are a few more people in the bar. Pretty and Dorothy are entertaining a middle-aged guy who seems to have refilled their glasses. The waiter from the restaurant side has started his shift and is balancing a tray with beer for two guys sitting at a window table.

"We do not want beer that gets warm," Never cautions. We raise our glasses to our lips. I open my throat and pour down the rest of the beer absentmindedly. It is now dark enough for me to exit the Contaz and catch a lift out of town without being spotted and having to explain myself to chatty people. It is fitting that Wilson, as a score to my imminent exile from this town, replays *Ndave Kuenda,* as I grab my backpack from the floor and slip out into the dusk.

5

Chenga Ose

I wake up in Chenga Ose. Early winter morning. The full moon is a floating glow at 03:23am. In the chilly stillness, I can hear a low rumbling. The railway line is less than a kilometre to the north. A low drawn-out blare from a locomotive horn disperses the last remnants of sleep. I step outside and into the toilet, then linger to stretch. I rub my arms briskly, the chill setting in. A second horn sounds louder, nearer; a long, lazy bellow from an iron bull. The blast rides over the crumpled sheet of houses rolling out in the distance. The luminous ball is high above me and the weak light reveals the unmade bed of asbestos linen, roughly slept in. Untidy dreams embedded in the creases. Roofs jut up on sharp angles and threads of power lines streak across and between folds. A haze settles between the peaks and in the distance, blends into the grey sky, still dark, and blurring the edge of the bed. It is a dusty, smoky fog. Cold and pressing in on me.

Each night I struggle with the uneasy broken sleep of new surroundings, a narrower bed. I rouse again, this time in a sweat. Too many layers, my body heat has steamed up the windows in the tiny bedroom. It is still dark outside. And the solitary light from the house across the road adds to the eeriness, illuminating the doorway like an amber portal. Leaning back on my elbows, I search for my bearings. The darkness is inside my room. My eyes do not adjust and it persists. I peel off a blanket and push it to the foot of the bed. It slides onto the floor. I reach towards the curtain-less window, open it a crack and lay back, feeling the chill crawl over my damp skin. After a while, I am dry. I pull the second cover back up to my ears and drift off.

I can't tell for how long I sleep, but the third time I wake up shivering. The room is filled with an incessant fluttering of numerous wings. A rush of air swirling above the bed. Unseen wingtips trace down the back of my neck, down my spine and down to my toes. An aerial presence is passing through the room. Its intent, however menacing, is not on me. Like a seething flock brushing past an insignificant obstacle, I am merely in its path. There are hauntings here which are not my own. The weakness in my joints, racing heart, blood rushing in my ears, all these feel familiar from my regular nightmares, but this hovering menace is something else, headed somewhere else and bound to someone else. Unlike the winter cold which I can curl up and cocoon myself from under the blankets, this iciness that this presence has brought in is transient, rousing me sharply as its trails slip out. In the darkness, it leaves me shaking and alert to every sound, the distant hooting of an owl, wind blowing through the rafters, the scurrying of a lizard along the walls. My own movements startle me. I inhale sharply and take in long calming breaths: I had been scarcely able to breathe as the presence had occupied my room. Time circles and circles, going nowhere. Relief shifts into curiosity as my breathing slows down, then apprehension, as I realise that the winged spirits may have located their target. Sudden yelping shrieks come in short bursts. My bedroom door faces my neighbours' bedroom window. It must be their little boy Shalom I'm hearing cry out at irregular intervals, his cries sliding in under my door. In the darkness, I can hear slippered feet shuffling on the floor and more doors opening and closing.

And then comes the mumbling of prayers. I am now fully awake but still in bed with the covers up to my ears. Breathing lightly and slowly, pausing at the top, and again at the bottom of each breath: I want to catch every sound coming from the house next door. What is going on? The steady fast-paced rhythm of prayers in tongues. A woman's voice exclaiming in Shona, Shalom's shrieks accenting the prayers every few seconds. Two more voices joining the ensemble: one deeper, male, and the other higher-pitched, female. The tempo is kept up, in the darkness the shrieks come at longer and longer intervals until they gradually reduce to whimpers and the murmur of low prayer. At some point, exhaustion sets in despite my tense muscles and I drift off to sleep again.

A long drawn-out moan from a distant train opens my eyelids but my fatigue from earlier almost makes me welcome the familiar terror. The sun's orange tint filters through bare glass. I reach for my phone to check the time then half-step into a pair of shoes and out onto the concrete slab outside my door.

This is the wasteland of Chenga Ose. I have been here for weeks but last night was the worst.

Standing outside, I feel exposed and almost naked on the bare concrete slab of this partially built house. I'm still trying to piece together the fragments from earlier. Inside, I had felt the walls closing in on me in the darkness. Outside, where I seek escape, the unpleasant details float out of reach. Now and again, I look across at my neighbours' house, hoping to get some answers. The air is cold and still. A light dust hangs in the air. I part my lips and breathe out. A puff of steam emerges and quickly dissipates. I have a slight headache, nothing outside of the usual hangovers, nothing an early beer cannot fix. Another bad habit. The sun's orange is thinning into a cleaner light and a ray of sun bounces off the solar panel on an angled roof in front of me. The crumpled rooftops now stand in sharp focus and the electrical cables become shiny loops racing in fours between bare, grey-plastered walls, piles of bricks and sharp asbestos eaves. Most houses are unfinished, started by newcomers with modest ambitions, but suspended for so long that they now lean towards decrepitude. Cheap building materials expose

their shoddy provenance in daylight. Shacks assembled
from deconstructed steel drums mushroom between these
structures and extend from others.

The manner in which the zvishiri floated through my room
has left me more curious than scared. Curious to know more
about these spirits that seemed to be under direction, to have
sentience, to know where to go and who to descend upon and
torment, and who to drift past. My experiences with men-of-
the-cloth of any design have left me broke, laughed at, and
with my own worsening nightmares. Shalom's visitations,
however, are convincing me to observe the kid from next
door, and perhaps get some answers.

I delay my trip into the city and spend much of that
morning lingering outside, hoping to have a chat with
Shalom, or his mother, and to put clearer faces to the praying
voices. I cannot bring myself to go and knock on their door;
I don't know how I would begin the conversation. So I wait.
The boy comes out first. Flannel pyjamas, fleece sweater,
fleece hat and a bowl of porridge in his hands. He walks
around the side of the building to catch the sun and comes to
an abrupt halt when he sees me. His eyes are large and clear,
his long lashes are more pronounced. Dark rings frame the
large eyes. We stand there, him sizing me up, me taking him
in.

"Hesi, Shalom."

He just looks down at his porridge.

"Uri kunzwa sei?" I ask.

"Ndiri bho."

His voice comes out stronger than I have imagined after
the whimpers I heard earlier. I think he sees the relief in my
face, because he drops one shoulder and shifts his weight.

"That cellphone, is it yours?" He asks, turning his attention
to the phone in my hand.

"Yes, it's mine. Do you want to call your girlfriend?"

He grins and squeals, "Aah, you, I don't have a girlfriend!"
"Not even anyone in your class?" I ask.

His eyes drop. "I am not going to school again today."

"Your porridge is getting cold." I decide to change the subject. I am still curious about last night, but not sure how to bring it up. The words just won't come out.

"I don't like porridge," he mutters while kicking a stone.

I stretch my neck while looking around and then do the same, looking into their kitchen window. He looks at me amused and a bit confused, then I gesture to the pile of garden refuse in my yard. He looks up at me, shocked, then a grin comes over him. He doesn't need a second prompt. In movements that take a bit too long and threaten to jeopardise the whole operation, he spoons out the entire bowl onto the pile and then places a handful of raked grass over it. When he is done, he looks up at me and I give him the nod. He returns the bowl to the kitchen and then we go our separate ways.

***

Overnight, heading into Friday, coming together in ghostly white clusters huddled around well-tended fires, the devout from Sowe ReChishanu begin lining up along Matamba Road, all the way from High Point Road, in their separate groupings, down to the bottom end of Chenga Ose, with the chain ending in the regional complex of the Joseph Manenji Church.[15] Stragglers in warm clothing drift in throughout the night with their white cotton nhava, containing their bleached-white flowing garments, slung over a shoulder. Their singing and praying are in rhythmical murmurs; it picks up when the morning arrivals surge in with the sun warming their backs. Across the tracks in Makombe Township, the nightly drumbeats from the Nyau ceremonies, funeral vigils and mbende dances tumble in

---

15   An awe-inspiring blend of Abrahamic and Shona spiritual practices. Also the erstwhile top religious refuge of those who had fallen on hard times. In recent times, most infamous for beating the crap out of a battalion of black-booted riot police, with bare fists, sandaled feet and Exodus-era staves.

wrapped in melodies exhilarating or soothing, depending on one's disposition. And if you listen keenly, just before dawn when only the eager cocks stir, you will hear the tail end of the mbira floating in from a bira ceremony, in that moment when an ancestor arrives and begins their dare consultation with those gathered in a circle.

It's a lonely place and time hangs heavy on my hands. I text some people from Miner's Drift that I know moved to the city but when I tell them where I'm staying, they pause. They have moved to the Avenues. Where one has to be if they want to make it. Where one is living to show that they are making it. Where I am not. If I could get to the Avenues, I tell myself, it would all be different.

Chenga Ose is an abstract concept to anyone now living in the Avenues. Some generic location south of Samora Machel Avenue, that represents things inferior and less affluent.

For them, it is where other people live. The bodies riding to work in the stuffy and packed commuter minibuses; the armpits with the odour; the anonymous faces peering into TV cameras behind reporters on the evening news; the swollen bellies affected by typhoid and cholera outbreaks; the multitude of faces and hands at political rallies; the legs running from teargas and riot police; gaping mouths that speak English with a bad accent; indiscriminate bodies that stand too close behind you in supermarket queues; the aching feet queuing for hours outside banks; those torsos bent over checking second-hand clothes from imported bales; the massed shoulders hunched together on sidewalks downtown; eager pavement barbers imploring, "Shall we cut?". Too numerous to deserve attention, so many scrabbling to make a living. Fruit and vegetable vendors taking over the pavements in the centre of town; the youths making a career out of installing WhatsApp on phones; those brash bodies driving cheap Toyota Altezzas; those learners that somehow slipped into private schools when the economy lost shape; the hustlers that landed in new money and almost became our neighbours; the thirsty, desperate mouths sucking for relief on the opening of a beer bottle or a Broncleer bottle and now, a glass pipe.

The statements, the assumptions, are casual and Chenga Ose is cast well: a pastoral name derived from an old saying, *Chenga ose manhanga, hapana risina mhodzi*, there is value in all things. Regardless, the residents of a new housing development refused to have a Shona name for their neighbourhood. When the city council jokingly advised that their utilities rates would be higher if they had an English name, the residents earnestly agreed to be renamed Westlea. The Westlea story might be embellished, but the facts do not change the truth.

Each city zone or suburb has its own self-created identity and I'm learning the stories about place fast, observing and listening. Highfield and Mbare, two of the oldest townships in Harare, have escaped ridicule. Enough politicians, businesspeople and popular musicians have come out of these two and speak so delightfully about them, that they are almost mythologised. There is a Mbare Club of successful people who were born or raised there. Forged in that crucible. Are your parents really achievers if they did not grow up in the streets of Mbare and then through sheer hard work and determination, make it out to the suburbs? Each generation keeps moving forward, across the railway tracks, then further north and ideally, north of Samora Machel Avenue. You had to start off in Mbare, you see, then your success was measured by how far north of it you settled. In *KuMbare,* Tanga wekwaSando sings a list of celebrated artists who emerged from that township.

Elisha Josam,
Ndewe kuMbare.
Chris Chabuka,
Ndewe kuMbare.
Madzikatire,
Ndewe kuMbare.
Fresh Dauti,
Ndewe kuMbare.

There are no songs about Chenga Ose. No heroes who have come out of here.

***

The past won't let me be. All this solitary time to process my thoughts, the hours spent drinking alone and, pertinently, the encounters with Shalom the kid from next door, all of it drags me back to the fight with Never, the green ribbon, Mr. Gumbo's marching songs and further back, the mystery of the train incident and the friends I never saw again. I can't tell which train rumblings are on the railway line running through Chenga Ose and which are echoes thundering in from my past.

Business has been brisk despite my low energy and daily hangovers. The power company has lines running in three sections of the housing development, eighteen sections altogether. In the three sections, only a few houses have power connected and so it is easy to convince a house owner to allow me to drop a line into their walls. I can't have cables running through sections into other sections and so, in the rest of the sections, I'm bolting solar panels onto roofs. Payment though is a problem, even with a deposit that covers all my materials, I barely have enough for the necessary quart or two a day. The residents of this place aren't high rollers but I'm getting by.

It takes me just over an hour to mshika-shika back to Chenga Ose from downtown Harare. I am living right on the edge of the city. My testicles and bearings are dangling over the line that runs between Harare Province and Mashonaland East Province. When I walk down the road to buy quarts of beer from the kiosk, I am making a border run. Or maybe I just feel like an alien. Or look like one.

I live exactly 38.4km south-east of the city centre and if I slip past the traffic police "spot checks" at Kamba Road, Chapungu Road, the car rally track, the Vehicle Inspection Department and Seventh Street, I can make the trip in under an hour.

I get home in the afternoon to find Shalom and a kid whose name I don't know kicking a ball around in the dirt that is their front yard. I made the ball for Shalom a couple weeks ago. Weaved and knotted it out of dry grass, an empty five-kilo plastic mealie-meal bag and discarded shoelaces. In truth, he started making the ball, got stuck and then asked me to finish it. I've never had to make a ball before but I did a decent job. Shalom sat quietly, watching my fingers working and only spoke again once I was done.

"You, you should give me that box of comflax when it is empty." He says.

"What box?"

"That one." And he pointed through my open kitchen door, at the Cerevita box on the counter.

"Okay," I said, "but why do you want it?"

"I want to make a car."

They are kicking the ball around and every couple of minutes Shalom grabs the ball and changes the rules of their game a bit to make sure he keeps winning. Shalom has a ringworm infection spread over his scalp. You can't really see it until he comes within a few metres and then the rings, little embossed circles, stick out in relief on his sharp little bald head. The rings came on as a parting gift when the zvishiri stopped tormenting him. After pulling him out of school for a couple of weeks, his mom finally found a prophet, Madzibaba Emmanuel, one of the many who gather along Matamba Road whom she believed could shield her son from the night visitors.

In the late afternoons, Shalom's mother often sits out on the raised manhole cover of the main sewage line that runs between our houses. She calls me "Mukoma" when I come within range and she will feign shyness: "Ah, Mukoma, this little one is so naughty. Don't hesitate to spank him if he wanders into your yard. He doesn't listen." The warm light flatters the tone of her skin and her thick woven braids. When she holds my gaze it is apparent who Shalom gets his eyes from. And yet, in recent weeks, she has taken to wrapping her head in a white scarf and covering her limbs entirely. I had guessed her age was somewhere around mine, late twenties, and our interactions had leaned towards flirtation, but recently, she has taken to referring to me through Shalom, as "older brother", and reduced our conversation to civilities. I have always called her Mai Shalom. She now carries herself with the sweeping movements of the middle-aged women in the street, her youthful face tugging downward in new lines. She only gets animated in movement and voice when admonishing her son. Throughout the day, she hums Sowe hymns and at times breaks into full vocals. Earlier, soon after I first moved here, she had a couple of visitors, but these dried up. And so, whatever conversation could have developed between us is completely gone: just polite greetings in the mornings and afternoons, the cordial clearing of throats if we both happen to step outside after dark. Seated outside now, she catches the fading rays of the dipping sun and watches her boy running around in the sandy dust patch. Every few minutes she warns him not to get himself dirty and threatens to beat him and bathe him in cold water. The sewage line under the manhole cover she sits on runs farther down between the rows of houses and under the main road. There are similar lines running at intervals from the different sections of Chenga Ose, all headed across the main road, across the railway line and to the sewage plant on the slopes a short distance from the tracks. Not all the sewage lines make the journey across.

A few have broken or disintegrated in the corridor between the road and the railway tracks. Scummy grey water collects in stagnant pools reeking of human shit and laundry soap. In one of the drier openings between the main road and railway tracks enveloped in the stench of leaking sewage, Shalom's mother found the Apostolic Second Rising Deliverance Church of Madzibaba Emmanuel.

***

Reaching out, I had spoken to Loveness on the phone a couple times soon after moving here. She was civil but distant. Which I understood, given that we had hardly kept in touch after she left Miner's Drift years ago, right after school. Two days ago, on Friday morning, she called in a cheery voice. She asked me how I felt, having grown up in a fairly comfortable town like Miner's Drift and now living in the unclipped toenails of the southern townships. Then she laughed and invited me for drinks in The Avenues.

Excited and even hopeful, I hired a rickety little Honda Fit from a mechanic a few houses down the street, and drove to the Tipperary Bar. The inside of the pub now doubles as a night club and so it is dimly lit, loud music blaring from the DJ's stage, sweaty, smoke-filled and packed with the drunk and horny. The pickpockets do not give you room to breathe and when they do, the working women take up the shift. Which is why the long outside bar with its low-hanging thatched roof, an addition to the overgrown garden and aged peeling facades all around, is better suited for conversation. We sat under the gazebo and talked tentatively about what we had been doing with our lives. She looked like I expected a grown-up Loveness to look. Certain and assured, wily and direct when directness was required, yet vague when vagueness was called for. Then she looked into my eyes and in an instant I was the dumbfounded boy in the classroom sweating, the love letter hidden in my pocket. She was a woman now and only the beer kept me composed. We drank and as we drank more, I loosened up and she smiled. Throughout the night, young women dressed in short skirts, tights and cropped tops would sway in through the gates and whisper in her ear. Some she would dismiss swiftly and now and again, she would allow one to sit with us for a while. I figured she was running something there on the side but it was none of my business.

I told her about my electrical apprenticeship, that I had abandoned it and how I now hustled a living fixing illegal electrical connections. I didn't need to tell her my reasons for leaving Miner's Drift. Nor she to tell me hers. It is a known thing that at some point that town squeezes, or the city calls, sometimes both and then one simply leaves. Either way, she was diplomatic and did not bring that up.

"You have skills, Jedza wema Stedza," she said. "You haven't done badly given the situation in this country."

She went on for a bit as the girls came and went and I started to feel my alcohol limit approaching. It was important I stayed clear-headed enough to pay attention because she had mentioned, in our phone conversation, that she had a few apartments in her name, including one in the complex where she stayed, that she might let me use for a while. The Avenues held such allure for me that I hung onto every word. Our last communication from my sister Natsai had come from the Avenues and I kept wondering if by hanging out there I might find out what had happened to her. And rekindle something with Loveness too?

Loveness didn't invite me over to her place that night. The point at which I could have had enough courage to make a move on her passed swiftly and I was now just keeping it together trying not to do or say something stupid.

"The apartment offer stands, Jedza wemaStedza, give me a call," she said, as she stood up and then told the barman she would cover whatever I drank after she had left.

**

The trains run on that central railway line that cuts down the middle of the country, dividing each town it slices through. The suburbs, the shops and the town centre on the left; the industry and high-density townships on the right, downwind, with the sewage dams and the zvishiri swirling around in obscurity. A running train is a rare sight these days, though, unless you live far south of the city and right by the tracks, as I now do. The human bodies, the dust, the stench of sewage, the loud voices and the indifference to personal space have moved further north. The railway tracks no longer separate North and South; they are now firmly in the South. The line that now separates the affluent from those merely surviving is Samora Machel Avenue, a long, broad road running parallel to the railway tracks, but a few kilometres to the north, cutting across the city centre of Harare.

***

Shalom's mother was not sitting at her usual spot on the sewage manhole when I got back this evening. The line is clogged somewhere downstream and it is overflowing here.[16]Frothing grey water is seeping out and the pool is spreading into my yard. The refuse truck comes by on Tuesdays – when it comes – but when it doesn't, Shalom's mother burns her plastic waste in a small pile in her front yard. Earlier I saw her lighting her pile and the acrid, thickly smoking bonfire has brought glee to Shalom. He is poking a stick into the fire and watching the plastic melt and burn on the end of the stick. Dark puffs of bitter smoke find their way into my bedroom, their pungent smell mingling with the odour of raw sewage.

"Hesi!" The little face pops up at my window and I know my solitude is over.

"Hesi shaa." I turn to face the little intruder. "What is that?"

"Chimuti changu! Huya!" The delight on his face could power my lights for three days. I have no option but to follow him outside. He is waiting at my door as I step out and then he drags me towards the fire.

---

16   As many as 4 200 people died of cholera in 2008. The Ministry blamed various shadowy forces for the tragedy. Who in their right mind would buy water purification chemicals or build water infrastructure for random civilians, when one can just spend the money on fancy cars instead?

"Why weren't you in school today?" I ask him while he scans around with all the seriousness of a crime scene investigator.

"I'm not feeling well," he mutters, without halting his search.

That explains the escalation in the prayers and singing I've heard coming from their house over the last few nights. I have also noticed Shalom's mother heading out for church service daily as opposed to Fridays. I have been staying up late and then crashing into sleep, only vaguely aware of sounds in the early mornings.

He bends down quickly and picks up a long stick and presents it to me. "This is yours," he says and proceeds to demonstrate how to poke a stick into molten burning plastic and then brandish the flaming end in circles. I decline politely and think about telling him not to play with burning plastic, but I'm still thinking about the attacks. I notice that he has lost weight and his skin has lost its brown lustre. It has taken on a tinge of ashy grey. He is still animated but running out of breath easily.

"Have you been to the hospital?" I ask him, knowing the answer.

"Uh uh," he shakes his head, "Muporofita ndivo vanouya nemvura." And he points to the bottles of the prophet's blessed water, which are dotted around their yard to ward off bad spirits.

This evening was the last time I would speak to Shalom. I was still up later that night, just after midnight, riding out the discomfort of drinking on an empty stomach. I felt the wave of unnaturally cold air, not as a chill going through my bedroom, but as a mass over the whole yard. I recognised it instantly. The zvishiri floated over my house and descended over Shalom's house with no regard for the bottles dotted across the yard and around the house. This time they were swift. There were no shrieks, no prayers and no hurried footsteps. A quick descent and when they took off, they took Shalom's light with them and left an empty shell of a boy. Mute, motionless and only able to stare into space.

"Cobra! Cobra! Cobra yema floor!"

"Chenga ose manhanga, hapana risina mhodzi" meaning there is value and reward in trying all things, even those deemed unworthy. And yet Chenga Ose is on the fringes of the city – one foot in the open grasslands, the other in the remnants of a defunct township. I stand in it. In the north, the city moves forward; companies are fighting to install fibre internet in homes. While down here in the south, on the edges long ignored by The Ministry, life floats in a bubble of soapy sewage.

"Mbaaaaaaatata! Mbaaaaaaaatata! Fresh mbaaaaaaatata!"

The air is still today. There are no clouds in the sky. Just the bare sun glaring down and the occasional slight gust of wind. But the dust still drifts into my rooms. As there is no regular transport this far out, every half hour or so, a mshika-shika speeds past hooting for passengers and sending clouds of dust over the road and the houses.[17]

"Hove! Fresh hove!" An old man rides past, pedalling strenuously, on his rickety bicycle with suspicious-looking fish heaped in a front basket.

My neighbour two houses down has a flimsy workbench in his front yard and he places a speaker outside the door as he grinds, drills and welds door frames, window frames and security screens. He produced the pole and stand for my washing line and that job taught me to get someone else. He plays old-school reggae and he is playing some song by Culture as two guys walk up to my door and peer in, hoping to sell solar power units.

An ice-cream man rides past on his tricycle. He is wearing overalls in the blue of the Dairibord we all love, but there is no Dairibord inscription on his hat or breast. The cooler box

---

17 Every time the city revives the public bus company, and there have been a couple of attempts, the institution's funds and operations are looted faster than it takes to refuel the first bus.

on his tricycle also has the Dairibord blue-and-white bands, but no words or logo. He doesn't need to shout; his distinctive bell draws kids from their play and sets them tugging at their mothers' skirts.

Two girls shuffle lazily past where the fence would be between my yard and the neighbour to my right. One of them is sucking the last bit of ice from a Freezit. She tosses the empty plastic wrapper on the ground. As they disappear down the street, the packet is nudged into my yard by small gusts of wind until it catches on a clump of grass.

Shalom's mother carries him out and places him on a reed mat in the sun, his back propped up by two pillows even though his neck is turned at a crooked angle. His vacant eyes do not blink. I turn and notice the Cerevita box standing on my kitchen counter. It is clear to me now that there are no men-of-the-cloth who can grasp what hangs over Shalom's head, just as there are none who can help me figure a path out of my melancholy. I have not put enough distance between myself and whatever these forces are that lie in another realm. I can't get Sisi Natsai's smiling face out of my head; I can't stop thinking about this little boy so listless on his reed mat. It will be difficult to collect all the money owed to me if I no longer live here but I'm willing to live with that. The Avenues might be my last chance to turn my life around. Or at least to try and find out what happened to my sister. I take out my phone and send Loveness a text message letting her know that I will be taking the apartment.

6

The Quill Pub, Harare

Natsai doesn't hang out often in the press club, but today she's looking for someone.

"How did I know that I would find you here, Thulani?"

"Hey, my neighbour who refuses to be my lover!"

"It's not even 11am yet, and please don't say that it's 8pm somewhere in the world."

"Do you want to know what the problem with the world is, Natsai? Positivity. There isn't enough of it these days. Shall I ask the barman to make it gin or lager for you?"

She sighs.

"Fine. Fine." Thulani raises an arm to get the barman's attention. "A Fanta please for the journalist here."

"What time did you start drinking?"

"Please be specific: back at the flat or in the pub?"

"Whichever, Thulani."

"In that case the question then becomes, "Have I stopped drinking from last night or have I started drinking this morning?""

"Thulani Sithole."

"Listen honey, if you're going to ask me wife questions then, the way I see it, we should just get married."

Natsai shakes her head. She looks around and catches a couple of guys ogling at her. Her skirt is mid-calf but she tugs down on it and then steps up to perch on the bar stool next to Thulani. "I worry about you. I'm sure there's something up in that head of yours that you'd rather not share with me, but just know that I'm here if you want to talk."

"Ah, Natsai, the likes of you will always try to make a brother out of me. Me, I'm here to marry, you see. Anyway, aren't you supposed to be at work right now?"

"I am." She takes a sip of her Fanta and savours the bubbles tickling her tongue. "I knocked on your door earlier when I was leaving the flat and got a bit worried when you didn't respond. Work is work. I was hoping I wouldn't find you here, but here we are."

"Oh come on, forget all that. Tell me what story Old Head has you working on now. That old man better not be trying to get his fingers on you."

"Not everyone is like you, Thulani. He's actually really helpful. He has me working on some story about the Rugby World Cup in New Zealand. Something about whether or not South Africa is eligible. Are you even listening to me?"

"Huh? Yeah, yeah, carry on, the Boers, rugby, New Zealand, sanctions, yes, yes."

"So yeah, I've got that story right now and then whatever else Old Head has in store for me this week. We'll see. I don't know much about rugby but it's better than what usually happens, when these guys who come in and tell me what to write and how to write it because they are from The Ministry or whatever. Usually Old Head deals with them but sometimes they just talk over him like he isn't there."

"I think they are here, in this pub." Thulani glances around, hyperventilating.

"What?" Natsai asks.

"The guys you're talking about. I'm telling you. They walk around in their suits and dark glasses and they'll abduct you in broad daylight."

"Thulani, I think we need to take you home so you can get some sleep."

"You haven't seen the things I've seen, Natsai. Your life can change so badly if they decide to come for you. Life is unfair like that."

"Iwe Thulani, what are you going on about? There's no-one here besides us and these guys over there."

Thulani takes a few deep shaky breaths while his eyes dart around. He pauses to take in each of the men sitting around the pub, then breathes out and relaxes his shoulders. He takes long gulps of his beer then hisses out a burp, his face turned away from Natsai.

"So, do you even have rugby fields in that little Miner's Drift of yours?"

"I'm not in the mood for your jokes today."

"You're just playing hard to get, Natsai. I know I'm hilarious after the second drink."

"Well, you're not funny after two hundred."

Thulani slaps the table. "Now, that's a joke!" And then he laughs until he coughs, then sighs.

"Well, if rugby articles don't work, you can always try stand-up comedy."

"Listen, I'm trying to build a career here. I don't want to be a robot that clocks in and out of work and then dies."

"You mean like your mentor?"

"I don't know why I tell you these things. Old Head may clock in exactly at 8am and be out at 4pm on the dot, but he holds that newsroom together. He has the most-read columns of all the newspapers in the group put together. He has CEOs and politicians and university professors calling him personally to give him press releases and exclusive interviews."

"If he's so important then why does he work for *The Tribune*? Why doesn't he leave the country or work for a fancy magazine or something?"

"Oh, it's not about the money, for him. He has turned down promotions and offers elsewhere. He likes to joke that someone must stay behind and turn off the lights after the chefes are done ruining the country."

"Sounds like someone has a crush on someone old enough to be their father. I'm warning you about these old perverts."

"Oh shush. Anyway, you keep interrupting me."

"The Rugby World Cup?"

"Yes, I'm not sure how they're going to go about it, but I think the organisers of the competition are going to replace South Africa with us, Zimbabwe."

"Well, well, well. How's that for irony? The South Africans bomb our railway corridor to Mozambique and in return we get their Rugby World Cup spot. Can't say it's a fair exchange though."

Uneasiness returns.

"Natsai, they are here. Spot the two ill-fitting suits that are walking in right now. They're here for me."[18]

"No one is here for you, Thulani."

"I'm serious, Natsai. You sisters from the sticks only have to fear Gule Wamkulu; here in the city, people are the monsters."

"Look, Thulani, you don't have to insult me, okay?"

Thulani unclenches his hand from his beer mug and slides it into an inside pocket of his jacket. He cautiously pulls out a quarter of brandy, looks around, then takes a couple of quick gulps. He burps harsh fumes and slides it back inside.

"You know the lawyer Ncube and his secretary were last seen leaving that hotel across the road and their bodies still haven't been found. That was fifteen years ago."

"Surely that isn't still happening? The Ministry can't do that to its own people?"

"Just keep your voice down, Natsai."

---

18   Abductions, tortures and outright disappearances are a perennial feature in Cecil John Rhodes' ongoing project. From the civilian intelligence of the 1970s to "the dreaded" military intelligence in today's Ministry.

"Maybe we should leave now. Besides, I have to get back to work."

"Okay, let me just finish this beer and then we leave together. By the way, what else are you working on? I might be a failed lecturer but I may be able to help you with something."

"You're not a failure, Thulani. You might want to stop drinking so much though. Anyway, remember that writer guy who caused a scene at the book fair? The one who won the international writing prize but just kept on doing all that crazy shit?"

"Yeah, yeah, him."

"Yeah, well I have to interview him for the Sunday paper."

"Is that what you're calling it now? I hear he's into white women."

"Oh, shut up. Can't I mention any man without you feeling jealous?"

"I do not know what you're talking about. Besides, why can't Old Head interview him, since he has important people calling him for interviews?"

"Old Head knows The Writer well enough to know he won't talk to him. He says he doesn't trust him because *The Tribune* is owned by The Ministry - and you know how much disdain he has for The Ministry. But, he thinks that the Writer might speak to me since I'm a woman and perhaps less threatening to him." "That dude is a lost cause, Natsai."

"No, no, no, that's where you're wrong. I mean yes, he seems to be a bit off-centre."

"A bit?"

"Thulani, ordinary people don't achieve extraordinary things. I'm just saying there is no need for a writer of his calibre to be such an outcast."

"Yeah, yeah, okay. Look, go ahead and do your story or project, or whatever. It's noble. Just remember to keep it professional."

Thulani's body goes rigid with his eyes frozen in a stare.

"Listen to that on the TV!"

"What?"

"That … that … announcement on the TV! Tell that barman to put up the fucking volume. Hey!"

"What, Thulani? What's going on? What did you hear?"

"Murderers. That's what they are. Bloody murderers and rapists."

The small TV is tucked on a shelf behind the bar and there is grainy file footage showing bloated bodies in civilian clothing, lying in awkward positions, and armed soldiers in berets and black boots standing over them. The clip cuts to the chefe in charge of national security, who is in the studio in Harare. Between white noise, he mentions "dissidents," the "state of emergency" and "high alert in Harare".

***

Tribune House, Harare

Natsai walks back along corridors into the open-plan newsroom. She looks at the clock on the wall and clutches her bag as she makes her way to Old Head's desk. He is slumped in his chair with a pen tucked behind his ear as usual. Then, unhurriedly, he stands up and in his automatic routine pats down his pockets for a cigarette which he always finds in the last pocket he searches. "Ah, there she is," he says through pursed lips as he lights his cigarette.

"I'm sorry I took too long during my tea break. I was helping a friend with a personal problem."

"Ah, the joys of youth. Enjoy it while it lasts." He takes a couple of puffs, then flicks his wrist to put out the burning match before tossing it into the heaped ashtray on his desk.

"I need to quit this habit," he says, then blows out a long chain of smoke while slumping back into his chair.

"Do you know anything about that broadcast they had on TV just now? What's going on?" Natsai asks.

"Oh yes. Trouble is brewing, Young Nats. I'm surprised they mentioned it on air so quickly. Seems we have some visitors who have come to cause some mischief in the city. You didn't hear it from me but it sounds like the state of emergency might spread to the city."

"Are you going to report on it?"

"Oh, are you trying to get yourself into the action? Careful, Young Nats, leave that to us old jackals."

"No, of course not. I'm just asking."

"Yes, I'll be covering it but military intelligence and state security are still keeping it quiet before they give us details. That's why I'm surprised that they aired that announcement on TV. Anyway, whatever they're releasing, they better do it before 4pm otherwise they'll only get a report from me tomorrow and it won't appear in the paper until the following day."

"You said I must remind you about The Writer this afternoon."

"Ah yes, indeed! The people's writer himself. I would go with you but I have to wait here for a call from my insider in The Ministry."

"So, I'm not sure how to approach The Writer. This will be my first solo interview."

"You'll just have to trust your instincts, Young Nats. Don't worry, I'm not going to throw you in the deep end. I'll give you a couple pointers. That guy though, what a chap. It's funny how these things go. So a couple years back, when I was covering that corruption case involving Chefe Dhivha Mudazvinhu and the famine relief funds, The Writer was quite vocal about exposing that looting. He would disrupt any press conference to shout out how the politicians are stealing public funds while people die from famine. Even down the road, there, in First Street, and in the park across the road, he would be there reading his poetry aloud and also naming corrupt politicians, calling them fake revolutionaries and all that. You were still in your little town unaware of all these things. I remember being asked to go and interview him, of course to discredit him, but I could never follow through with it. Chefe Dhivha, as you will remember got exposed and his cronies, those flashy young chaps who fronted his deals, ended up being convicted. Chefe Dhivha did not go to court, he wasn't even arrested. Do you know what happened? They just reshuffled their cabinet and sent him to another department. Guess who is now the big chefe at state security and whose call I'm waiting for right now? Chefe Dhivha. I will teach you a lot of things you don't know, Young Nats. These guys will steal anything. Torturing and killing civilians is keeping them too busy to loot at the moment."

"Ah, Old Head, you have started your stories again. So, how do I approach The Writer?"

"Oh, The Writer, yes-yes. Ah, that one is simple. Actually, I'll give you a bit of homework so you can practise researching and preparing for an interview. If you ask around, people will tell you that you should go to Blackwood Park. They'll tell you, 'Ah, that one, he's always sitting on a bench in the park, writing.' People tell each other so many falsehoods. In some ways the Writer feeds into the romance of it all: his image as the poor artist facing the dilemma between bread and paper and choosing paper. Sometimes pencil. Which is all fine, but I think we have a problem when this is the official version from the Writers' Association, who really should know better."

"So, how should I go about finding him and what do I say to him when I do?"

"Start by calling his publishers. You'll get his latest residential address. I remember it as some apartment block a couple of streets down from the park, but you'd need to confirm that. It also won't hurt for you to check the park. He does tend to frequent it."

"Okay, but what do I actually say when I see him?"

"Oh, don't you worry about that. I can never prepare you for that. You'll just have to go with the flow."

Old Head stubs out his cigarette in the ashtray, then slides his chair back and rises to his feet. He pats down all his pockets in turn, starting from the shirt and finds his pack of cigarettes in the last pocket he searches. He taps out one, then lights it while settling back into the seat. He takes a couple of puffs then exhales a long stream of smoke.

"Hmmm, yes, 1983, that was the year. Those chefes were really stealing that year." He slumps deeper into his chair as Natsai rises to her feet. "Now I have a whistleblower telling me that these chefes are buying and reselling state-subsidised cars at Willowvale Motor Industries. Those guys..." He shakes his head.

***

Natsai was aware of one thing mentioned by Old Head, that even though the media and people holding important positions stay away from the Writer, they love to talk about him. To start with, she hung about the park looking out for him. She was there for only a few minutes. It's not a large park and all the benches are lined up along the pathways so anyone can easily make out a shabbily dressed man plonking away on a typewriter or scribbling in a notebook. She then walked back into the office and called his publishers and they directed her to the University. They in turn suggested she speak to the Danish Cultural Society and a woman there gave her his address.

She found him. Flat No.8, Sloane Court on 6th Street in the Avenues. No security guard there, for a change. She knocked on the door and a voice barked at her to "Come in already."

A framed photograph of him and a white woman. Books. A couple more photographs stuck on a wall and scattered across a desk. Empty alcohol bottles. A typewriter. It is a crummy little place but strangely comfortable. Sunlight warms it from a window above a writing desk. More books. Russian tomes in translation and English poetry anthologies. She doesn't know what to make of it.

The Writer was gangly, stooped, dishevelled. His dreadlocks were a mop of thin strands branching out from thicker trunks that have long forgotten from which follicles they sprouted. They were entangled fibres of ideas, bawdy rhetoric, postmodernist prose, failed assimilation with ends split by mindblasts of ungovernable revolutionary energy. He was incredibly there when he wanted to be present, but not there the rest of the time. And that was her first time with him. She thinks he might have found her annoying. He seemed agitated by the interruption. Not by her though. But Natsai could see she was getting in the way of whatever he wanted to do and so she got up to leave. He asked her if "they" had sent her.

"They who?"

He looked her square in the eyes. He rubbed his face with his open palm and then turned away.

"I know they sent you! Tell them to bloody well fuck off!"

She thought about Thulani in that moment and her eyes lit up as she made the comparison. Paranoia.

He noticed the shift in her countenance and glared at her. He turned sharply away from her then spun round to face her again, "But I can see you're not one of them. You may well be from *The Tribune* but you're okay, whoever you are. But I'm afraid I must leave you now. I need to find a warm bar with quarrelsome yet intelligent minds to argue against."

***

Natsai bumps shoulders with pedestrians along the city's pavements and weaves through gridlocked rush hour traffic. A reddish sunset filters through the city blocks. Commuter buses grunt fumes in the slow-moving traffic. Overnight sprinklers are fizzing and spitting across the park and light shimmers in the spray. Natsai feels uneasy as the spray lands on her skin, a light spattering of drops. The hairs on her skin rise and goosebumps crawl up her arms and legs. She rubs her arms briskly and quickens her steps. The fountain in the centre of the park, where all the paths converge, is in full spray with the jets of water rising and falling, shooting up in sequence then dropping. She feels a burning sensation on her ankle. She looks down and raises her leg, expecting to brush off an insect. Instead, she sees the marks on her ankle glowing, pulsating, throbbing. The atmosphere all around her is like a radiant mist. A figure forms and beckons to her from the fountain. Fingers of water extending out to her and inviting her as they draw back. She leans in.

"Sister, sister! Are you okay, my sister?" A voice calls out to her and a hand shakes her shoulder. She rouses out of her trance and looks around her. "Ah, sister, are you lost? Are you new in town?" Then the man, a passerby, laughs and walks on. A few more pedestrians glance at her as they pass by. She shakes her head and takes a deep breath, then sets off towards the office.

The guards at the entrance to Tribune House are getting ready for their shift to end, lively in their chatter and shedding their work jackets. The offices are now empty and only one or two people are still working in each department. As she walks down the long corridor to her open-plan office, she hears a phone ringing. She's not sure at first which phone but becomes more certain as the ringing gets louder. That is the phone on Old Head's desk. Halfway down the corridor the ringing ends, then starts up again. It rings on until she arrives at the desk and stands over the phone unsure what to do. She lets it ring. It is now well after 6pm and Old Head is long gone. She doesn't answer his phone unless he asks her to, usually when he is eating lunch or avoiding someone. Natsai has only come back here to drop off her work bag and clock out but now this phone is ringing on and on. Stopping and starting. It ends. Then it rings again. Without pause for thought, she answers the call.

"We need a reporter at Earl's Court along Prince Edward Street in the Avenues, urgently. A bomb has gone off and we need this in the paper tomorrow morning. Bring your press identity card."

Earl's Court, the Avenues

The sun has set and streetlights are on. Natsai hails a Rixi Cab from the pavement and shrinks into the back seat. She clutches her bag to her chest and checks it often to make sure that she has her notepad and pens. The cab driver is mouthing off about how he would never let his daughter "roam the streets of Harare by herself at this time of the night." Natsai runs through possible scenarios in her mind. *What has been blown up? Has anyone been killed? What will she write? Who will she speak to?* She thinks about Thulani's reaction to the announcement on the TV. What will Old Head think of her if she messes this up? The cab crosses Samora Machel Avenue and a couple of speeding ambulances force them to give way. Their flashing lights are blinding and the sirens blare into the cab. Natsai wrings her hands and clutches her bag even tighter.

There is a police cordon one block before Prince Edward Street and so Natsai pays her fare and disembarks. Traffic police drums have been placed across the road, blocking access, and there are soldiers and police officers scurrying about. Pungent scorched odours hang in the air and sting her eyes. Up ahead, dirty plumes of smoke are rising into the darkened evening sky illuminated when the swivelling emergency lights from the many vehicles and the mounted flood lights flash their beams into dense, gritty clouds. At the boundary of the cordoned off area is a mine-proof military personnel carrier chug-chug-chug-chug-chugging away.

"Comrade, do you live here?" A police officer asks, holding up an open palm to warn her off.

Natsai glances around her. "No, I'm with the press," she replies.

The officer then glances around and asks a female police officer to search her. Natsai holds out her arms and the officer pats her down. She reaches for her bag and rummages through it.

"Let her in, Constable. These are our comrades from the press." A voice with an authoritative tone barks from the shadows.

"Thank you, Officer. I don't have my press card because..."

"Ah young sister, come in, come in and do your work." An officer with stripes on his shoulders steps into view and leads Natsai towards the bomb scene. They stop at an inner perimeter next to paramedics and police officers in white latex gloves.

"So, Officer, what happened here?"

"Apartheid agents in cahoots with dissidents, my sister. They have struck again, spreading panic and alarm."

"The call I received at the office mentioned a bomb blast?"

"Yes. The racist Boers have killed an innocent civilian."

"Why?"

"Mabhunu have no reason for their callousness, comrade, it is in their nature. They just want to spread fear and anxiety. Look up there. That is the flat they bombed. They killed a young wife while her child was in the next room."

"What time was the bomb set off?"

"This evening, a short while before 6pm."

"How many casualties?"

"Just the one female occupant. The explosion blew off the entire wall and roof of her flat. Do you see those two sections of the durawall?"

"Yes."

"The explosion was on the first floor. It ripped off the roof and the wall of the flat and then blew off two sections of the wall over here in the garden. Now you tell me, what is the intention behind that? They wanted to kill everyone in the family!"

"Who is the victim, Officer? Why was she a target?"

"She was just an innocent civilian. They will look for excuses like they always do. They think that we are harbouring ANC activists in this country. They are just an evil regime out to terrorise our people. Remember that they are arming dissidents in Matabeleland and MNR bandits in Mozambique."

"Is there any evidence of what type of device was involved?"

"At the moment it looks like a device was planted in the living room and activated when the racists saw the victim enter the room."

"Any suspects in custody yet, Officer?"

"No, the perpetrators of this barbaric attack are still at large but our intelligence sources at The Ministry assure us that they are racist Apartheid agents working within our borders in cahoots with dissidents."

"One last question Officer, have the next of kin been informed?"

"Er, not yet, but we need this story in print for tomorrow morning before other sources report it in an unpatriotic way."

"Thank you, Officer. Is it okay if I take a closer look?"

***

Through the smoke and glare, loud groans filter through to Natsai's ears as she makes her way past stretchers and huddled service workers. It is a messy scene.[19] Broken glass crunches under her feet with each step. In the driveway, two cars are juxtaposed at awkward angles, windows either blown out completely, or shattered into a mosaic of tiny cracks. As she makes her way around the cars, she stumbles on a piece of porcelain bathroom sink with one tap still intact. She looks up to see where it could have come from and sees a large gaping hole in an apartment wall on the second floor, the middle apartment. She can look right up through what is left of the ceiling and roof, also been blown away, broken roof trusses sticking out like frayed nerves exposed, all opening out into the night sky. Her throat feels constricted. Her fingers begin to cramp from the grip she has on her pen. A flood light is swung across the yard and she sees military, police and state security agents picking over the garden and up in the flat. Behind her, the neighbours are milling in the road, shocked,

---

19 The Apartheid regime besieged and bombed Mozambique, particularly the port town of Beira, to economically choke and pressure newly independent Zimbabwe into stopping aid to South African liberation parties.

too scared to go back home. Everyone is whispering. Gloved and masked police officers are inching around the garden and now and again one bags bits of flesh. Natsai feels her stomach lurching and she swallows hard to keep it down. She takes a couple steps forward and then steps into a puddle. The ground ahead is wet and she traces the wetness to the gushing noise of a broken pipe somewhere in the darkness. Closer to the apartment building now, electrical cables are sparking like severed neurons misfiring out of sequence. There are small piles of smouldering debris, some bursting briefly into flame. She stops in her tracks, unable to move, when she realises she is standing in water. A tingling sensation slides over the partially covered mark on her ankle. She taps her fingers on the bag seven times, tap-tap-tap-tap-tap-tap-tap and breaks the spell, steps to higher ground. Following the hazardous waste workers and photographers, she tiptoes through to the staircase, on the way, stumbling over bricks and rubble and debris strewn all the way up the stairs and into the apartment. She takes a couple of steps into the flat and realises that she is staring back into the street below. The living room simply opens out into the night. What's left of the interior of the flat is an untidy rubble-strewn cranium. Clothes are scattered all over the floor, over sheets of corrugated roofing metal, bricks and remnants of couches, beds and other furniture and appliances. She smells the faint rusted-iron scent of wet blood, notices red smears on the walls and on broken furniture. A series of camera flashes go off and the sensation overwhelms her nerves. She feels her knees giving in but she manages to compose herself and make her way back down the staircase and out into the street. She composes herself, looks around for someone to interview. She won't let Old Head down.

"Excuse me ma'am, I know you're going through a lot right now. I'm from *The Tribune*, do you mind if I ask you a few questions?"

"Well, I don't know if we're allowed to talk to anyone. They told us not to say anything to anyone."

"It's okay ma'am, I've just spoken to the Officer over there and he says it's okay."

"Well, if you're sure, you know this is a bad, bad thing that's happened here."

"Yes, it is ma'am, so do you live here?"

"Yes, I live right next door. It's quite shocking what's happened to her."

"You mean you live in the flat right next to the bombed apartment?"

"Well, yes, and I was in the kitchen making a cup of tea for my Angus when this really loud bang went off and shook the whole building. My Angus fought in the war you know and he says it was just like those times."

"How well did you know the victim, ma'am?"

"Oh, she is such a sweet girl. I don't remember her name too well, one of these African names, I just used to call her Tracy."

"What was she like?"

"Like I said, very sweet. I didn't talk to her much though. She was always inside her flat. Her little one and her, oh, and her gentleman, who used to come in and out."

"A gentleman? Her husband?"

"I guess so. Oh, I don't know. You know how things are these days. He would come for a few days and then be away again."

"When did you last see him, ma'am?"

"Oh, I might have heard a male voice coming from their flat this morning, but I can't be too sure."

"Okay, thank you, ma'am."

"You're welcome, my girl."

***

Tribune House

The sergeant arranges a car to take Natsai back to *The Tribune* offices. Each pair of flashing lights sends her mind reeling back to the flood lights and revolving emergency lights. The driver helps her out of the car and she is startled when he bangs the door shut. The city is silent. The pavement is empty. The echo of her heels startles her as she hurries past the shadows. The overnight guards greet her and say things she cannot hear above the ringing in her ears. She is nervous walking down the dimly lit corridor to her desk and her nerves detonate when the fluorescent light bulbs stutter on. Blinding surges of panic race through her. She turns into the bathroom and she jumps at the flicker of the fluorescent lights again. She stares at the basin and taps, afraid to touch them. The drip-drip-drip dripping of a leaking faucet ratcheting up the tension in her like a tick-tick-tick ticking time bomb. She only has brief respite when she settles into her chair. Fragments of her memory are scattered around the newsroom and they keep appearing, disappearing and then reappearing around her of their own accord. Images blast through her mind like shrapnel laced with adrenaline. Her pen shakes in her hand, she can't hold her notebook still, she cannot type. Flashbacks crack in with each flutter of the overhead fluorescent bulbs. The report is not adding up. She cannot connect the narrative given by the sergeant to the eye witness interviews. How are dissidents involved if there are no suspects? Old Head is not here to give his overbearing yet wise guidance. Who is the deceased woman? Why would anyone target her?

Somehow, she gets the report done, though some elements are missing: she can't bring herself to recall too much. The printroom staff sends someone to pick it up. After submitting the story, she decides to take a nap in the office and wait for sunrise. It is almost 2am and she's sure as hell not coming back into the office later in the morning. Her nerves are fried. The same stimuli that tormented her now orchestrate her crash into a deep slumber. She awakens as the first rays of the sun hit the tops of the trees in the park.

Memories from the previous night flood her mind and set her on edge. She walks into the bathroom to freshen up and

splashes water on her face a few times. She pauses, forgets
how many times she has done it then begins to panic. She
grips the tap, turns it back on, then counts seven splashes.
The water in the basin drains away. She feels relieved. She
gathers her bag, grips it against her chest and heads out.

Standing on the pavement outside Tribune House and
looking out into the park, she remembers The Writer.
Early morning buses are rumbling by and the noisy engines
reverberate long after they have passed. It is still too early for
the morning rush into the city. That will kick in after 7am or
so. Newspaper vendors are out on the street corners. She sees
a section of her report on a folded part of the front page. The
byline says "Staff Reporter." She checks to see if her notebook
is in her bag then sets off for Sloane Court. There is a film of
dew on grassy stretches of the park. Nothing moves. It has a
calming stillness barely disturbed by the crooning of doves.

The fountain breathes and hisses, showers of falling
water cast a misty haze over the ponds in the centre. Unease
descends upon Natsai. Again, she cannot seem to resist some
unknown force that beckons mysteriously in the water-
spangled morning light. She leans in towards the sudden
whirlpool and spinning vortex of the fountain, as if straining
to hear a whisper, as if she is receiving a summons from
beyond the spray. She wills a foot to move up off the ground
and taps with her heel to ward off whatever pulls her towards
the shining body of water so deep and turbulent within, on
the seventh tap she loosens the binds. Her ritual works for
now. She shivers, crosses her arms tighter across her chest
and quickens her pace. She comes out on the Second Street
end and crosses over with the Sports Club buildings dozing
stiffly on the left. A Harare United bus trundles by without
giving her right of way at the crossing point.

Sloane Court, the Avenues

As she walks along the side streets, the sound of traffic
quietens and the morning snoozes. Tree canopies lean

over the pavements across the street. Ah, the Avenues, she thinks. How happy she was to move here once, how it all still seems so normal on the surface, how the Avenues shimmers and slips in and out of your sight, a mirage of a place.

The night watchman at Sloane Court is still there, slumped inside his warm little box. She decides not to rouse him but he stirs when the lever clangs as she opens the side gate. She pauses but he just sighs and nods off again. She has a different approach today. Her jangled nerves have made her sensitive to The Writer's own skittish disposition. She might have been a bit too confrontational when she first saw him the day before. So, she figures a softer approach will work better. Let him do the talking. She could start with a diversion. A story that's doing the rounds perhaps. If she starts waffling or small talk, she's going to spook him. Maybe mention the book fair. That's a good starting point with any writer. She missed the event and therefore his readings so she's not sure what to say about that.

What if *he* asks her about her opinion on his disruptive presence at the book fair? What if he tests to see where her loyalties lie? Old Head was at the book fair and he told her what happened. About him being drunk and sleeping overnight in a gutter, disrupting the session the next day and claiming to have been abducted by agents from The Ministry who were clad in ill-fitting polyester suits. This guy. Or maybe she could mention Chinua Achebe. She hasn't read Achebe but she's heard enough to be sure everyone loves Achebe. Every African writer must love Achebe. But Old Head also told her that this guy is a contrarian. That he doesn't even like being referred to as an "African writer." She doesn't know how he feels about Chinua Achebe.

"Well are you going to come in or stand on my bloody doorstep all day long?"

"I'm sorry. I was just..."

"Oh, bloody hell, if you're going to be rude don't be apologetic about it. The world has no use for indecision."

"Uhmm, I was just…"

"Passing by, again? In the neighbourhood, again? Where's your originality, woman? At least show some creativity."

"I'm sorry, I didn't mean to…"

"Oh God, there is no hope for you. What can I do for you, dear lass?"

"I was just hoping to, uhmm, talk to you, hear your thoughts on literature in this country, maybe have you on…"

"They killed my sister."

"I'm sorry, what?"

"The bloody Boers killed my sister and this incompetent caricature of a state has the gall to print the story without bothering to inform me or anyone in my family. And they're carrying on about dissidents. What the hell do their fictitious dissidents have to do with this? What manner of animal prints a front-page death without informing the next of kin?"

"Are you saying that…?"

"There is the damn newspaper on the desk. Read it."

She can't bring herself to look at the paper. She's appalled at herself and shocked to the core. Weakness cuts through all the joints in her body. The pit of her stomach churns and spasms and it is as if her insides, her heart, her lungs, her mind, all drop down into her bowels. She starts tapping-tapping-tapping her foot. She loses count. She can't count. Slowly she regains focus in her eyes. He is shouting and spittle is flying, flinging out phrases and words that make no sense. He is shaking the newspaper in her face, pointing to the front page with its terrifying headline. She leans towards it and checks for a byline. Her name is not given. The relief is fleeting, swiftly overwhelmed by guilt. She is light-headed and cannot process what is going on, cannot stay in the present or make sense of the recent past. He unfolds the paper and she sees a photograph of the bombed-out flat. The bitter ashy smell of the smoke, the flashing lights, the gloved hands, the chug-chug-chug of the military vehicle: all of this overwhelms her senses. She taps and taps. He wrings his hands and rubs his eyes with the heels of his palms. And then he jumps up. As if he has been waiting to vent before gathering the courage to go and face the tragedy. She shakes herself out of her daze. He just says, "Well I'm off now," and twists into a tight-fitting jacket with a printed floral design.

***

The bombings around the country had never affected her personally. As far back as she could remember, there had always been news stories and headlines of attacks happening in the Eastern Districts or in the Midlands and Matabeleland.

Two guys would come into the newsroom and speak to the editor. After they had left someone, usually Old Head, would get instructed to write an insert about a mysterious and dangerous dissident. No sources, no witnesses, no references. Sometimes, after the guys had come in, the editor would just slip a note with the insert to the layout desk. Last week they had run the same insert and the dissident had a different name and they also had a blurry mugshot that could have been anyone.

Natsai had run the story of the bombed flat. She hadn't checked for any relations. The Writer had been torn apart, shattered into pieces by her negligence. His sister had died.

A couple of days later, *The Tribune* has another large photo on the front page. In this image, The Writer is standing outside the bombed flat, positioned next to a group of Ministry officials. In his floral jacket, he looks out-of-place, disoriented, helpless. The bomb damage looks even more horrific in daylight. The photo must have been taken that same morning he walked there from his flat. The official story is still the same. They are blaming agents from the regime in South Africa. The South African regime is arrogantly saying they cannot be held responsible for what happens to "ANC terrorists". The headline story now says that the target was the woman's husband who is an ANC activist and that the bomb was planted in a television set he had brought back from a trip to Mozambique.

She is dead.

***

Tribune House, Harare

"You see, Young Nats, you remind me of the time that I spent a few weeks writing "AIDS-related" as the cause of death of some of our chefes. The resulting heat that came down on me from The Ministry was all fire and brimstone, I tell you. I was much older than you of course, but I was still learning how to navigate these corridors. You see, we now write "short illness" or "long illness" but that came at my expense. Are you with me, Young Nats?"

"Yes, I hear you."

"Don't beat yourself up about these things. It's all part of your journey to being a decorated member of our profession. I could tell you more stories but you would say that I'm lying."

"So, they are not saying anything up there in the offices?"

"Oh, don't worry. You're not getting fired for this little mishap. I sorted it out with those suited clowns."

Natsai sits upright at her desk across the aisle from Old Head. Her tapping has been incessant the whole morning; shifting from one foot to the other, from the feet to the fingers, and back again to the feet. Each time she reaches the seventh tap, her anxiety ratchets up a notch, making the next seven taps more crucial.

"You don't look convinced. Don't worry, you will forget about all this by the end of the day."

"So, did The Writer not complain to anyone here?"

"Is that what you're worried about? Young Nats, you can't get attached to your sources, my girl. I doubt he will come anywhere near this place. There isn't enough of an audience here for his antics. Besides, the chefes don't take him seriously. I can tell you stories about how they claim to be best friends with him when they are hosting foreign dignitaries but you will say I'm exaggerating. No, don't worry about that one."

"Have you ever been to a bomb scene?" Natsai asks after a brief silence.

"It is you who is the bomb scene, my girl." He chuckles.

"First you spill water all over the tea room, now I'm noticing that you don't have any mirrors in your flat, eh?"

Old Head clears his throat and nods at the misaligned buttons on Natsai's blouse. She fumbles at her blouse and corrects the mishap.

"Bomb scene? Ah, those ones are easy. Are you forgetting that I worked at the Manicaland office soon after Independence? Those ones are easy. I've seen so many of them. You just go in and out, write your report and you're done. The report you wrote up is better than my first bomb report but you'll say that I'm lying now."

Old Head yawns and stretches. He then pushes his chair back, pats his shirt pocket, then stands up and pats the front then the back trouser pockets, pulls out his pack of cigarettes, sits back down, lights one up and flicks the burnt out match in the ashtray. His coping ritual, thinks Natsai. Not unlike my tapping and Thulani's habit of drinking every day. He draws two quick puffs then slumps into his chair while blowing out a long chain of smoke.

"Bomb scenes, yah those ones are easy. Remember to call the National Rugby Union offices to follow up on the final teams announcement."

***

Blackwood Park, Harare:

Natsai has no intentions of going to the National Rugby Union offices nor of doing any work at all. But she needs to relieve the tension in her shoulders. Her back muscles have knotted painfully: the more she has ruminated over the events of the last few days, the tighter the knots in her back, arms and legs have twisted. She packs up her bag and walks out of the office desperate for some fresh air and sunlight. She steps out onto the pavement and is surprised to see Thulani pacing up and down the entrance with his shoulders stooped, deep in concentration. He begins to mumble an apology but Natsai brushes it off and leads him across the street and into the park. The park has its usual pedestrians in polyester suits and georgettes but in addition, police officers positioned at each of the exits and a couple of soldiers at the fountain in the centre.

"They are all over, these policemen and soldiers," Thulani says after they take a seat on one of the benches. "I cannot breathe."

"I can't help you if you don't tell me what's going on, Thulani. You don't look like you have slept at all."

Thulani is restless. He keeps glancing up and down the pathways and glancing over his shoulder. His left leg is shaking and now in concert with Natsai's relay of heel-tapping and gripping her bag more and more tightly. "I can't bear seeing them all around like this," he says. He searches inside his jacket and his trembling hands emerge empty. He draws a sharp breath of air and shakes his leg with more intensity.

"I need you to do me a favour please, Natsai. I promise I'll pay you back soon."

"You can't keep doing this to yourself, Thulani. You have stopped paying me back and I can't just keep buying you alcohol."

They sit in silence. Natsai shifts from one aching buttock to the other and Thulani with his shoulders still stooped, and his hands on the bench by his sides, rocks back and forth. He takes two sharp breaths then opens his mouth.

"I know you mean well, Natsai. You think I'm just this drunk with no cares in the world." He pauses.

Natsai begins to speak but Thulani holds up a hand and carries on.

"I have meant to tell you all these things so many times but I don't know, I just end up saying some stupid nonsense." Natsai places a hand on his shoulder.

Thulani shuts his eyes and a tear rolls down. He sniffs. "I've always meant to tell you about my grandparents and aunts and uncles and cousins and how they were driven from their homes by soldiers in red berets – The Sixth Battalion.[20] That is all true. But even when I was trying to tell you about that, I was not ready to tell you that I was also there. It wasn't just my relatives. My family was also beaten and insulted. I was there."

Tears stream down both cheeks. He heaves. Natsai rubs his shoulder and he begins to sob.

She vaguely remembers him bringing up the topic at The Quill Pub on yet another evening that she had been trying to talk him into going home. She had been talking about the weird dissident columns that Old Head had been instructed to write up. Thulani had looked at her in an unsettling way. He had held his gaze and then when she had asked him what was up, he had looked away. He had then mumbled under his breath but she had not paid much attention to his words.

He wipes the tears from his face with the back of his sleeve and then composes himself.

"There are soldiers burning our villages, but I don't know about these dissidents you guys write about," he says grimly. "My grand-parents' homestead, where my father was born, was completely burned down. My grandfather, one of my uncles and a herd boy, were beaten and dragged away and we never saw them again. One of my aunts..." He started heaving again.

They sit on the bench attuned to one another's emotions yet also feeling the pulse of the city throbbing all around. Delivery trucks rolling up and down, turning into service lanes, drivers leaning out of windows talking to clerks with clipboards. People walking briskly up and down the

---

20   Gukurahundi: that six-year-long "moment of madness" where the former gallant comrades raped, tortured and killed up to 20 000 civilians who they referred to as "cockroaches" in the process, so they could establish their unopposed one-party state.

pavement. The sun well up, now directly overhead and its rays now landing on the tarmac. No shadows on the pavements or in the alleyways. Another regular day in the city centre. A newspaper vendor across Second Street, standing at the entrance to the park. The headline on the front of his papers says something about a meeting on political unity talks being held or postponed. Thulani bowed and lost in thought; Natsai leaning into him. She has known Thulani for months, ever since she moved to the Avenues and yet this morning, she truly sees him for the first time. If what she has felt over the last couple days is any indication, then she is only beginning to understand the turmoil in his soul. She has been trying to push her own distressed chaos to the back of her mind. Trying to convince her mind that the bomb scene was "easy" as Old Head had told her, but it has been this constant loud humming in her skull. And when Thulani was opening up to her, even though she held it together, inside her head tiny explosions were going off with each emotion he shared.

***

She's not going back to the office. She ponders aloud: "Old Head can lecture me about missing the rugby announcement. He can also tell me his stories 'you-will-not-believe' about how he would have done things differently. He can also let the chefes fire me if he wants." There is an emerging lull at the office. Something is brewing in The Ministry corridors. The political unity story and all the noise around it is drowning out everything else. Natsai is not involved in that. Old Head seems to be writing that up himself. She has seen the memos on his desk and watched him speak on the phone in a hushed voice. Whatever is going on in the newsroom, she is not going back there this afternoon.

She pats Thulani on the back: "Come, let's go to your favourite spot. But you better pay me back this time."

***

The Quill Pub

They take their seats at the bar and Thulani asks the barman to pour him a "proper" brandy. Natsai receives her Fanta and then twirls the straw in the glass while watching the bubbles rise and burst on the surface. She starts counting each rising bubble and her anxiety builds when she can't keep the multiples in check. Her foot begins to tap against the stool. Thulani, on the other hand dilutes his double brandy with minimal Coca-Cola, takes a short sip and then two longer gulps. He rests the glass on his thigh and closes his eyes while the liquor flows down his gullet, into his stomach, absorbs into his bloodstream, and warms his heart, floods his brain, and trickles into his extremities. "Hayi, hayi, hello my friend!" His lips draw into a smile while he shakes his head slowly from side to side. Natsai takes her eyes off the bubbles and watches his transformation.

"Barman, please give this woman exactly what I am having?" Thulani says with his usual mock seriousness.

The barman, aware of the game they play and Thulani's companion's usual shake of the head, still casts a glance at Natsai. She has a look of indecision, which makes the barman halt. She nods. The barman looks at Thulani. He has a look of mild amusement on his face.

He calls her bluff. "Pour it, my friend," he says to the barman. The barman responds to the order with a humorous smile. Natsai raises her glass while Thulani watches her with no attempts to hide his amusement. She takes some of Thulani's Coca-Cola and empties it into her brandy. She smells it. She takes the straw from her Fanta and stirs the drink, then takes a small sip. She contorts her face, shuts her eyes and swallows it. Thulani laughs out loud and claps his hands, "Nazo ke! You have finally broken your virginity!" Natsai recovers from the first sip and coughs once while thumping her chest. "I don't know how you drink this stuff."

"Easy, like this." Thulani empties his glass in one go and orders another.

Natsai takes another drink and doesn't twist her face as much. Her next sip is longer. Warmth rises in her chest and then spreads out into her limbs. Her cheeks are tingly. The reproachful, accusatory voice she has been hearing in her head the last couple of days drops lower in volume and then falls silent. She relaxes her legs, the shaking gone. Her hands are steady, no desire to tap. She does not count bubbles. She does not count anything.

"How are you feeling? Everything okay there?" Thulani cannot help himself.

"You have been keeping the good stuff from me, Thuls." Natsai laughs. "Let's move over to one of those window cubicles."

"I've got an even better suggestion. Let's have the next round in the cubicle, then we can leave this expensive place, get a bottle of brandy from the bottle store and have it on my apartment balcony? Sundowners, Nats."

A surge of emotion rushes through Natsai. She wants to share all the things that have been weighing heavy on her. She wants to hear all the emotions he has been keeping inside him. She wants to feel it all. The tension in her shoulders has dissolved and her mind is free, set adrift. She feels a warm tingling sensation building up each time she looks at Thulani. She needs to resolve it. She looks into Thulani's eyes: "I'm all for it."

***

The view from the pub window is electric, the city buzzing with activity. People fly past on the pavement in a blur of office wear. Vehicles zip by with light bouncing off chrome and glass. The warmth of the sun awakens sensations in her skin. Natsai is sensitive to the warming touch. She touches Thulani. She likes it when he touches her.

She floats through the late afternoon. She realises just how funny Thulani is. She hasn't laughed this hard in … in a long time. For an instant, the face of her little brother Gerry flickers into consciousness, his teasing grin. How long since she went home to Miner's Drift? They cross city streets in fits of laughter. Car horns honk at them and she cautions him to be careful. In and out of the bottle store. They have their bottle which she carries because she wants to "see how it feels" and he holds the bag with the Coca-Cola and a couple of brandy quarters. "You are happy, eh?" a passer-by comments. They burst out laughing. Inside the complex, they head to his flat. It is now early evening. She feels briefly nauseous but it passes. "Have some water," he says. "I'll drink water tomorrow," she replies. They fall onto the couch laughing. The tension in her body peaks. When he leans into her she responds readily. They fumble at each other's buttons and belt clasps and giggle through sloppy kisses.

"Are you sure?" Thulani asks.

"Yes," she replies without hesitation. Tension rolls away from Natsai's body in wave after wave. As the tide recedes, they both pass out.

***

Sirens wail and the rotating emergency lights spin round and round making her head dizzy and her stomach queasy. Hot acid rises up her throat as she opens her eyes. The room is in darkness but there is enough light to make out the upright edges of furniture. Curtains. A chest of drawers. The source of the light is a TV test screen with its vertical bright-coloured bars. The sirens align into the monotonous sine tone from the TV. She stares at the screen and makes out the time - 23:07:51, 52, 53, 54, 55, 56, 57. A bitter hot liquid rushes into her mouth and she stumbles off the bed and vomits into the curtains. She purges and purges then regains her breath while on all fours. She wipes her mouth with the curtain. The nausea begins to subside. She takes a few more gulps of air and then looks around.

She is in Thulani's bedsitter. She now recognises it. He is lying on the bed naked, legs entangled in bed linen. She realises that she is also completely naked. She clutches at her body, covering her breasts, then crouches to hide her bare crotch. The noise from the TV persists. She now becomes aware of Thulani's soft snoring. Slowly, she grabs the bed and rises to her feet. Blood rushes from her head and she steadies herself against the bed with her thighs. Blood rushes around her body, pulsates through her ear canals. A pounding within throbs through her limbs.

The punitive voice in her head is back, louder: "Stupid. How could you? What have you done? So stupid." Flashbacks from the bomb scene return, this time more vividly, scenes of fragmentation and strobe lights. She taps her foot seven times to get moving. She touches each item of her clothing seven times before she can pull it on. She gathers together her shoes and her bag and slithers out of Thulani's flat and down the corridor. She puts on shoes and braces herself for the short walk to her own flat.

Back in her apartment the voice is louder still. She splashes cold water on her face, rinses her mouth then brushes her teeth. Electric light, the glare of neon, hurts her eyes. Her head is boiling, a turbulent steaming mess. She takes three painkiller tablets and swallows them with water. Her stomach cramps and gurgles: she burps a brandy-infused stench. She decides to rest for a bit before showering. She lies down on her bed and instantly falls into a deep slumber.

**

Natsai wakes up feeling thirsty. She checks her watch and it is after 10am. She is feeling less nauseous than earlier and steadier on her feet but is a nervous wreck. Memories of the previous afternoon and night flit through her mind and she feels flushed, mortified, even distraught. Surging over these emotions is the amplified guilt of her betrayal of The Writer. This too: it is too late now for her to simply walk into the newsroom empty-handed. She needs to have some pretext for her absence. While showering, she resolves to visit The

Writer. Not easy and she has no idea what to expect. Should she confess? If she talks with him she can have a cover for her lateness, but also to quieten the accusing voice in her head.

Natsai summons the strength to slip out of her flat. She constantly glances around her to make sure she doesn't bump into Thulani in the street. Shame like a cold trickle of dirty water runs down her spine with each memory that rolls into her mind from the pub and his flat. She notices police officers standing in pairs at every other street corner. Her heartbeat quickens with each sighting. A military truck drives by slowly chug-chug-chug-chugging away. Her head begins to spin. However troubled her thoughts and emotions were before yesterday, they are now much more chaotic.

"This is all my fault. But where was Old Head? I'm still a junior reporter, he knew they would call him to the bomb scene. You're so stupid. Why did I drink so much? Why did I drink at all? I need to confess to The Writer. It's your fault. I must just apologise. How do I avoid bumping into Thulani? That friendship is over. I'm never drinking alcohol again."

***

This could be any other morning in the Avenues, traffic stalling and the hustling-hustling on pavements, the deep shadowy places under the trees, the streams meandering through parks. Even in bright sunshine, Natsai doesn't feel safe, she is looking-looking around her, feeling as if she has lost her way. What was here before the Avenues, before this sinister crowded city came into being? Deep unstoppable waters are rising here on these sunbaked pavements and hot tarred streets: she could be swept away at any time.

***

The guard at Sloane Court is awake today. It is almost noon. He's stretched back on his rickety chair and leaning against one side of the guard box, squeezed into the last sliver of disappearing shade. His knees have a spot of sunlight hitting them, but his head is flush against the wooden wall of the guard box. He hears Natsai swing the gate open but doesn't lean forward into the glare. His eyes dart towards her. He waits for her to speak.

"Elder, allow me to visit."

"Eh, how far are you going?"

"I'm going up to see this man, The Writer. Is he around?"

At these words he swings forward and squints into the full blaze of sunlight. He shields his eyes with a hand and then slowly drops it as his eyes adjust.

"What do you mean you are looking for The Writer? Have you not heard?"

"Heard what, elder? Has he moved?"

"The man left us. He is not with us anymore."

"What do you mean? Has he…?" Natsai's foot begins to tap the ground.

"He passed away. That young man who writes books passed away yesterday."

7

TIME SWERVES BACK

Before the Avenues, 1892

VaDziva:

"Mbuya Dziva, you who are in the air above and the waters below. Birther of these wetlands. When you sneeze, the ground itself quakes. You whose tears flood the earth itself. We seek passage through these fields yet fear to tread with our cracked feet. We who fear your wrath. We who are not ready to join you.

[To the tune of *Nhemamusasa*]

This is our home,
Home! Home!
And to our kin,
Come! Come!

Show us the musasa trees here so we may lay our offerings. Where we take, we will replace with more. Where you guide us, we will guide others and tell them your name. May our meagre offerings not offend you. Where one tree falls, we will plant ten more. Our offerings are here, at this and that tree, as you guide us through your land.

This is our home,
Home! Home!
And to our kin,
Come! Come!

For holding your water, we give thanks. For saving our offending villages from your tears, we give you thanks. You who may flood us on a whim. And yet you water us in the dry season, for this we are thankful. We are forever undeserving. For quenching our thirst always, we are beholden to you.

This is our home,
Home! Home!
And to our kin,
Come! Come!

From your lands we see far beyond our humble villages. From your peaks we see all you protect from your anger. In your treacherous pathways, we seek refuge."

***

What happens when you drain a wetland in Fort Salisbury that is not yet Harare? When you play god and cut off a stream. Dry out the very medium of life. Change its course from Mukuvisi such that it doesn't flow beneath the ground and can no longer tribute into Mazowe such that the Mupfure no longer receives this tribute which does not then forward it into Sanyati whose mouth stops emptying into the Zambezi down at the bottom of the escarpment? Do the great spirits of the Land fold their arms and sigh? Does this stir the wrath of gods who are quick to anger?

And this elevated land, bound by the Limpopo at the bottom of the plateau, and the Zambezi River frothing and swirling along the top northern rim. The Zambezi rising from a black marshy dambo in dense undulating miombo woodland, and irreverently threading through the narrow

Batoka Gorge and then, like a teetering messenger to the gods, tracing the northern edge, in a clockwise direction along the floor of the Zambezi Escarpment, before flowing eastwards towards the Indian Ocean.

As it was for two-million years, a river settled into its rhythms and over millennia, wildlife and human communities living within and around and adapting to the river and its seasonal flooding.

Until 1956, when work began to dam the Zambezi River at Batoka Gorge, by men from faraway lands, under instruction from colonial administrators, whose forebears had rolled in on trains of beast-drawn wagons only fifty years before, and been captivated by their apparent success at controlling patches of wetlands and a stream, hundreds of miles upstream of the Zambezi, in a place they named Salisbury, forever shifting the landscape of the Zambezi Valley.

The flooded valley remains haunted by the ghosts of drowned animals and souls of villagers washed away. Fossilised bare tree trunks jutting out from the shallows stand as unmarked graves. More than 55 000 BaTonga people separated and displaced from community and rich alluvial river soils, onto higher sandier less fertile soils on either side of the lake.

***

The South Anglo Company, represented here by Lord Fifefingers, hereby agrees to the following articles and conditions, whereby peace and amity shall continue forever:

Know all men by these present, that whereas Charles Dumb Rudderless, of Kimberley; Rockhead Magwheel, of London; and Francis Robert Tombstone, of Kimberley, His Honour Stephanus Johannes Paulus Preposterous, State President of the South Anglican Republic, represented in this by Pieter Johannes Gobbler by virtue of a power furnished him under date 6th June, 1887, in the name and on behalf of the people and the State of the South Anglican Republic,

Her Majesty Queen Vexatious, represented in this by Lord Nutsforth, one of the Queen's Principal Secretaries of State, hereinafter called the grantees, have covenanted and agreed with said Lobengula, and do hereby covenant and agree to deliver on the Zambesi River a steamboat with guns suitable for defensive purposes upon the said river [guffaws and jeers from the gallery], or in lieu of the said steamboat, should I so elect, to pay to him the sum of five hundred pounds sterling, British currency [more jeering and laughter].

Whereas the British way of life is the very precept upon which civilization shall be built in the primitive margins of the globe.

Whereas, not in a thousand years, is it in the best interests of the childlike native races, just emerging from barbarism, for them to be left in a permanent state of independence.

Whereas it is known that wherever gold is, or wherever it is reported to be, there it is impossible for native races to exclude white men, and, therefore, the wisest and safest course for them to adopt, and that which will give least trouble to themselves, is to agree with one approved body of white men, and arrange where white people are to dig.

Whereas the Company is indefatigable as ever in its exertions for the good of the colony and its inhabitants. To wit all Christianising being done here on just principles, and the best of order; and we are determined to make a way for the spread of the glorious Gospel of our Lord and Saviour Jesus Christ. Wherein it is the Company's duty to seize more territory, meaning simply more of the Anglo-Saxon race, more of the best, the most human, most honorable race the world possesses.

Whereas it is incumbent on the Company to manage districts on the edges of civilization and to extend the blessings of civilization – the roads, telegraph and railroads – through these dark regions, this land of Ophir.

Whereas other civilised powers have ousted the savages from all their possessions, and very often under circumstances of cruelty and massacre which have left a permanent stain

on the name and reputation of those nations who boast –
and justly boast, no doubt - that they are the pioneers of
civilisation.

Whereas the selfless burden of civilisation shall require
that Lobengula grant and assign unto the said grantees, their
heirs, representatives, and assigns, jointly and severally, the
complete and exclusive charge over all metals and minerals
situated and contained in his kingdoms, principalities, and
dominions, together with full power to do all things that they
may deem necessary to win and procure the same. To take
all necessary and lawful steps to exclude from his kingdom
all other persons seeking land, metals, minerals, or mining
rights therein and to grant no concessions of land or mining
rights from and after this date without the grantees' consent
and concurrence.

Hon. Goodfellow (Backbencher): "Are we to understand
that the South Anglo Company, by way of Royal Charter,
patents to deprive natives of their rights to their land and of
an opportunity of living in their own country?"

Lord Fifefingers: "Hon. Gentlemen come here apparently
as the friends of savage races. [guffaws and laughter] My
right Hon. and gallant Friend, after full consideration of the
question, the South Anglo Company, under consultation
with the Secretary of State for Colonial Affairs, came to the
conclusion that the expansion of Her Majesty's Empire was
to the interest of the natives, burdensome as that duty may
be."

***

South Anglo Company:

Colonel MacIlwaine Pennyfeather:

Rally round the flag, boys! Backs against our wagons. Move
the Maxims into place. Test the .303 rounds on native rump.
One Maxim for each thousand naked savages. Act the part,

boys, we're not your average thieving prospectors, we're here for the Crown.

[sings]

"Whatever happens
We have got
The Maxim gun
And they have not!" Rat-a-tat-tat. Rat-a-tat-tat.

Military band strikes up, discordant and offkey: [To the tune of God Save The Queen]

We shall build here,
Hear! Hear!
And those who resist?
Hang! Hang!

Major Reginald Oswald Moffat:

"Dynamite, go carefully there! More fragile than a crate of Cape brandy, you fool! Nothing like dynamite for a good demolition job. Set the wires and take cover at a distance. No coaches run through trees. No rail runs through a hill. Plunge and take cover, Johnny ol' boy! Blow the fish into the air. Blow the hills into powder. What species of fish is that? Drain this causeway, pull up those trees. Hoist the flag here. Where shall our Houses of Parliament stand if not here? And we'll have all our chums over for the opening of Parliament. Chums and cronies! That's how the Empire is built, chums sticking together through thick and thin.

Lieutenant-General Thomas Boyd-Tomkins:

"Law courts with a statue of Good Queen Vexatious in front. Nearly Jubilee time. Rotten Row? Then a market square, of course and some fountains, men will be thirsty governing the colony so a bottle store or two, a tavern tucked out of sight, a theatre for some Gilbert & Sullivan, music hall burlesque to cheer us up. Brothels of course, but don't tell the ladies.

Dr Figaro Macmaster, pigsticker, impresario, land surveyor and lawyer:

"It'll all be legal, signed and stamped. The More Fat Treaty, the Rude Concession, the hut taxes, the cattle taxes, the acquisition and apportionment and husbandry of lands anywhere and everywhere. The Commission into Ancient Ruins to loot the Zimbabwe Ruins, that Phoenician palace of Ophir. The Forestry Commission to raze hardwood forests and miombo woodland, plant up timber for the empire, plantations of wattle, eucalyptus and pine. Pillage and looting is all perfectly legal if you have a valid document wheretofore whereas above mentioned clause into claws hitherto known as the undersigned the underdogs on this day of grace."

"Whereas there shall be peace and friendship between civilised men and these fellow creatures.

"Whereas there shall be no violation of territory on either side."

Military band, still offkey but louder:

We shall build here,
Hear! Hear!
And those who resist?
Hang! Hang!

Legislators, judges, architects (in unison):

"Let's put up some company buildings. The Dutch style will do. Put them on wide grounds and have them on two levels. But now we've chopped down all the local trees and cleared away woodland, the streets look too bare. Sprinkle in some imported jacaranda saplings. Then sprinkle in a lot more. A park or two, streams into ponds and fountains, can't have too many patches of clipped lawn in a city."

Military band, deafening volume to be heard over shouts and cheers:

We shall build here,
Hear! Hear!
And those who resist?
Hang! Hang!

Salisbury City Founders:

Name this street after a soldier, a banker, a painter and a mercenary. Name this school after the Prince and the General and that fort after the King and the Queen. But leave that park there, we'll stroll around it after dark. Brick up the swampy bits, stick in some roses! A gazebo or two, a band playing.

Prisons, no point in law courts and Houses of Parliament without a decent gaol or two. Lock 'em up! Gallows behind the cells, all neat and tidy. Grass verges in front, some bedding plants.

Military band, roaring away:

We shall build here,
Hear! Hear!
And those who resist?
Hang! Hang!

Field-Marshal Edward Pilkington:

What we really need is a jolly inland sea for recreation, a dam for boating, rivers stocked with bass and tiger fish. More settlers of the right sort, more trains with supplies of bully beef, more munitions, rum as well as rotgut brandy. Thank God for steam!

Chaplain to Her Majesty's armed forces:

What puts the wind up me is witchcraft, I don't mind admitting it. Those figures on the kopje, just watching and waiting for us to bugger off. Insurrection. Poison. Devilish mischief. Hang them, shoot them. It has to be biblical, or at least legal. A Witchcraft Suppression Act, that's the ticket.

Military band in disarray but shouting still:

We shall build here,
Hear! Hear!
And those who resist?
Hang! Hang!"

South Anglo Company Men in Unison:

"Whereas a future of boundless industrial development now opens out for this land which, less than a decade before, had been one of the waste places of the earth.

Whereas a great part of these dark lands may be still in the twilight, but there too the glare of civilisation, and the railroad on which it shall ride on, is gradually driving back the shadows which only yesterday shrouded the country in seclusion and mystery."

Hear, Hear!

VaDziva:

"Mbuya Dziva, you who are in the air above and the waters below. Birther of these wetlands. When you sneeze, the ground itself quakes. You whose tears flood the earth itself. We seek passage through these bloodstained fields yet fear to tread with our cracked feet. We who are left, we who fear your wrath.

We who are not ready to join you.

We ask that you speak to us, that you forgive not only us, but those without knees. We have stained the earth from which your breasts rise and from which all emerge, with our blood, and are bound to, at your will, return. We ask that you hear us.

You have been silent for a harvest, we ask that you hear us.

You have been silent for two harvests, we ask that you hear us.

You have been silent for three harvests, we ask that you hear us.

You have been silent... "

8

TIME SWERVES BACK

Whispers in the Deep, 1991

Norman Geoffrey Oswald Moffat lands at Harare International Airport on the British Airways' direct flight from Heathrow. In the terminal he soon spots an elderly man in a dark-blue chauffeur's uniform, flashing a white cardboard placard with 'NGO MOFFAT' printed on it. They drive out of the airport and from the rear of the Land Rover Discovery, Norman gets down to business.

"Say, are you with the embassy or a private shuttle?"

"Embassy."

"Splendid. You got some refreshments in here?"

"No."

"What's your name, fellow?"

"Takawira."

"Taw-ka-ri? Alright then, T., ol' chap, you got an envelope for me, yes?"

"Your envelope is at the apartment."

"Right. Right. Let's get a move on then, shall we?"

Norman folds his arms across his chest and then releases them again with an exasperated sigh. He rolls down a window and loosens his collar. He can't sit still. He leans over and checks the time on the dashboard clock, then sets the William Wood on his wrist to the local time. He stares at it, places it against his ear, listens, taps it with his finger, then

places it against his ear again. It has stopped working. He
sulks back into his seat.

"Say, ol' chap. How about you speed up a bit?"

***

The Queen will be arriving for a Royal visit in four weeks'
time.[21] He's there to make sure it all goes smoothly, schedules
on time, dignitaries seated according to Whitehall protocols.
A lucky opportunity, him being in the right place at the right
time to land a plum job. Previously there had been woman
trouble, an affair with a friend's wife, a clumsy seduction
attempt with police involved. September last year he was
crawling out of lowlife pubs and puking on pavements
around his digs, trust fund under threat, mummy not paying
any more bills, yet now he is on a Foreign Office internship
at the British Embassy in Harare.

***

The old man looks up at the rear-view mirror and Norman
Moffat catches his gaze in the fading daylight. A piercing,
impersonal appraisal. He cannot tell if the old man hates
white people or if he is just rude. Surly or sycophantic,
that's what he has been told to expect. They drive through
the centre of the city and Norman cranes his neck at pub
and nightclub neon signs, skirts in the evening crowds of
pedestrians. He taps his fingers on the arm rest. He checks
his watch again then frowns and leans forward to check the
clock. They catch the last of the traffic leaving the city. They

---

21   The King-in-Waiting visits former and current colonies from time
to time to check that Royal portraits are hung up straight and dusted
regularly. This former colony decides to clean up the capital city, in
preparation for Her Majesty, by evicting people from nineteen "squatter
camps" around the city and dumping them at one big squatter camp about
thirty minutes' drive outside the city.

drive away from the high-rise buildings and up a broad tree-lined street with branches hanging over the road to form a leafy green tunnel of canopy. The old man makes a few more turns and then parks in front of an apartment building with the name Rembrandt Court in letters painted white above the entrance.

The old man grabs the bags and they head into the building. In the lobby, a woman behind a desk greets Norman then asks him to sign for a brown envelope. They go up to apartment 408 in the lift while Norman opens the envelope. Not too shabby.

He tries his luck once more.

"So, you know where a bloke can go to find some girls that want to have some fun, eh?"

Takawira shakes his head.

"Urgh, come on T. ol' chap. Surely you know a couple good spots around town?"

Silence.

"You're a tough one, eh? Don't worry, old chap. Thanks for the ride: I would give you a small tip for your troubles but I don't have any local currency."

Takawira gestures at the brown envelope.

"Oh, it's just twenties in here, sorry. But I'll make sure to put in a good word for you at the embassy."

Takawira sucks his teeth, then turns to walk away but Norman calls out to him.

"So, are you picking me up tomorrow?"

The driver nods, then walks through the door. He almost shuts it behind him but pauses and swings it open again. He lifts his face up to Norman who is still standing near the door and says,

"Women here, daughters and sisters, are not for you to play with."

He slams the door shut.

Norman goes blank for a moment. His feelings shift from confusion to fear, then anger.

He storms to the door and pulls it open. He peers down both ends of the long corridor but the old man is nowhere to be seen.

Norman steadies himself against the door. The last time he felt this shaken he had just started boarding school. In chapel he suspected the Anglican priest had been directing his warnings about the sin of masturbation at him. The same fierce accusatory stare. How can this elderly African man say what he said to him? How could the old chap just disappear in the passages like that? He must ask for a new driver, someone more congenial.

***

In her dream, Natsai is trying to find a way out of Pioneer Park, but her feet keep getting sucked into the muddy grass, a squelchy undertow that feels like a quagmire. Three nights this week she has had this dream and it grows more vivid each night.

Tonight, she did not make it out of the swamp and onto the concrete path. A cold slippery hand grasped at her ankle from the mud. The fingers dug into her skin and the sharp pain forced her eyelids open. Her ankle throbbed as she lay in bed.

***

Months have passed since Natsai encountered the Writer. Her genuine, platonic friendship with Thulani ended the night she allowed the brandy to flow through her veins. That night began a tumultuous cycle of liquid euphoria and a frenzied passing of time between drinking buddies, always followed by self-loathing, regret and hungover shamefulness. The relief, each day, waiting for escape into euphoria either in the Quill Pub, in the bottles in Thulani's apartment, or in her bed. Whatever they had had faded as Thulani withdrew into himself and she sought stiffer relief beyond what they shared in their doomed spiral.

***

Natsai is working late in the offsite archives of *The Tribune*, a building on the corner of Fife Avenue and Second Street. Staff and researchers finish work at 4pm but today she stays behind so she can type out her C.V.

She needs to look around for a new job. Old Head is retiring but she has fallen out of favour with him. He says she is unreliable. That she has wasted her potential. It is unlikely that he will recommend her to take over his desk at the end of the year. She has consistently refused to take on certain assignments, avoiding scenes of political violence or investigations into disappearances. Inside her she carries craters, rubble, cracked and gaping walls, air thick with dust and cordite, and, like some pieces of falling sky, the din of breaking glass. Arriving at any crime scene, she hears the warning cries of wild birds shrieking and beating their wings. Regardless of her recent work record of absenteeism, she has a solid block of experience that most agencies around town will appreciate.

She isn't quite done with the typing but she can't stay too long because then she must walk through the Avenues alone at night. Muggings are rare but she doesn't want to tempt fate. Cutting across Pioneer Park is also dicey once the last shoppers from the Fife Avenue Shopping Centre have passed through and the expanses of grassy lawn and thoroughfares lie deserted. She will get there well after dark and then must cut across the winding paths to her flat in darkness. She is not afraid of the dark but there is a stream that meanders across the park, right down along the middle, and it conjures memories of the footbridge back in Miner's Drift. A stream that has spills over its banks, a boundless unhindered flow of water, a pool with depths unplumbed. The dampness and the wet chill crossing over this city park stream makes her uncomfortable. She has felt the skin down her back prickle and her arms tingle as she steps over the water.

A recurring dream has further set her on edge. In the dream, she is suspended, out of time, dangling over the water as the grey form breaks the surface. Lately, she wakes up in a sweat, unsure of where she is or when it is. Damp chills like tides washing out to her fingers and toes, like the slow concentric ripples radiating out to the water's edge. Something inevitable in those widening circles.

***

Norman looks around the apartment in Rembrandt's Court. He scoffs. He darts into the kitchen and swings open the door of the small fridge. It clicks into a soft whirring. The only contents are a sealed jug of water in the lower half and a tray of ice cubes in the freezer. He slams it shut and swears under his breath. Drags his luggage into the larger bedroom and opens his bags on the bed. He checks out the wardrobe space and hangs up his drip-dry suits and then arranges his underpants, vests and socks in the drawers, in boarding-school style. He sees a telephone beside the bed and decides to call his ex-fiancée in the UK. He looks at his watch and frowns when he remembers that it is not working. He can't figure out the time difference between Britain and Zimbabwe.

It is late afternoon or early evening, he can't understand that it gets dark so early here in summer. A country without winters. He rings the exchange and gets a line out to the UK but the phone rings unanswered; his ex-fiancée must be out. Or still miffed. He decides to take a shower and turns on the water as he undresses, the water spurts out from the showerhead and he can't turn it off. It smells like river water, is tinged reddish as iron, cold, with a bitter unchlorinated taste.

He will complain later but now he just wants to get out of the place.

He goes back into the sitting room and turns on the television set, switches between channels. There are only two. Both are showing news bulletins, one in some local language and the other in English. He switches off the TV and fully takes in the apartment for the first time. He chuckles at the thought of the more secretive agents who had been here before him. The clandestine meetings they must have held, the covert operations they would have conducted. More exciting times. Norman looks around for the brown envelope and spots it on the kitchen counter. He fetches it and pulls out a handful of notes. He does a quick mental calculation to estimate how much it is in English pounds. Unimpressive but enough for a decent time tonight. There is a business card in a folded note with the name Patricia Phillips and the logo of the British Embassy. There is no designation under her name. The writing on the note has an urgent flourish and reads,

"*N.G.O. Moffat, for your convenience. 8am pick-up.*"

He flips the twenty-dollar bills between his fingers then folds them into a wallet and leaves the apartment. The prospect of a little adventure brightens his mood.

There is no-one in the foyer so he heads out onto the pavement. Balmy weather, clear skies darkening. Not as tropical as he'd thought. There are distant city sounds, traffic and sirens. Music throbbing nearby from two separate venues but he cannot tell if they are around the corner or on the other side of the city.

A relief to be out of his rooms, he had had a bad moment there. He feels surprisingly energetic for someone who has been on a longish flight of eleven hours. He's not particularly hungry but knows a good meal and a little fun are what he needs. A car turns the corner down the road and starts coming up towards him. He can see the orange taxi light on the roof and instinctively raises an arm. The taxi pulls over right up to him. He is on the passenger side and the driver leans through and shouts, "Good evening, sir!"

Norman bends down and peers into the taxi and responds, "Know where I can get some decent food around here?"

The cab driver nods his head and says, "Yes. Hotel on the street after this one. Terreskane Hotel."

"How far is it? Can I walk there?"

The man inside the car responds quite cheerfully and tells him, "Go back there. At the corner you turn left. Go straight and then after the second road you will see it on the left side." The driver pauses for a moment and then adds, "I can find for you a girlfriend."

Norman catches on instantly. He rubs his palms and reaches for the door handle. "Just the man I'm looking for. I wish you had picked me up from the airport."

"And you can just give me twenty dollars, isn't it?" The taxi driver smiles up at him.

Norman utters a nervous laugh and stands up straight. "Oh no, my friend. I thought you were just doing me a favour?"

"Yes sir, it's a favour for you. And you can just give me a twenty?"

"Sorry to trouble you, my friend."

Norman frowns and steps away from the cab. He doesn't want to end up paying exorbitant fees to a pimp on his first evening here. He can find someone himself, never has trouble accosting likely prospects in strange cities.

He watches the cab drive away and sets off walking to the right along the pavement. The music is loud now and clearly coming from a venue on the street ahead. He can make out a number of cars and a fair amount of movement outside the venue. An orange neon sign glows into view on the left side of the road. The Terreskane Hotel.[22]

As he approaches the hotel, he makes out the shape of a woman coming out through a gate onto the street. She stands under the light at the gate and is having some difficulty getting it closed. Norman sees her. Luck, he thinks, opportunity

---

22   British-themed pubs have gone through many hands and patrons since the colony ended. Their location has allowed many a bumbling coloniser to unwind from a long day of colonising by pouring himself liberal quantities of brandy or gin and taking women, sometimes with their consent.

knocking! He begins to move in on her, conscious of her youth and something tentative in her movements. He increases his pace, leans forward, his upper body tautens, he assumes a reassuring bland smile and moves in ahead of her to open the latch.

"Hello. Are you okay there?"

Natsai is startled. She had been engrossed in trying to slide the shackle through the slots in the gate and hadn't noticed the man walking up to her. She turns around sharply and stutters a greeting.

"Hello, sir."

"Need a hand?"

"No thanks, it's okay."

"Oh, you don't have to call me sir. Here, let me help you with that."

Natsai isn't sure what to do but she finally gives in. He's just being helpful.

"Now, let me see. What do we have here? Hmmm, where does this go?" He snaps the rod in and it pops back out, misaligned. "Oopsie daisy! Silly me." He scratches his head then has another go with the same result. He glances sheepishly at Natsai then digs in again. "Bloody hell," he mutters under his breath then apologises to Natsai. He props his knee against the gate, aligns it with the frame and then as he figures out his next move, the rod shoots in and the gate holds. "Ha! There it is!"

Natsai hears the click of the mechanism and smiles while looking directly at him. He stands there blinking and grinning, for a moment secretly amused by her confident stare.

"Thanks for the help but I need to get going."

She swings round and takes a couple of steps towards Second Street.

"Wait. Uhmm, so what's your name?"

She carries on walking and turns but not all the way round. "Natsai, but you can call me Petronella."

"Oh, that's an interesting name. What does it mean?" He pulls up level with her on the street side.

"Which one?"

"Well, both I guess."

"Natsai means reparations, but I'll understand if your tongue can't wrap around that."

"Oh my, I can't say I was ready for that answer. I'll see how flexible my tongue is."

Norman shrugs and looks helpless, ready to present himself as a butt for her amusement. A well-practised technique.

"Aren't you going to ask what my name means?"

"I get the feeling you are going to tell me anyway."

"Oh no, I wouldn't impose on you. I'm just a regular old Norman. Did I just say that out loud?"

They get to Second Street and she turns right to avoid walking past the entrance of the Terreskane Hotel. Norman trots up to her, moves ahead and walks a step ahead of her while looking into her face. She's quick on her feet, this one. He'll have to head her off before she gets away.

"Listen, uhmm, Petronella?"

She looks into his face.

"I'm really trying here. Okay, Nasy, Nasy... oh my word, I'm so bad at this."

She stares at him.

"Uhmm, silly me. I was wondering if you would join me for a meal. I was just going across to that hotel there."

"No thanks, Norman. I have to go home. It's late. Maybe next time."

"Where do you live? Maybe I can drop you off there later?"

"But you're walking. How can you drop me off?"

"Oh, we can get a cab to your place. I mean, to drop you off at your place later. I hope you don't think I'm being too forward. I've just landed from England and I just wanted some company."

"Listen, I live quite close, no need for a cab. However, this isn't the place to be strolling around this time of the night."

"I don't follow. Why can't I walk you home? Is this a dangerous neighbourhood?"

"Not really. Not in the way you think. There are loitering laws, women can't be seen walking around the Avenues at night. The police will arrest me."

"Arrest you, just for walking?"

"Let me try and remember the exact charge: *'Loitering with the intent to solicit for the purposes of prostitution'.*"

"That's bloody absurd."

"Indeed. They just want money though. You pay them a bribe and they'll let you go."

"Has it ever happened to you? Being arrested?"

"It happens to all of us at some point. That's why I don't want to walk past that place."

"Good heavens."

Natsai looks at him again and notices how young he is, how gauche. Harmless. The street lighting softens his face and even though she's a bit uneasy, his mention of not being a local makes her curious about him. His eyes light up as he watches her considering his proposition.

"Okay, just for a short time and then I must go home."

Norman Moffat can't hide his excitement. She is dressed so conservatively that she could pass for a woman working behind a desk somewhere or maybe as a teacher at a prep school. The hem of her pencil skirt is just above the knee but no higher. Just the slightest hint of a thigh. Maybe two fingers of a thigh. He should get an exact measure. Not just yet. Maybe after she's had a couple of drinks in her.

They set off across the road and the brighter lights as they get closer to the hotel allow Norman to notice her slight limp. He asks her about it, lowering his voice to sound sympathetic, *you can tell me anything.*

"Oh, it's nothing," she says. "It's just an old injury, the pain comes and goes."

There are working girls strutting back and forth at the entrance to the Terreskane who cluck and suck their teeth when the couple walks in. They sneer at and taunt Natsai. One of the girls says, "Mister, come here. I can give you a nice thing," as she reaches out and strokes his forearm.

"Oh dearie me," Norman grins, clearly embarrassed.

***

The path to the entrance passes a perforated cinder-block garden wall through which Norman glimpses a garden and pool area. They enter a wide lobby with a restaurant on the left side, a small bar on the right and a reception desk straight ahead. More people, more activity, on the pavement outside the hotel than inside, Norman notes. They are all staring at the newcomers. The two women behind the reception desk, the barman and the guy wiping down the counter, the man and woman at the bar, and the waiter who is shuffling towards them with a wide grin on his face. Too much attention. Norman wants privacy, to stay unobserved.

"Hello, sir. Welcome to the Terreskane Hotel. Would you like to have dinner in the restaurant or maybe drinks in the garden?"

"Hello, we're here for dinner. Dinner and a couple of drinks."

"Very good, sir. Please follow me inside the restaurant."

"Eh, Wilfred, is it?"

Norman leans forward and squints at the badge on the waiter's chest.

"Yes sir, Wilfred."

"Right, could we perhaps have dinner in the garden? Is that at all possible?"

"In the garden, sir? Yes, sir. I can bring the food out to you. This way to the garden."

Something to drink and a meal at last. Privacy.

Norman remembers his companion, ushers her ahead of him. He notices her leather heels. Classy, he thinks to himself. Quite unlike the bold bevy with the bright-coloured faces at the entrance. Even in the shadows, with the streetlight falling in patches, the scarlet lips had pushed right under his nose. The rouge on the cheeks and the darkened eyes made him think of Soho walk-ups. They also aroused him. In a manner he couldn't quite figure out, their skimpy dressing and comical sexiness stoked an urge in him. As he walks behind Natsai, he notices her restrained duckwalk and remembers what she said about her ankle. A hint of vulnerability, never a bad thing.

Wilfred leads them along a short passage and they emerge in a walled garden with a swimming pool, thick lawn, garden chairs and tables arranged near the poolside. The air smells of chlorine. Band equipment has been set up on a platform, but no sign of a band and the music is playing through the speakers from a stereo. Wilfred asks them if they want to have drinks at the garden bar next to the pool or if they want to take their table right away. The pool is a kidney-shaped old-style pool, tiled blue with steps at the shallow end and a fountain in the form of leaping dolphins shooting jets of water through gaping jaws, at the deep end. Norman chooses a table near the fountain end of the pool and they weave through and scan over the menu while Wilfred stands at a respectful distance.

"Norman, I will be late if I eat. Just one drink." Natsai reminds him.

"Oh, come on. Don't be a spoilsport."

"It's way past 8pm now. I must go in five minutes."

"But you must eat. Let us order you something and then if you don't feel like sticking around, Wilfred here will wrap it up for you. How's that sound?"

"Okay, that might work."

"Fine then. I'm having this whole spring chicken in a basket. What will you have?"

"I'm stuck between ordering a salad to impress you and stuffing myself with a full chicken."

"Are you trying to impress me, ma'am?"

"You're getting ahead of yourself, my dear fellow."

They both laugh at her attempt at a British accent.

"Okay, why don't you have what I'm having, that way we both suffer if it's bad?" Norman chuckles. It's going better than anticipated.

She agrees, "Okay."

"Very good then. Wilfred?"

"Yes, Sir?"

"Two spring chickens for us and what local beer do you recommend?"

"We have Castle Lager, sir."

"Very well, a Castle Lager for me, and you Natasha?"

"Double brandy and coke for me."

"Oh, I didn't expect that!"

"What did you expect? A girl who says, "I don't drink"? Or who says wine or cocktails? I'm a journalist, Norman."

"Oh, that's interesting. I didn't take you for a journalist."

"What did you take me for?"

"Honestly, I hadn't given it much thought, but I'm pleasantly surprised."

"And what do you do, kind sir?"

"I work for the government."

"On Her Majesty's service, yeah? Double 'O'-seven, innit?" They both laugh again at her accent.

"Yes, well, I'm not a spy or anything like that."

"Is that so? So, are you a teacher or something like that?"

"I work for the Foreign Office, as a cultural attaché."

"Oh, interesting."

Norman gestures to Wilfred who jumps forward and leans over with his ear close to Norman's face, hands clasped behind his back. Norman leans forward and spells out their drinks order to him. The latter grins and nods before turning around and dashing off to the garden bar. He is away for a short while and then comes back with the drinks.

"You're calling me Natasha."

"I beg your pardon."

"My name is Natsai, not Natasha."

"Oh, is that so? I'm sorry. Natasha just sounds easier."

"Just think of reparations, that might make it easier."

"Okay, Nat-sai it is then!"

Wilfred takes an interminable time to bring two whole spring chickens. During that time he sips his beer slowly while watching Natsai liven up and chat more vivaciously, off her guard.

Norman gestures for another round of drinks and Wilfred moves with the swiftness of a waiter expecting a tip to retire on. Wilfred gives Norman an inquisitive, "Something stronger?" look and winks at him; Wilfred nods and shoots off. He comes back with a round of tequila shots. Norman watches Natsai slide lower in her seat and loosen a button on her blouse. He makes small talk and when she gives him elaborate, slightly incoherent answers, he nods and beams, oohing and aahing at appropriate points, making no unexpected moves as yet. Watching himself. She ignores the finger bowl and tucks into the chicken. Wilfred comes back with yet another round of drinks and she takes a break to address him.

"You are very busy at this table, eh uncle?"

Wilfred grins obsequiously and glances at Norman. Norman is chewing slowly and in no rush to respond, his eyes on Natsai. Natsai fills up her brandy glass with Coca-Cola and takes a sip. "Is this still a double shot or are you now pouring with a loose wrist?" Wilfred blinks and grins, moves away.

Natsai gulps down a long draught. The evening has turned oppressive. She tries to get some air between her thighs but the skirt she is wearing is rather tight and so she tries to hike it, but her hands are now greasy, so she slumps back in her chair and carries on eating. Norman Moffat watches her pulling the chicken apart with her strong hands. He follows the movement of the light reflecting off her jaw line and swallows when she swallows. He watches her licking her lips.

She points a gnawed drumstick at him without taking her eyes off her plate. "You know what I'm going to call you from now on? *Watchmore.* That's your new name."

Norman gives her his blandest smile.

Wilfred is hovering when she gets up to go to the bathroom. He moves towards her but she steadies herself and waves him away. The men's leering expressions suddenly make her feel less safe.

"Say?"

Wilfred turns to Norman Moffat's voice.

"She's a good one, hey?"

"Yes, sir. Very good one."

"Say, how much do you reckon she'll ask for? You know, for the night?"

"To marry this one?"

"No man, to take her with me just for the night."

"Ah right, ah this one I don't know, sir."

"But you know what the others charge right? Surely?"

"Ah sir, there outside, on the road, they are… maybe you can pay $5."

"Right, right. Well, we'll see how it goes with Lady Natasha here."

***

There was a swimming pool brimming with dark water and she wanted to slide into it. She devoured a small roast chicken and when she was finished, the bones got up, rolled to the edge of the pool and started chanting:

She dances,
Come see,
In her watery den,
She dances...

summoning the njuzu to the surface. She wanted to shout at the dancing bones and tell them that she wasn't scared of the njuzu. They could do nothing to her. Besides, the njuzu were stuck deep in that muddy stream far away in Miner's Drift and there were always reeds for them to hide in. Here there is paving and mown grass. She is not afraid of those that cannot live out of water. The chicken bones fall at her feet and tell her the njuzu want her. She starts laughing and she kicks them far into the darkness.

Who cries for you, Natsai?

She is startled by this new yet familiar chorus of voices. She feels these voices, more than she hears them. Natsai closes her eyes for a moment and when she opens them again, she's stepping out from the shadows, amber street lights outlining the fence of Pioneer Park. How did she get here? Her heels tap on the concrete path and then she steps onto soft grass and her heels sink in. She hears the same voices whispering.

Who are you?

"I … I … I am Natsai."

The voices breathe in her ear. *What do you find sacred? Who are your people? Why do you pour grief into your troubled spirit?*

As she ponders over these questions, a load begins to lift off her shoulders. Burdens that have dragged her down and weakened her joints. Leeches that have supped from her soul loosen their bite and drop off. She looks down at the ground, towards the source of the voices. Soothing.

Did we not touch you with our hand?

"But … but … you did not take me."

She doubts us. She walks around bearing our mark yet never acknowledging us.

She has the mark. One ear tingles.

There is the mark. Again in the same ear.

She is marked. And now it is the other ear.

The voices unite into one bold enquiry: *Are you not of VaDziva?*

Guilt and remorse and shame flood her senses. The burdens halt their departure.

Your people did not call out your name when we reached out and grasped at you.

Indeed, they still have not pleaded with us. Your people never cried out for you, nor asked us our intentions.

Why did no one lament you? Who leaves their own daughter to seek her own solutions to these troubles of the spirit?

Natsai leans in towards the voices, drawn by the lure of release, physical and emotional.

"I am here. I am here now." She whispers.

The voices disappear.

Everywhere is stillness, cold and silence. She feels the coolness of the earth and then realises water is sliding up over her feet and creeping up her ankles. The cold water burns over the mark on her ankle and it throbs. A hand places webbed fingers over her ankle mark and it's a fit. The throbbing stops.

Fingers loosen the buckles of her shoes and she steps out of them. The soles of her feet are cooled as they contact the soaked earth.

Step forth, child.

The ground gives as the cold water creeps up to her legs and her waist. With her knees now level with the ground, webbed fingers rise up and unclasp her skirt, pulling it down and off to the side.

Leave it all behind, child.

Now up to her waist, the fingers peel off her underwear, rising further up and unbuttoning her blouse.

She gasps.

Enter as you are, child.

Then her belly and her breast, blouse cast away and brassiere unclasped and discarded. Her troubles of the surface world bound in the removed garments, the long cool fingers rise up to her neck.

The njuzu whisper in her ear:

She dances,
Come see,
In her watery den,
She dances...

There, in the darkness of the park, a medium forms that is at once a murky pool and a spiritual being. In a cold embrace, the njuzu drag her body downward. For a brief moment she sees herself outside her body, hovering, suspended and weightless. A tingling numbness washes over her body and then the descent begins. She is dragged from the surface and right down into the soaked earth. Mud squelches around her, lets her pass through.

Her passage into the underground covers her nakedness in the sackcloth of the forlorn. The one-piece garment of those who seek atonement.

Grass goes wild and drifts up through the soles of her feet as she sinks down. Down through buried roots of trees, boulders, veins of ore she tumbles. She falls through rain, fountain, spray, chlorinated water, sewers, the polluted stream, the rising river and buried wetland. She falls like spilled water or a fragment of grit, deeper and deeper, the njuzu holding her limp hand in their grasp. The earth is not solid, it gives way, she is a chip of small grain fallen off a grinding stone, she is both germ and seed, she is still herself but falling and following. Water rises to meet her, gravity has no force in this domain. She forgets who she has been, she remembers what might have been, she sees clearly despite the murky depths. The njuzu's grasp speaks to her as flux, as memory, as resistance. She is, at once, here in the now, and also back in time, suspended in that void over the stepping stones at the small pool. Down further through conduits, weirs, the river bed, down into caverns and spiraling passages, coil upon coil shaking loose.

Who sings your lamentation, child?

Another swift tug and she submerges further, sucked into a deep water-filled labyrinth. She asks the njuzu where they are going but they ignore her and drag her down through the watery maze. In the darkness of this downward journey, she shivers and breathes in a new, fluid medium; deeper water chills through her and she is now in tow, turn after turn along flooded passages and tunnels. Again, she pleads with the njuzu to tell her where they are going but they do not respond. The sensation she felt walking across the stream as a child crawls over her and once again she smells the muddy water of the stream and steaming white bread in its packet. Time slows down, circles and widens. They drop deeper, into a cavern and settle, she is now at her destination. She sits in the darkness weeping now, a child again, a grown woman, someone in flux. Her salty tears diffuse into the water as they seep out. *If she doesn't return home, then her mother will think she was out acting irresponsibly and bringing shame to the family. And what will her mother tell the other church mothers?*

She weeps in the wet darkness. She weeps for answers. Her face always upturned, looking up to the surface high above. That distant iridescent surface is the future. Time passes and she waits. She begs for release. She weeps. She longs for the surface and more time passes. She is weighed down from the inside. Unchained but bound to the bottom of the cavern. Now and then mbira notes drift in, accompanied by ngoma and hosho, descending from the surface and echoing through the passages, with voices ululating, calling and responding. Endless loops pass and the njuzu select a captured spirit and sometimes a body from the many caverns spread throughout the channels. Those captured spirits whose people sing, dance and imbibe for them. Those who call their names.

Now in her den the sun rises,
She dances,
There she glides out,
As she dances.

As the sound of dancing feet reverberates through the maze and the music reaches a crescendo, the njuzu free a spirit or a body from the cavern floor and they rise towards the surface, towards the voices summoning them. Natsai stays rooted in her place at the bottom looking up as looping notes float down towards her, waiting for her name to be called.

9

Green Notes, 2016

You are sitting in a mshika-shika with your bag on your lap and open armpits on either side. You've made it. You, Jedza, are finally on your way to the Avenues to take up the flat that Loveness has offered you. The place where Sisi Natsai vanished. Mystery and opportunity beckon.

Your mind has been hemmed in by the dark winds spinning through Chenga Ose and you now free yourself of them with each exhaled breath. The journey is familiar: you've shuttled often between Chenga Ose and the city but this trip has the weight of a final departure. Excited about starting over again, yet anxious about starting over yet again. Andy Brown's song has been looping in your head all morning. It began with the hwindis shouting "Toenda here? Brothaz, toenda here kuTonaz?" as you waited in the road for a mshika-shika. Since then you have been humming the chorus to *Ndoenda* and, as the song goes, *you have no intention of going back*. None whatsoever. You send Loveness a Whatsapp text letting her know that you are now in the city.

The mshika-shika drops you off downtown in the Market Square area and you weave through the crowds up to Rezende Street to catch a kombi to the Avenues. You hope that Loveness has not changed her mind, send her another message just to make sure. Is she seeing anyone else? You try to picture the flat in your head, assure yourself that

anything is better than Chenga Ose. You grip the straps of
your backpack, keep up with the flow of pedestrians. The
fast-moving feet on uneven pavements. Raucous banter. The
car horns hooting. You're glad Chenga Ose is behind you.

***

We who traverse these city zones year in and year out have
vague memories of Rezende Street being an orderly bus
terminus. What we see now is a congested commuter taxi
rank adjacent to shops selling tightly packed and haphazardly
arranged cheap clothing imports, hair-grooming products
and electronic gadgets.

***

Dhindindi Dreams Drink-And-Go Pub comes up on your left
and you consider walking in for one or two beers to numb
the usual hangover but the stench from a waste skip near the
doorway catches in your throat. A choking sensation. You
cough, come close to retching and as you move your hand
away from your mouth, you see an open casket leaning against
the skip, empty, with its frayed satin lining hanging out and
blowing in the wind. You blink at the image and turn away. On
your right, a spool of Christians unwinds from the first floor of
a corner building at the northern end of the street, the Upper
Room of Our Saviour Ministries, and you shake your head at
the elation in their voices. It takes concentration to thread one's
way along the pavement, twisting this way and that between
vendors whose wares unroll from shop windows and spill
over into the road. Men and women with narrowed eyes scan
passersby like long-beaked herons stalking insects, dart forward
to coax the gullible into getting a set of passport photographs.[23]

---

23   Depending on The Ministry's mood, priorities and the corruption
levels of the prevailing chefe, and how much you pay, a passport may take
anything from three days to two years before it's ready for collection.

***

Harare city is this living and breathing thing. It has a pulse, beating to its own rhythm, offbeat and setting its own time. The people on the street, vending and shouting for commuters, dance to the tune. The faceless councillors in the city hall break the rhythm, they drum colonial marches in a city that is pumping out a new vibrant beat, daily.

We here in the city have constant thoughts of leaving the country for any place that is habitable. For us, anywhere else is a step forward, staying is a step backwards. Will this city, or anywhere within these borders, ever be far enough away? We ask, "How much for a set of photographs?" The women we address give us a quick keen-eyed sweep and then, with no emotion showing, venture: "$5." We mumble, "Thank you," and start off. They trail us for half a block and only turn back after we still don't relent on their last offer of $2.

***

The Rezende Street rank in the morning, shortly before noon, when the sun is directly overhead. There is no shade cover, no respite from the glare. Bus shelters were vandalised long ago and what remains are skeletal frames of smooth round poles. Street kids hang from them like hanks of drying yarn shaken by wind. In dimmer light, they might have been starving birds picking at a bony carcass. You walk across the concourse at the bottom of the street and skirt around a few benches placed around a barren musasa tree. Leafless shattered trees in a dusty lot. The area is bare and gritty and does not receive any shade from the buildings around it.

***

The city may be falling to pieces but the hustle and vitality of the desperate is undiminished. We remember the Facebook posts and Whatsapp forwarded messages from a few months ago, when protesters set off on marches along the city streets. Recorded on shaky handheld videos of people peering from the side of the street, from parked cars, in shop fronts and doorways, videos taken from cell phones as onlookers stared down from high-rise office buildings. We remember the weary faces of pensioners who had been queueing outside banks for hours for their monthly stipend, turning to look at the spectacle.[24]

"WE REFUSE, TO BE TOLD, WHAT TO DO, BY HALFWITS!" The protesters chanted, as they evaded teargas canisters and raised police batons.

***

Your humming stirs up the hanks of yarn hanging on the skeletal frame of the bus shelter. They take off from the metal piping and flutter into white storks. You recall the beating of the wings from your nights in Chenga Ose: your chest tightens. The birds scatter in different directions opening out into a widening spiral. You squint at feathers falling out in their wake and trace them floating down onto the hot tarmac. You reach out a hand to receive a falling feather. It spirals down into your open palm and crumbles into a fine powder on contact.

A hwindi is touting, "Those going to Mount Pleasant, come here! All passing through The Avenues, come!" The broad-faced woman you shall soon come to know as Sisi Stella hands you one of her two plastic shopping bags then positions her frame at the opening of the sliding door, trying to figure out which seat to heave onto. *You have to ask men to help you these days*, you hear her mutter. She tells the hwindi

---

24   Once in a while, for shits and giggles, and also to put USD in their pockets, and the pockets of their buddies and family, The Ministry will print money and crash the entire economy. Good folks will lose all their income and savings, moan and groan, then carry on just like they did the previous time. A few will protest.

that she is getting off close by, "At the maize," so she doesn't want to sit too deep into the kombi. She tells you that she wants your window seat as she is an older woman and you back down when she glares at you. The vehicle sways to the right slightly when she pulls herself in, then steadies again. The hwindi yells and beckons to other likely prospects and the sun blazes down. A girl in the seat behind you fans herself with a pamphlet advertising Huawei phones. She brushes your ear with her pamphlet, whispers an apology which might possibly be an opening to approach her but you're uncertain of your chances. The girl taps Sisi Stella on the shoulder and greets her with a small wave.

"Ah it's you," says Sisi Stella and turns back to the front.

The rows fill up steadily with the tout peeking in at intervals and urging you to cram yourselves in four per seat. You fight off nausea, inhaling the sour odours of midday sweat, dirty upholstery and boiled salted peanuts. The sun's glare on the window glass is barred and harsh, blinding. The hwindi calls out to the driver and he saunters over and gives him a wad of notes with the assumed value of US$0.50. The driver gets behind the wheel, ready to get his show on the road, make up for lost time. A different tout worms his way into the full commuter taxi and, while leaning just inside the taxi, reaches behind him and tugs at the sliding door. The door grates reluctantly, before jamming in its tracks. The leaning man bucks his behind against the door and on the third movement it jumps off its hinges and crashes onto the street. The new tout steps backwards out of the kombi and with the help of a passing boy who keeps demanding payment for his labour, they lift the door back onto the track groove and manage to slam it shut.

Silence follows. A weightless interlude: some passengers have their notes ready in their hands and some stare blankly ahead; some sit still, drowsy in the heat; some fidget on their phones. You hear a chorus floating in from all around you. Music filtering in from above and below; it drifts away as swiftly as it came in. Your ears pick out mbira notes and you

wonder who might be playing mbira in the city at this time
of day in the glare of noon. Then you shake your head; these
are just lingering memories from the broken place you have
left behind. The empty casket appears again, this time laid
out on top of the skip, strips of torn satin lining hanging
out in ribbons from the inside and crumpled in a pile on the
ground. A pair of wet footprints appear from invisible feet,
the prints drying up and disappearing before your eyes.

***

We sit in silence as the kombi driver takes one look to the left,
sees a wave of traffic bearing down and then swerves into the
road anyway. We passengers grip the edges of our seats and
pump imaginary brakes as the taxi cuts across four lanes of
oncoming traffic and comes to a sudden stop at the Julius
Nyerere Way intersection. The guy at the sliding door breaks
the spell: "Let us put the bus money together, my parents."
And so we move our hands in and out of our pockets; notes
are exchanged and taxi fare is passed forward to him. Moist,
browned and crumpled dollar bills are unfolded and handed
over. Green notes assigned the value of two dollars are pulled
out and passed forward.[25] Bills are dropped into cupped palms,
shifted across seats and passed backwards and forwards. The
tout is hunched over by the sliding door with the length of
his body following the curve of the roof and his eyes peering
closely at the exchanges, hands flicking notes as he counts.
He asks, "How many on this? How many on this dhora? How
many on this ten dhoraz? How many on this Bond note?" He
straightens up and neatly stacks the notes together. He notes

---

25   When the former governor of the Reserve Bank of Zimbabwe was
asked how the state funded a farming inputs programme, he boasted
about vague "internally generated resources". They printed, ladies and
gentlemen. They printed bills on paper worth less than single-ply toilet
rolls, in the process shooting the exchange rate and inflation into the
highest rates ever experienced by a country not at war in the history of
humankind. Internally generated poverty is what that was, if you ask me.

who has paid with what and who is owed what change, then turns his head forward and starts chatting with the driver through the gap between the two front headrests. Turns back and while staring at us, enquires in a low threatening voice, "And those ones who have not yet paid?" We do not flinch. We also refuse to be told what to do by half-wits. He swings back and picks up his conversation.

***

You begin to relax as the kombi weaves up Julius Nyerere Way and then across Samora Machel Avenue. Your eyes are drawn towards the spurting fountains as you pass Blackwood Park. Bodily forms, sinuous and wavering, rise and fall in the spray in that glimpse of time's dissolve. You pass the National Gallery and then turn left onto Second Street at the NSSA building, without pausing at the STOP sign. The spire of the Roman Catholic cathedral, over to the right on Fourth Street, flashes in between buildings. Further down behind the kombi, from the town end of Second Street, the Anglican Cathedral spire pierces the horizon. Sun hot on the back of your neck, window glass blurry. More tricks of the light?

You have now entered the Avenues district of the city.

You pull out your phone and text Loveness. Tell her you hope she's at her flat. You watch the blue ticks appear and wait for a reply. She is online. She has read your message. She doesn't respond.

Now on Second Street, the driver crosses Herbert Chitepo Street and then slows into congested traffic outside the old Terreskane Hotel. You have heard of it. The older guys still call it "paTK", even though it has changed names over the years. They still joke about some girl who spent or stole their entire paycheck in one night in that hotel. Even now, in the middle of the day, women in short dresses linger at the entrance. One flashes her thighs at a passing car.

The left lane is blocked by stationary kombis, mshika-shikas and pick-up trucks. Vendors, pickpockets and

commuters with maShangani or Ghana Must Go bags, are
milling around. Groups of young men running and yelling
after kombis; touts pursuing travellers with requests to
get into this or that kombi; drivers yelling at each other;
passengers snatching back their luggage from overzealous
hands; irate drivers hooting at the commotion. Vendors
shove their takeaways through the window, right into Sisi
Stella's face and she curses at them. An ice-cream vendor
selling two ice-creams for one dollar thrusts his arm in your
direction and you jerk back, turn your face away. Across the
pavement can be seen two municipal police officers leaning
against a wall, uninterested in the disorder.

   The council tried arrests, harassment, bribes and have
now run out of ideas. Kombis are not in the rule books they
inherited. The kombi guys are dancing to a new tune and the
Harare City Council is fiddling around with a broken turntable.
Harare is bursting at the seams while the city fathers stuff sleep
in their pipes and smoke away the city's possibilities.

                           ***

We stare out of kombi windows into the broken light and see
gunnaz standing along a high wall behind a line of jacaranda
trees. Silence descends on our kombi as we pass this stretch
of road. Our eyes glance nervously at the gunnaz, the security
wall with its visible surveillance cameras and the rooftops
jutting through at intervals. The Ministry of Goats, Green
Maize and The Girl Child.

                           ***

The driver's in a hurry, muttering and slamming his steering
wheel when forced to slow down, and with Chinamano
Avenue coming up you clear your throat and direct a bold
"At the maize," to the hwindi.

   He looks back and asks, "Did someone say, 'At the maize?'"
which you confirm. He gets the driver's attention, repeats

your stop and then reaches out to thump the roof of the kombi twice. The driver doesn't reduce speed until you are right on Chinamano Avenue and then he swerves to a stop. The hwindi slides the door open and hops out. A couple of other passengers step out of the kombi so you can make your way out. One of them is Sisi Stella, and she instructs him, "You can give me my change now." He asks her, "Mathaz, are you dropping off here?" and she replies yes and that she wants her change. You have stepped out onto the pavement. The girl with the Huawei pamphlet has also stepped out and is walking into Chinamano Avenue. Sisi Stella stands unmoving between the scrawny fellow and the open sliding door of the commuter taxi. The driver, keen to get on his way, peers back towards the two of them with his arm slung behind the front passenger seat. The tout looks Sisi Stella over, sucks his front teeth loudly and then counts out a mixture of green notes assigned a value of two dollars and one-dollar bills. He thrusts the notes towards her and attempts to step past, but she stands her ground.

"What is this? Give me real money, do you hear me?"

Frowning, she places a firm hand on the door and ignores the handful of notes held out to her. The hwindi glances around him and then withdraws his hand while mumbling into his T-shirt.

"What did you just say?"

Sisi Stella stares him down. A stare implacable as the sun in your eyes.

He continues to replace the green notes with US one-dollar bills while assuring her that she did not hear anything. "We all have to use this new money. This is the money that is now here, mathaz."

"If I give you real money, you give me back my change in real money, little boy."

Triumphant, she then steps out onto the pavement. The tout hops back into the kombi and slides the door shut as the driver pulls off. The girl with the Huawei pamphlet has slowed down and Sisi Stella catches up with her. You stand there watching the two of them talking at the corner. They appear to know each other quite well and the indomitable Sisi Stella seems to be instructing or chastising the girl. You cannot make out the words.

Another kombi pulls up next to you and a hwindi beckons to you, "Shall we go, brother? Shall we go? One who is travelling alone?" The hwindi shouts at the driver, "He doesn't want, this one" and the kombi pulls away. You're left gagging in a cloud of exhaust fumes, coughing as a bitter taste rises up in your throat. Which route to take now?

You pull out your phone again. A belated reply from Loveness; she's waiting at the flat. Your heart sinks, the optimism and resolve you had in the mshika-shika now a rancid taste in your mouth. The roaring bustle of the city streets clashes with the rising chorus of doubting voices in your head.

The question you have been asking yourself over and over again takes on more urgency and fear: *Where are you going?* You have been humming to yourself, "*ndoenda, ndoenda*" but now you are not so sure about your destination. The song in your head is about departure. At this moment, you are faced with arrival. Further down the street, your fellow passenger with her Huawei pamphlet is now on her own and has stopped to look around and get her bearings. Another newcomer in the Avenues? There's a light box with the Castle Lager logo and the name *Jacaranda Vibes Bar*. Dry-mouthed, you swallow hard at the promise of relief. The quarreling voices in your head simmer down in anticipation. You swing your backpack over your shoulder and tell yourself you're going to have just one drink, only one, before going to the flat.

10

Names & Faces:

The Avenues, 2016

This place is different. Not as slow and backward as Miner's Drift, thank the ancestors, nor as desperate as Chenga Ose. Your flat in the Avenues, sublet from Loveness, is a cramped hole in the ungainly red-brick compound at the end of Fourth Street. Its location allows you to brag that you now live in the city, as long as those you're bragging to don't know the place and never visit. Rastaz loiter outside, at the corner of Chinamano Avenue and Fourth Street, from mid-morning to late afternoon. And from dusk until a short while before sunrise, two or three working girls patrol the junction. The rastaz do not bother anyone. Neither do the girls. The latter will sometimes greet men walking by.

"Ko ndeipi?"

And if they respond, one of them may suggest,

"Ko handei ka kushort time?"

***

I walk down to the corner and there are five or so rastaz milling about. One in a black graduation gown, who proceeds, without ceremony, to tell me the prevailing black-market rate for US dollars in each of the three forms of local currency, together with the reasons for yet another overnight change.

Two rastaz are sitting on concrete blocks and another two are selling ironing boards and water-heating buckets. The lingering sweetish odour of cannabis greets me on my approach. A glance around and I notice the droopy eyelids, red beady eyes unfocused, the lazy smiles. The graduate is holding a pack of airtime cards and so I nod to the rest, and ask him,

"Ndeipi rastaz, ndipo $5 yeCallnet?"

Quick exchange and I'm walking back to the flat. The rastaz keep the corner tidy. Sure, the council bin is overflowing but the excess rubbish is piled up neatly at the base. Strewn along the path though, in the wall recesses and in between the protruding roots of the jacaranda trees lining the road, are plastic Broncleer bottles, empty condom wrappers, broken beer bottles and cracked blackened glass pipes with white crystal residue.

After a few trips I start greeting the rest of the corner rastaz. It was bound to happen, I walk or run past them two or four times a day. My pattern has been consistent for the past couple months: I'm holed up indoors, usually listening to vinyl records, sometimes fixing and most times juicing up electrical connections and walking to the corner gives me a break from my thoughts. There are two regulars. The rastaz who sells airtime in the black gown – if he wore glasses he could pass for a third-year student.[26] And then there is the rastaz with the banana cart. The airtime rastaz has the hint of a chiChewa accent to his Shona. It comes through in his lengthy explanations of treasury bills, nostro accounts, arbitrage and the folly of the reserve bank's official exchange rate. I ask him for his name and he replies, "Professor." He stands there grinning in his gown waiting for me to get it. He is high as fuck. The next few times the other rastaz hear

---

26   In an alternate universe, or a better life, Profe could have indeed been a university professor: he could have done his PhD in economics or something. In this lifetime however, his best bet would be to join and rise up through the ranks of The Ministry and receive his doctorate by making a highly-placed phone call to the University Chancellor.

me call him Professor they laugh and insist that I call him "Profe" as they all do. I also learn that Professor is indeed his real name.

Profe and Banana Cart Guy are the mainstay of the group. The other two or three positions seem to be reserved for random visitors. It becomes something of a routine: as I approach, Profe starts smiling as he reaches into his pouch for Callnet vouchers while updating me on the shortcomings of the Reserve Bank governor's monetary policy. Banana Cart Guy has taken to addressing me respectfully as Mukoma – it fits, I'm noticeably older than them. Banana Cart Guy is high more often than the rest.

***

One morning, you wake up with Mapfumo's *Mugarandega* stuck in your head. Another one of those records that your old man played when he was in a melancholic mood. This is not your first time living alone, but being in this city gives the song new meaning. The lyrics roll off your tongue as you lean into the warmth of the sun on your small balcony:

Tell me where the others have gone,
I am left here, living alone,
This is poverty, forebearer of us children,
Now that I am left here, living alone,
Now I long to go where others are,
Left here, all alone.

You walk down to the corner to buy airtime but Profe is not there, absent for the first time in months. Banana Cart Guy isn't there either, but it is still early. He usually arrives after 10:30am or so. Two temporary rastaz are there. You don't recognise these faces. You enquire about Profe but they are too high to understand my questions. One is barely standing, meaning he is on his feet but teetering on the tips of his toes. "Aka sticker," as Profe puts it. Barely sticking to the surface of reality. The high has a fistful of his knotty hair, pulling him up into the sunlight, his ancestors reaching from below the earth, keeping his feet on the ground. One moment he is square on his feet, the next he is almost tipping over his toes. He recovers from the forward position and in the next breath he is almost tipping over sideways. He carries on this delicate swaying dance with his eyes closed and jaw clamped shut, the angled lines of the muscles in his jaws etched in sharp relief. He couldn't open his mouth if he tried. His fellow is sitting on a concrete block in similar condition, rocking as if shaken by winds, but the seat allows him to dance less precariously. An empty bottle of Broncleer cough syrup lies crushed under one foot. The culprit, this time though, is musombodhiya, that short-tempered moonshine in the water bottle of the seated rastaz.[27] You go down two streets and buy airtime from the guard outside The Pointe Restaurant instead.

Later that day you walk past the corner again and Banana Cart Guy is now there. You ask him about Profe and his face turns sad. He says that Profe is not feeling well and that he has decided to go home. Home is somewhere on the outskirts of the city; he doesn't know where exactly. A sombreness hangs over the corner crew. The two dancers are now both seated on the concrete block, leaning lazily against each other for support. Profe is so ill that he has had to go back home. The story sounds morbidly familiar – he had complained about a persistent headache the previous week. You leave the corner with its solemn inhabitants.

***

---

27   The youths of the city will always find substances to blow their minds open. If it's not a distilled spirit of unknown concentrations – zed, kachasu, musombodhiya or tototo, then it's sniffed glue or smoked mbanje, bronco for the codeine, or the baddest and most recently arrived fucker of them all, kranko, mutoriro or guka: crystal methamphetamine. In the parlance, any gun can shoot.

Back in my flat I text Never. I have kept him updated on my move from Chenga Ose to the Avenues. He and Loveness may well mention me in their chats but I let him know what's happening, nonetheless. The alliances on this street corner remind me of my friendship with Never. If we had grown up in the city, would we be hustling together on this corner? If I had not left, would I be with him passing time in the Contaz? It is no secret that between the two of us, Never has his life sorted. He is a young guy who *has his things together*, as I so often overheard from the women about town. He could have any girl he wanted and there is no shortage of eager ones lining up to be married by him. Never's main concern seems to be choosing where to spend his money and with whom. It would be nice to not have to worry about money. To not have him tell me that I worry too much about everything, while he buys our beers and decides how fast we drink and when.

***

On the ground, in the Avenues, beneath the canopy of jacaranda trees, the commerce is personal. Girls sell sex wrapped in Rezende Street fashions, taxi drivers chat outside bars that have seen better times, vendors sell fruits and vegetables from their carts and sweets and cigarettes from upturned boxes, airtime vendors stand at every other corner, ice-cream vendors cycle and ring their bells on hot days and sometimes on cold days, while middle-aged men guard the entrances to residential complexes.

***

On the third day of Profe's absence, a guy stands at the corner in an orange bib selling airtime. I reckon he is one of the two swaying faces from a couple days before. He seems awkward in his new position. He doesn't have adequate stock and I watch him run out of Cellutel vouchers. Despite my own low-grade hangover, I'm patient with him. I wait for him to calm down and to stop being confused and then I buy my airtime and stroll back to the flat.

The gloom at the corner persists. I cannot shake off the heaviness that lingers in my heart from Chenga Ose and at times I feel as if I have brought it along with me. A familiar despair that I feel in their presence.

I take to enquiring about Profe from Banana Cart Guy and this is easy because over the past few months I have made sure that I only buy airtime and bananas from this corner. The news is the same. No news. A bad wind has drifted in and settled. An air heavy with foulness. An air the elders would say needs to be cast out. Air like sickness that rears its head when you neglect your guardians, forget your ways and leave the gates open for malevolent spirits to wander in.

Two more weeks pass. Time is not on my side.

**

Profe comes back on a Wednesday. Banana Cart Guy is ecstatic. His excitement breaches the numbness of the cannabis and the Broncleer. The stand-in airtime guy is not wearing a bib. He is clowning around with Banana Cart Guy.

"Profe is back, Mukoma, look at him!"

Banana Cart Guy grabs your arm and pulls you around to greet the returnee. Someone has brought a little portable radio, one of those jobs that run on solar power and Killer T is screeching out:[28]

Of those who stand around me, who are my friends?
Show me, So I see,
And when you hear me plead, Glory to the heavens,
Answer me, So I know,

---

28   If one identifies as a rastaz then it is only fair that one also listens to Zim Dancehall, the quintessential beat of the disenfranchised urban youth. Appropriated from Jamaican dancehalls and repurposed for the city that never sleeps.

Who around me has that love, Of Mother Mary,
Show me, I need to see,
Who is on my side, In these dark times?

Profe is slouched on one of the temporary seats. Head recently and crudely shaven. His face is hollowed out. Gaunt. He looks years younger, not in a good way. A kid brother to his old self. His eyes are clear and large but they hold long vacant stares. You stand in front of him and Profe stares at nothing. Seconds tick by. At a stroke, recognition lights up on his face and a weak smile strains through. Profe tries to state the exchange rate but his mind draws a blank. He attempts to tell you the latest motivations of the Goat Department of The Ministry, but his brain is weary. You joke and tease and then Profe tires of the smiles and just sighs and leans back in exhaustion. His face rests in a spot of sunlight but that does not mask the ashen pallor dusting his skin. He leaves the corner early.

Later, after he has gone, you walk back and chat with Banana Cart Guy.

"Profe varwara," he says. "He is weak. He is not himself."

***

The heaviness in your heart now clouds your thoughts. Troubled sentiments on the street echo within you and words form from the sadness. Profe labours to reach his corner for three more days and then he disappears again. You hear your melancholy as a chorus of sombre voices. Death halts its retreat, turns around and stares back at the corner. It starts creeping back along the broken pavement under the jacaranda trees; this time not caring to hide in the shadows. It takes bold steps over the large roots which have erupted through the pavement. Jacaranda branches sway and creak in its wake on this windless day, then cease to gesture and take on the stiffness of pallbearers. Wandering spirits tug at the branches and dance on the leaves. Drifting homeless spirits of the migrants from foreign lands, whose journeys led them to what is now the Avenues, now marooned here as mashavi. They blow a chilled breath in your face and even though you look away, you concede in your heart that there is no hope left here. Defeat weighs down the branches. It drops down onto your shoulders and crawls into your shirt and down your spine.

As Mapfumo laments:

This is the strife of the landless,
Those whom the ancestors have abandoned,
Where are they to lead us?
Who shall whisper advice in our ears?
And now our sisters are departed, dying in poverty.

Banana Cart Guy confesses to you, "Profe rushed his return. We could see that he is not well yet. He should have stayed home a while longer, recuperating."

***

A week goes by. The replacement rastaz comes back and this time he is more confident. There is permanence in his posture at the corner. Pungent cannabis fumes blow up from the corner every day. And from the small speaker, Killer T sounds louder:

This darkness is relentless, we need some light,
Show me, So we see,
Our cries do not cease, we need change,
Answer us, So we know,
Now we cannot tell what is good and what is evil,
Show us, So we see,
Give me the blessings, that others receive,
Show me, So I see.

***

Banana Cart Guy arrives at 11am, is blown and singing along by 11:30am. His face lights up when he sees me and later in the day, he trusts me to trade with pedestrians while he attends to motorists who are inching by in slow rush-hour traffic.

"Mukoma, these ones, these ones here you can sell six for one dhora."

"These small ones, my guy?"

"Those small ones, Mukoma."

"But my guy, how does that work? How can I sell the smaller ones for more money than the bigger ones? You're now playing clever town games, eh?"

"Ah Mukoma, trust me, the people know these small sweet ones. They are called manzarayapera, the hunger-finishers. Just watch."

"Horaiti, and these regular ones, how much?"

"Ah those ones, sell ten for one dhora, as we do every day."

Our conversations get longer and I start to recognise what I thought was a temporary or transient gang is more than that; no, it is the same four guys coming together day after day.

***

Profe reappears after three weeks. He looks much better than he did when he left the second time. His cheeks, neck and head fill out over the following weeks. I give Profe a while to settle back into his rhythm. I don't want to seem intrusive. We are not friends though I do feel a fair level of familiarity. Even after all these months Profe is still skittish, distrustful. Banana Cart Guy is more relaxed and lets me operate his cash till. His is a blend of trust, drunkenness and a laid-back personality. Profe shares the drunkenness but not the trust and nonchalance.

He pulls up a beaming smile. It comes up easily and sits on his face comfortably. But it has a narrow range and when I carry an exchange beyond pleasantries, his exchange-rate dissemination and a purchase, an anxiety reaches up in Profe's jaw and draws the smile down into an awkward grin. I can't muster up the courage to ask Profe about his illness. The sterile grin comes up early in every exchange – until one day when I get to the corner to find him animated and talkative. I am unsure what substance or combination has him this cranked up but there is a clue sticking out of his pocket. I come down to the corner and find him floating on cannabis fumes in a bid to come down from the glass pipe. I ask him to turn down the volume of Shingirayi's chanting:

I almost died!
So close to death!
So close to death, but by grace I'm raised!
A dead man walking!
Oh Mother, I came close to dying!

and tell me about his illness and disappearances. Something about his fortunes resonates with my own wanderings.

"Mukoma, you know the old woman who sits on that corner … apo pana Third Street apo?"

I ask, "Which corner?"

Profe leans backwards and then crouches before pointing through the narrow band of midday jacaranda shade to the corner down the road.

I nod in exaggerated recognition.

"Ah, Mukoma, the day I fell ill a second time, it was a horror movie, I tell you. There I was, walking down to catch the kombi into town when that gogaz called out to me to stop. 'Let me bite your ears, my child,' she said. And I thought to myself, 'ah'.

"Now you know kuti that muchembere uya doesn't just talk to anyone ka, so I was a bit startled, and I start thinking to myself, 'Which one is this one?' So, I stop but leave a distance between myself and her. She just says it straight out, that I am not well and the hospital medicine will not fix the pain in my head."

Profe pauses, drags on his joint and then exhales a long plume of smoke before settling down on one of the concrete blocks.

"Are you with me, Mukoma?"

I mirror him absentmindedly and sit facing him.

"Mukoma," he continues, "muchembere uya told me that there are swirling waters beneath this place and that they are rising. And that when they rise then we must all know this is happening and be careful where we walk. She told me that she is an old person and she has seen a lot of things in her life. She told me that those from below are trying to speak to me, and that is why I do not feel well."

Profe pauses.

"You see where this is going, Mukoma?

"I was now confused and I heard this whining sound in my ears. You know how your ears can just go 'nswiiiiiiiiiii' sometimes when you hit that top guka? Yah, like that. I carried on standing there looking at the gogaz on the crate and I didn't know what to do. She told me that if I don't believe her, I must walk on to the Second Street corner and look for the odd tree at that corner, the musasa tree.[29] 'Look around the tree, see if the ground around it is wet,' she said. 'Rub your hands on its bark and make an offering to it.'

"You know me, Mukoma, I was now thinking what are these horror films that this gogaz is getting me into. But I was just stuck there. I opened my mouth but she leaned over quickly and placed her hand over my mouth, and then removed it to whisper, 'They will not rest until they have taken many.' Then she turned away from me and dropped her head forward over her knees. Nothing to see but the top of her head. I was dismissed. After that I thought to myself, ah Profe, there is no harm in trying this, all that we do eventually leads to death anyway. I turned and hurried down the street. I got to the corner of Second Street and waited for any kombi going into town.

---

29   The myth of the musasa tree from whose branches Mbuya Nehanda was hanged is one that is so strong that when the tree was finally felled by yet another car crashing into it, the State provided a slow-moving police escort following the chopped-up tree to its final resting place. P.S. She was not hanged from a tree.

"Do you want to know the funny thing? While I was standing there, with these horrors circling in my head, I couldn't resist taking a quick look across the road. You know me, I *know* these trees. I didn't grow up in a town like these 'born locations' I spend the whole day with here. I've spent my life keeping company with trees. The first tree on the other side was a jacaranda like all the regimented trees lining these streets. Then I saw the odd-shaped smaller tree next to it. My jaw tightened and I started to turn away, but then I saw the girl who was standing next to the tree reaching into her bag. Same time, a kombi slowed down and pulled up right in front of me and the hwindi jumped out and told me to sit in front. You will not believe me if I tell you that I couldn't even move. My eyes were just stuck on this girl and when the kombi pulled away, I remember the pissed-off hwindi shouting at me. I didn't care. I set off across the road."

Profe stares at me out of his beady red eyes and then he bursts out laughing. "Mukoma, are you hearing this story?" Just as suddenly, he coughs twice and resumes.

"It's like she was a magnet pulling me across the road. That time it was still afternoon and she was dressed how these girls dress when it's not yet dark: black tights and a small top. She looked okay but that's not why I was going to her, Mukoma. I couldn't even see her face, you know. She was digging into her bag and her face was hidden by the weave falling down to her shoulders. I just thought, ah, let me approach this one. You know me, Mukoma, I know how to talk to girls. So, I asked for her name. She just looked at me. I think she was just used to guys just saying 'ndeipi' and the next thing out of their mouths is, 'Marii short time?' I asked her for her name and she was surprised kuti I was good with talking to girls. Ah, so she tried to think of a fake name but she made the mistake of looking at me and she got herself confused. So she just asked me straight,

'Toita sei rastaz? What do you want us to do? Do you have money to pay?'

I don't know, I replied.

"Ah, then she said, 'Mxm, don't waste my time, you young boys must stop wasting our time. Don't you have a girlfriend?'

At that time I just said to her, 'That gogaz there said I must come to this tree,' and I pointed towards Second Street to the old woman and her box stacked with cigarettes. The girl looked to where I was pointing.

'What do you know about her?' she asked.

'I don't know, she just said I must come to this tree.'

"Ah, Mukoma, I looked at the ground around me, unsure of what to say next. Then I remembered what the gogaz had said. I rubbed the soles of my sneakers to gauge the level of dampness. This should have been a dusty patch of ground and yet it was shadowed with moisture as if liquid was seeping up from beneath the surface. I thought to myself, *ah, there is something not making sense here.*

"And then the girl said, 'Stay away from this tree.' This she blurted out and immediately looked down at her feet. 'There is something dark going on here, if I was you, I would stay away.'

"I looked at her for a moment, then looked at the tree, the rocks placed around it and the ashes of recent fires, and then walked up to it. 'I'm not feeling well,' I remember mumbling to myself as I placed my hands on it. I placed both palms on the trunk and rubbed up and down slowly for a few seconds. It was a young tree and felt smooth and hard. It also felt cold, like a polished stone.

"She watched me but stayed rooted to her spot. Then I stopped, turned to her, and said, 'Ah, sorry,' and then I walked away to catch a kombi into town."

Profe sighs deeply, his eyes closed. The joint has gone out and the stub hangs from his fingers. His whole body has ground to a halt and he sits there, suspended, leaning to one side. After a moment, he lifts his eyelids and grunts, barely audible, "Yah, Mukoma, I need to walk to my people for these things. There are things here that need me to talk to my ancestors."

11

Outrunning the Train

Highlands is aptly named. The bypass now tilts in earnest. I shut out all thoughts of wires, burns and circuits and set down to work. Face down. Back straight. Shoulders relaxed. Short steps. Drive from the glutes. Breathe, Jedza, breathe. I breach the crest and turn left onto Listlessness Road.[30] I walk. A short parade. Brief relief. If I drop my breathing and heart rate too low; if my muscles cool down; then this motor will struggle to get going again. And so, I count twenty paces and set off again. The road undulates. I bob and weave. Come up onto Freedom Way North. I shall not go farther.

***

The bathroom tap drips steadily in the darkness. I stumble off Loveness's bed and feel my way to the bathroom. I switch on the light, take a moment to inspect my sweaty face and then open the basin tap. My chest is still heaving and my throat is parched. We weren't loud today. We never get that far. A hoarse whisper floats out of the tap and a distant gurgle hints that there may be water in the flats below, or not. This little

---

30   When they named the streets, the colonisers wanted us to walk under the gaze of their financiers and pioneering mercenaries; the chefes renamed them after their idea of heroes: in both instances, we walk under Fear, Anxiety, Panic, Alarm, Listlessness and Despondency.

thing didn't really perform tonight. It was too distracted. So it tells me.

Again.

I have been counting down the days. It was either Monday or Tuesday. I passed by the corner downstairs and bought the 7-Day Sexy Coffee and had it that same evening when I got to Loveness's flat. I cannot remember which day it was. Things went well that night. It has been weeks full of my excuses and I have finally managed to coax a moan from her.

***

I chop my stride down Tongogara Avenue and my feet scratch a sharp sound. There are no other runners on the road this morning. I have missed the gang of police recruits on their morning run from their training base.[31] Scrawny, bald-headed, blue-clad chanting bobble-heads in white Tommy canvas shoes. I can set my clock to them. They chant call-and-response morari through the Avenues and down into Milton Park. I keep my music volume low. The birds are quiet. Only the lone rumbles of an early commuter taxi and a Lobels bread truck break the silence. The gunnaz at The Ministry corner on Fear Street shifts from one foot to the other. I dread this moment and the next 90 seconds as I run past the precinct. It is not the same dread as facing an incline or a mess of tangled live electrical cables. On this stretch I dread a whistle from the guards.

At the main thoroughfare, two more gunnaz and a police officer are exchanging loud banter. The officer is getting ready to remove the barriers. At the corner, I see a man doing push-ups under the attention of the bayonet ends of two AK47s. He has a shopping bag next to him and looks much like a regular bhlaaz going about his business. And yet there he is, straining on his hands and toes.

---

31 I understand (as opposed to excusing) why the police in this place are so violent towards citizens. Their training is horrendous. Nothing beats the time The Ministry was so corrupt and bankrupt that new police recruits had to buy their own uniforms.

**

The water is regularly cut off on a Friday and returns late on the Sunday or, at the latest, on Monday morning. Unless The Ministry sends out a maintenance warning. When that happens, it's usually four or five days until there is water again. What comes back is brown filth. It sputters out and belches more air than liquid. Black gritty particles flow in and when the water pools, sediment collects at the bottom with those black particles and a finer brown silt. There was a burst pipe along Baines Avenue a few weeks ago. That length of pipe has burst a few times in the past few months. The water flows freely down the streets and over blocked storm water drains for a few blocks over a couple days before The Ministry maintenance guys pitch up and stand around looking at it. Then they go away and a few hours later the torrent reduces to a trickle. Depending on the phase of the moon, they can come back the next morning, or the next week, and then they replace that short bit of decayed asbestos with PVC piping. During those days, water flows down the street while filth and dirt around the burst section swirls around and is sucked into the pipe. When they fix the section, allowing the water to flow again, all the filth is pushed along and flushed out in every kitchen sink and bathtub down the line.

At times The Ministry receives mysterious reports about water pooling and overflowing into the Avenues but when the maintenance guys get to the location there are no burst pipes to repair. They cannot find the source of the water leak. They stand around scratching their heads as the water seeps back into the earth. Out walking, I steer around the edges of the pools of water, briefly glancing into the shadowy reflections peering back up at me. If I stare long enough, I peer back into a past where Natsai stands in the rain, water pooling at her feet. Standing drenched in the downpours that she seemed to draw to her, cloudbursts that would just as quickly churn up the red mud of Miner's Drift, before flowing away downhill carrying plant debris and handfuls of grit. Ingrained memories of my sister float by, then lodge in the earth as the puddles dry up, only to loosen and rise up again in the next swell.

***

The refrigerator stutters to life. It rouses me from my sleep. 4:02am. Electricity is back.[32] I can make my 10km route and squeeze in a bucket bath before the power and water go out again at 5am. Water starts gurgling back into the pipes. I pull on my running shoes, shorts and a T-shirt, plug in my earphones. The Avenues are serene at this hour. No airtime guys, no fruit and vegetable vendors with their carts. It is that sweet brief hour between the break of dawn and the daily electricity cut-off. The last working girls have left their corners. All that is left are the torn condom wrappers and empty Broncleer bottles. Cool morning light casts the broken lamp posts as stiff weary overnight guards keeping vigil. It looks like rain.

***

Today is either day seven or day eight since I took the coffee. Everlust swears by his coffee and I have no reason to doubt him. He has a daily stream of cars lining up to buy from him. It took me a while to realise that the guys standing at the Avenues corners with ironing boards were selling sex enhancement stuff. Lust, as the other rastaz call him, laughs when I ask him how long he has been running this game.

"Ah Mukoma, did you really think people could iron this much?"

---

32 Energy is hard to come by in the Republic if you're not in the Eating Circle. Fun times are had during periods when the city only has power for four hours per day. Or when you queue for days at the fuel station. My energy highlight was The Ministry believing that a questionable diviner from Chinhoyi could produce refined diesel from a spiritual rock on a hill.

I initially thought that Lust was a bit of a charlatan. That he was just a salesman punting his product so that of course he would say anything to push a sale. He proved me wrong. I am pleased. Loveness was pleased, briefly. The flat I moved into, owned by Loveness, is in the same complex and one floor above hers. She doesn't really expect me to pay rent, but I do anyway, when I can. To make up for the rent shortfall I bypassed her electrical meter so that she has free electricity whenever there is power. Lust and his gear became necessary when this matchstick failed to light up with her. This had never happened to me before and still only happens when I'm with her. Her power to intimidate me has not lessened and much as I desire her, the stick threatens to burn, then swiftly fizzles out. When I brought the subject up with the corner rastaz, I did at first pretend I was asking for someone else: they immediately caught on and it was only after their laughter at my having been "fixed" by Loveness that they called Lust over to show me his pouch. I started off with the blue diamonds, generic and not-so-legal Viagra. After weeks of Loveness twirling my twig with her fingers for what seemed like hours on end, for which she started calling me "Tamba Tamba", it finally burst into flame. The blue diamonds cleared my pipes but constricted my nostrils; and then I breathed like a bull with a cold and Loveness couldn't get going with all my wheezing.

***

It's a steady rise from the Newlands Shopping Centre traffic lights on the bypass, up to the traffic circle. I run on the shoulder of the road. The tarmac gives purchase on the incline. I step off the road whenever I hear a vehicle coming up behind me. You can never trust Harare drivers. I crunch gravel. The traffic circle looms closer, comes into view and then sinks away behind me. Two days ago I got a shock from a live circuit and it left a patch of tender skin on my arm. Sweat runs down the rawness and burns. "Yes," as my artisan used to say, "a shock or two is a reminder that one is working with electricity, but you, Jedza, you, haa you must go and pour beer for your ancestors." He would then slap my shoulders and laugh.

***

There is an open bucket filled with tap water and a jug standing next to it. I fill the jug and splash water on my face a few times. I look up into the mirror and run my hands over my face. I suck in my belly and puff out my chest. I was leaner once and had more definition in my upper body.

Loveness suggested I start running again as I did in primary school. She also believes getting fitter will spark my damp squib. I have mapped out a route and have been going out onto the road early in the mornings. It's still not igniting with her but the running allows me to get that out of my head and to stave off the recurring train visions. Each day I get surges of nervous energy and can't sit still. Tension mounts in my chest and between my ears: I find myself out on the road steaming up inclines even if it sometimes feels I am just trying to outrun that train gaining on me.

I suck in air and my belly goes concave, pause my breath counting to seven, with my breath paused, then let out the air just before my lungs start screaming. I'm not sure I can light up another round. I have no idea how this coffee works, no idea as to whether I need to rest for an hour or for a day. If Loveness wants to fuck again, I will have to find an excuse. Anything will sound better than standing before her with a burnt-out curled match between my fingers, yet again.

***

It takes a while to hit my stride. I huff and a-puff and a-huff and I puff and I lug myself up the road. My pace is off and then I wheeze. I wheeze until my throat constricts. If I cannot breathe, my limbs will cease.

I raise my palms and push the air, my body brakes to a gentle stride. Slower and slower my gears turn. I hear the traffic rumbling past and yet in the distance, my ears pick up heavy metal wheels clanging in hot pursuit.

My body struggles to make the adjustment from rapid eye movement to rapid foot movement; the dreams I left behind are bearing down on me. I step on and off the pavement on the uneven running path and all this does is slow me down. I feel it at the back of my neck, drawing nearer with every stride, the steamer charging and a-chugging and a-charging and a-chugging.

It's a laboured run onto Resilience Road; past the Police Clothing Factory Shop; past the Central and Remand Prisons; past the old drive-in cinema that is now the Kebab restaurant. I'm wheezing and a-heaving, lungs expanding and a-screaming, limbs are aching and a-pleading, train a-looming and a-clanging and a-choo-choo!

I go weak in the knees just as the rise begins. I am now just stumbling along. I will have to move fast when I get back to the flat. The layout of the electrical distribution boards in the newer apartment complexes appears fancy but I've seen a workaround. It all comes down to electricity going in one end and coming out the other.

***

When I step out of the bathroom, I see that the kitchen light is now on and catch a glimpse of Loveness's shadow sliding along the walls. I toss a roll of toilet paper into the darkness of the bedroom and then follow her into the kitchen while swinging my receding glory.

"Are we finished, already?" I ask her while slapping her bum. She has slipped on her panties and looks tiny in a huge golf shirt. I have noticed a couple of these in her bedroom but have kept my mouth shut because I may find what I am looking for.

"If I say let's go back onto the bed, what will you do?"

"Ah you, then we will pick up our hoes and carry on ploughing where we left off ka!"

"I only have Castle Pilsener, will it do?" She ignores my impotent threats.

"You know that we dance to whatever song is playing, let it come." I reach out for her bum again, but she swerves out of reach and then adds, "But you, you don't get enough, what is it with you?"

"It's your things, I can't get enough of them." I reach for her waist and she pulls away again.

"You seem to want to put angry sex into me, is everything okay?"

"Ah Loveness, it's your things, shaa, why don't you just accept being desired?"

"Mxm, anaJedza, oh." She hands me a bottle of beer and then leads the way out of the kitchen and into the bedroom. I follow her and start dressing while she reclines on the bed checking messages on her phone. She texts back and forth and then looks up at me.

"I guess this means that I must leave now?" I say.

***

The way back is mostly downhill. My knees are strong, but my endurance is waning. I haven't run in fourteen days. I am four kilometres out and fatigue is setting in. I grind. I spot another runner on Peace Crescent, paused while stretching. Instinctively I put on speed to catch up. I cross Comrades Avenue and I'm almost striding. Twenty paces out and the runner turns right and off my route. The folly of a chase has put me off my rhythm. I barrel down and cross Mayhem Avenue. Yet another incline looms ahead. Legs get heavy, fatigue creeps back in. Rate of breathing shoots up. I draw in my arms and swing short. I feel strong on the declines and crushed on the inclines. I am not in control.

***

"Shaa, I would like you to stay over but..." she looks at me apologetically. "My situation, you know it. And also, it's not like you're catching kombis to Chengaz shaa, handiti you're just going upstairs?"

"Asi he's on his way here right now?" I ask.

"Jedza, act properly, you hear me?"

"It's fine. Does this mean I'm not going to see you this weekend?"

"I've been meaning to tell you. If you want Chefe Dhivha to help you, then we have to stop this. Otherwise what we want won't work. He is possessive."

"But Loveness, our fire is burning nicely right now, is it not?"

"True ka, but, it's different, if you're going to be working with him. I can't introduce you two and then we carry on doing this."

She gets back up off the bed and brushes past me with the door keys in her hand. I feel the sting but I brave it out.

"So, that's the last round we've hit?" I call out to her. She doesn't respond.

I grab my beer and follow her to the door. One thing that hasn't changed about Loveness: regardless of what else is going on, however high she gets on feelings and fantasies, she always deals with matters as they are on the ground.

The light from the corridor outside and the bright shaft coming in from her bedroom casts her in silhouette. The folds of the shirt sit on top of her bum and gather in the small of her back. The curve downwards makes me pause. She sighs and then leans into me and places her palm just above my belt. The match strikes the side of the box. The head bursts into a ball of flames. She kisses me and bites on my lower lip. My heart starts racing. We have been here before, where we start something and then I can't follow it through. I slide my hand across and check if the fire has caught on; I singe my fingers. I push the door shut with my foot and pull her back into the bedroom.

***

I just want to get home now. Exhaustion has set in. My legs are heavy. Lungs sore. My nose is running. I roll down past the last stretch of eucalyptus trees and start to feel better with each step. I have broken into a second wind. It is also downhill all the way from here. I now ready myself to make it past the first section of The Ministry.

***

Loveness introduced her sugar daddy to me as Chefe Dhivha. She calls him Dhivha, short for David. She put the "Chefe" in there because that is how everyone, including myself, must refer to him, simply as Chefe. The Chefe of The Ministry of Goats, Green Maize and The Girl Child. She told him I'm just her mupfanha, her little brother from Miner's Drift, even though we are the same age. He didn't seem to care, or if he did, he was too arrogant to show it. She suggested I meet him and then, if he took a liking to me, he could start giving me some work to do at The Ministry. That's one of the ways she makes her money, handling small contracts that he passes down to her. That's how Never got the little core house that I squatted in for a while in Chenga Ose; Loveness had cut him a supply contract.

***

This front route is okay except for the higher number of eager gunnaz. I lower the volume of my music in anticipation. I don't want to hear the whistle, but I would rather hear it than miss the whistle. The whistle comes in, short and sharp and I pull one earphone out and look around. It sounds again and I look across the road. A gunnaz in full gear shouts at me,

"Move, you! This is not the place to drag your feet as if you have been bitten by an STD!"

He then simulates a brisk jog for a few paces and then waits for me to follow suit. I do, briskly.

I plod on at my faster pace and in between gasps I notice a car that has stalled in the turning lane at the corner of Fear and Tongogara. The doors of the car spring open and two guys set about the task of pushing their little hatchback across the intersection. The dreadlocked driver sticks to the task of guiding the car out of the danger zone with admirable resolve. Two gunnaz appear and start trailing the car while limbering up for a spot of fun. The dreadlocked fellow surely has strong ancestors on his side because one of the sentries at the corner recognises him and calls back the two gunnaz just as they are about to summon the men pushing the car.

"If this homeboy with the dread was not here, we would have made you very busy!"

***

This week was a challenge. Loveness had organised everything. We met up at One Try Leisure Centre, kwaTry, just outside the city. The place has lost its lustre. Once a strip mall, it is now a sand-strewn meagre cluster of beer, meat and grocery outlets. There is no chance of Chefe's wife ever driving down that way. It is the perfect spot.

En route I had sat in Loveness's car with two young women whom she called her girls. Similar to the girls who had come and gone that evening we sat at Tipperary Bar. One, fidgeting with her wristband, looked familiar but I could not recall where I knew her from or where I had seen her before. We arrived at kwaTry and circled until we found Chefe. His companion briefly stepped out and waved to catch our attention as we searched the car park. Hidden behind tinted windows rolled up, Chefe was waiting in his grey Land Cruiser with this younger guy about my age. An open cooler on the seat with two bottles of Johnny Walker Double Black whisky, a bottle of Glenfiddich 15-year-old single-malt, and three cases of Red Bull energy drink. There was a fair amount of activity all around us. Food vendors, their big black pots simmering on open fires, were almost done. A band was setting up their equipment at the entrance to the old night club, amplifiers forcing sound into the midday heat. Rastaz were milling around the parked cars selling pirated CDs and

DVDs, cell phone chargers and sunglasses. Loveness pulled up next to the Land Cruiser in a pale plume of dust.

She stepped out and got into the other vehicle. The windows were lightly tinted so I couldn't quite make out what was going on. I was trying not to let any of this get to me. After a short while the guy in the front passenger seat slid down his window and gestured at our car. The girls in the back seat left to join Loveness while I went over and stood by the passenger window. Loveness introduced Chefe's companion to me as Derek. He suggested we go together to grab ciders for the girls and to order meat and sadza with the woman at the cooking area. I leaned in to get a look at Chefe as Derek was exiting the car but Derek obscured my view. "You want to see everything, eh?" Derek said to me as we stood around. I guess he caught me stealing a glance back into Chefe's car a few times. "Ah, you know, I'm just looking out for my sister." He looked at me and shook his head. "Your sister?" Then he laughed and walked away to check on the food. Chefe did not once leave the car and I hardly spoke to him. His seat was positioned far back from the steering wheel to give his ample stomach room to breathe. Between gulps of whisky his arms would either gesticulate the size of his financial deals, new mansion, his ideal woman's bum or his other cars, or rest atop his belly. He had a running joke the whole time we were there, that he would drop in regularly when he wasn't bragging about something else.

"You know what the news headlines would say if we were to all perish here suddenly? Heh, young men? Heh, girls? The headlines would say, "Chefe Dhivha ... and others ... perish in an accident.""

And then he would laugh and wheeze and laugh and wheeze. "Chefe Dhivha and others," he would repeat and laugh even harder. He would then take out a handkerchief and dab the dampness from his forehead all the way over his bald head.

"You young boys can drink this Johnso. It goes with your young age. Us big people have earned the right to drink this teenager." And then he would stroke the bottle of Glenfiddich. "Yes, in life you have to sacrifice to make a name for yourself. Some of us were very active in the struggle, you see. But, let us drink and have fun because it is a weekend, eh? These are the fruits we fought for, eh?"

"Others … hahahaha!"

At some point, he and Loveness drove away for about an hour. I stayed behind with Derek and the girls, who moved off to talk privately. The girl with the wrist band would snap it repeatedly once in a while and that would prompt me to rack my brains to remember why she looked so familiar. I had hardly interacted with any women since coming to the city so I figured I had encountered her before my move. I however did not want to take my mind back to Chenga Ose or Miner's Drift. Neither of the girls was chatty beyond what was absolutely necessary so I just pushed it to the back of my mind as best I could. Didn't extend my conversation beyond boozy banter. I drank faster and stared hard at the ground. Derek noticed my discomfort and it amused him. More than once he made a remark about how much of a good brother I was. I refilled my glass before it was halfway. Loveness and the Chefe rejoined us and we stayed on until late into the night. I didn't really get to speak to Loveness and I tried not to look directly at the Chefe. On the way back, Loveness assured me that it was all good. She said Chefe thought that I was a clever guy, whatever that meant.

***

I turn right and head down Panic Drive with the forgotten end of The Ministry on one side and some sports fields on my left. This last section is quieter, but not without its share of excitement. The gunnaz here tend to reserve their delight for the drunken patrons walking out of the pub inside the clubhouse.

***

Not yet midnight. I am heated, drenched in sweat and have a raging fire in my balls. I lie gasping next to Loveness. My heart is racing, the vibrations are thumping against the base of my throat. For the first time in this relationship, or whatever this is, I have left her motionless. The couple of times that I've managed to get a blaze going she has whispered clan names into my ear, "Pale beast. That is the spot, You who leads," and then of course I could not hold it in and I bellowed swiftly and shuddered. Today I was a different animal. Perhaps spurred on by the bittersweet desire for what will soon be lost.

"Shaa, if you're found in here it's going to be horror," she pleads.

I put my clothes back on, I also grab two beers from her fridge and hurry up the two flights of stairs to my floor. I feel light-headed by the time I get to my door. I go out on the balcony for a moment, take a deep breath and look down at the line of people filling up their buckets at the communal tap in the parking lot. It's a small parking lot with far fewer parking bays than the number of tenants' cars. I pull my phone out and check the time: 22:45. I walk into my place, use one beer to open the other and then recline on the bed to catch my breath. I have not taken two sips before the smouldering log in my underwear starts to fire up again.

***

It is turning out to be a bright morning with sunlight streaking through the tops of the pine trees lining Fear Street up ahead. My complex is coming into view in the distance. I can't tell if the gunnaz have changed shifts. All of them look the same. I run past them and they are unusually silent. Maybe it is the coolness of the shade. Kombis and cars are now streaming down Fear Street and so I run along the pavement on the sports club side. I am on the home stretch with my mind already on finishing off the distribution board bypass to Loveness's flat, when I trip over a protruding root. For a moment, I just lie there winded. The smells of a hot tarred road at noon, oil and steel fill my nostrils – odd against the morning chill. Face pressed into red clay soil, heart thudding with terror. I look up, shake my head from side to side and the piercing train whistle fades into a whistle from across the road. I have caught the attention of the two gunnaz at the corner. When I get to my feet and stumble, one of them whistles again. Then they both burst out laughing and one shouts,

"You had almost gone again, ka!"

I get home at 4:50am and flop into the armchair. But it has all been for nothing, the power has already been cut. Fatigue hits me and the walls start closing in on me. The approach starts off as a deep rumble. Low and distant. It gets louder as a train appears and looms closer. And now the ground trembles where I'm standing at some corner in the Avenues. The train is rushing past with its intermittent clanging and the horn blaring. My throat constricts and when I try to swallow, suddenly I am fully awake. Fresh sweat from the nightmare pours into the soaked running clothes clinging to my skin.

12

Tormented Souls

The second pilsener has one more sip left in it. Franco's *Kinsiona* is turning softly on a turntable. Loveness' flat was a partial storeroom and came with essential furniture as well as this working turntable and a stack of old vinyl records. I wondered and almost asked her where all this old stuff came from, but the more I have become reacquainted with Loveness, the more I've learned not to ask questions when the answers may upset me. I have the seven-inch single on repeat. From the moment I walked in and saw the dusty contraption, it transported me back to my parents' living room and Father's old reggae, chimurenga and Congolese rumba records that the adults would dance to on Christmas Day and Independence Day.

Voices from the corner of Fourth and Chinamano drift up to my balcony. The earlier cooking sounds, clanging of pots, the sizzle of oil in frying pans, the opening and shutting doors, the hooting in the car park, the stomping up and down the stair well, kids screaming at bath time, bath water running, moaning and grunting from the neighbouring flats; all the evening sounds have died down. I walk up and down the silent dimly lit corridors to get the blood back in my legs and at each unit I pass, the scent of carbolic soap alternates with the lingering smells of burnt food. The situation in my pants is still urgent and beginning to cause some discomfort.

I step back inside the flat and go out onto the balcony. It's after midnight and the wind on the second floor rustles through the leaves of trees leaning in from across the alley. The rustling and murmuring sounds like a whispered conspiracy. The air has cooled down. The heat coming off the tarred road and the walls is long gone. No mosquitoes. The whining tonight is from cars speeding down the deserted avenues.

Women at the corner are haggling with customers, heckling one another and hurling insults at time wasters. I pick out three voices. Two of them are to the left of the intersection and one to the right. Voices are bouncing back and forth, right and left, like shots lobbed at a tennis match, broken only by the hum of a passing car. The whispers are still animated in the leaves. In the darkness, larger trees loom like shadowy phantoms, towering spirits sucking me into the night. The tension in my balls is excruciating. I put on my slippers, grab a handful of notes and shuffle out of the flat in my sleeping shorts and a T-shirt. I take the unnecessary route past Loveness's flat. The light outside her door is on but no lights inside. In the car park below, Chefe's Land Cruiser is in her parking bay; her car is halfway up on the curb, his car squeezed in behind it.[33] The proximity of these two vehicles sends a sinking sensation into my balls. The guard on duty is still awake and raises a hand at me as I slide the gate open. Colder than expected: I should have pulled on a sweater, but can't turn back now. The pavement is a black tunnel so I stick to the amber glow of the road. Cool air creeps over my skin and sobers me up a bit. Hairs rise on my arms and I rub my hands briskly over the goose bumps. As I approach the intersection, the voices I heard from the balcony return,

---

33   The new Republic rationalised offering huge salaries and even bigger cars to lure and retain needed professionals in the civil service and parastatals. That was more than forty years ago. Employment since then has shrunk to 15% but the size of the cars in The Ministry offices stays HUGE.

sharper. The corner is a different country after midnight. It is reduced to a single amber spot of light under a streetlamp with a border of darkness leaning in around it. My presence looms out of the blackness and the girls' voices go quiet.

"Ma sistaz, ndeipi?" I step fully into the light so they can see me. The corner gang's office is in neat order at this hour. There isn't a scrap of paper, a banana peel, cigarette butt or plastic bottle in sight. I can't see the concrete bin; it is somewhere outside the circle of light. The concrete blocks are within reach and so I rest a leg on one.

"What's up, little husband?" a hoarse voice responds from the darkness.

Walking into the amber zone, I'm temporarily blinded. I had made out vague figures and voices and now I hear a voice scratching in from the dark. I also quickly realise I have no idea what to say next.

"Shall we have a short time?" The voice comes back.

I step across the threshold towards the voice and wait for my eyes to adjust.

"Brother, do you want for the whole night?" The second voice comes in.

I'm between them.

The second voice is stronger, clearer. There is an ease to it. A suggestive nonchalance.

"I'm coming from these flats here." I say it hesitantly and I start to feel stupid.

"So, are we going? Let's go?" The hoarse voice outlines a body before me. She is only slightly shorter than me. I make out a slender frame, tight clothes; I hear the heels click as she paces, long hair, maybe braids or a weave, and a small bag slung over a shoulder.

"Can you please finish seducing each other, dear people of God?" The second voice floats in from the darkness. "If you were other people, you could have gone and come back already."

The indifference in her voice slides up my thighs. We could go up to my flat and she could be back down within fifteen minutes. Or I could be done with it down here in five. The scent of Loveness is still on me. Even as I left my flat, I was hoping I wouldn't have to come all the way down here. I was hanging onto this silly hope, so stupid in this instant, that Loveness would be in her flat and that Land Cruiser wouldn't be outside and we could pick up where we left off.

"Brother seems to be thinking about his lover." The hoarse voice calls across to the second voice.

A car pulls in along Fourth Street, from the town direction and swings around the corner into Chinamano. The headlights are on full beam and in that brief arc of light, the second voice is revealed, wrapped in deep brown skin, a gold micro mini-skirt, matching bikini top and studded heels. She has long thin black braids tied back with only a thin curtain covering her ears. Her face is turned away to avoid the glare of headlights, but the light powder foundation is somewhat visible. As the beam swings towards me I turn my back and step towards the pavement. The hoarse voice walks in the opposite direction, head tilted downwards, towards the car. The car turns slowly towards the second voice but she in turn moves down along the road, ahead of the car. The hoarse voice walks towards the driver's window. There is a sliding sound, a pause and then a series of bright camera flashes from the rear window on the passenger side of the car. The flashes illuminate the canopy of leaves, the matt-grey road, pale jacaranda trunks and branches, and the dazzling gold figure before it scurries onto the pavement and behind a tree.

"Fuck you, asshole! Child of a whore!"

The curses shoot in from both voices on either side of the road and from a third voice further down. There is laughter from the car and the flashes stop as it speeds down the road and turns right and disappears into Third Street. There is shouting after the car and calling up and down between the three voices and from further down across Fourth Street and from further down Chinamano. Amidst the excitement I turn and start to walk around the corner, heading back to the flat. Before I get far a voice calls out to me.

"So, Brother, what were you saying we should do about it?"

***

I wake up in a sweat with the sound of the train rumbling into the distance. It takes a while for the tremors to cease. I get out onto the road and push through my circuit in the early morning chill. I only managed to sleep for an hour or so and the run is tough. Every beer breath is a laboured purge of the previous night. All the tall blocks of flats along my route lean in to crush me onto the potholed road. I stumble back into the car park. The front of Loveness's car is still hoisted over the curb but the Land Cruiser is gone. Two or three other 'shared' parking bays are also empty. At some point the drivers creep out before dawn to drive back to their wives.

Once inside the flat, I turn the bathroom taps and water comes out. She might have seen me coming up the stairs, or maybe it's coincidence, but a text message vibrates in from Loveness,

"Hanzi naDhivha u mst go 2 hs office 1st thing ths mrng. Tek your I.D."

The corner of Fourth and Chinamano is in full swing. Morning traffic crawls by with the usual unnecessary confusion and kombis edging into the lead. One stops at the corner and two women in kitchen whites cross the road towards the Bolano Hotel. Profe is there at the corner, garish in his orange bib, waving his airtime vouchers at the traffic. Chatting to him is a guard from the law firm across Chinamano Avenue. No Banana Cart Guy. Two new faces are seated on the concrete blocks and I can't tell if they have just started drinking something, or they haven't stopped since last night. Profe sees me and is uncharacteristically excited,

"Mukoma, the rate has picked up today. Today it is ugly."
"Profe Ndeipi?" I greet him.

"Heavy, Mukoma, heavy," he greets back.

"So, what has raised it?"

"Mukoma, can't you hear that 'Ye Ye' song playing everywhere today? The Big One who changes the bag at The Ministry has stopped breathing so no-one is changing the bag." The little wind up radio is indeed tuned in and screeching out the wailing song that The Ministry plays on repeat whenever some important person in The Ministry dies.

It is almost 8am and a woman is pacing the corner in the spot where the second voice was coming from last night. I can't tell if it's her. The limbs, the hair and the heels could be hers. I didn't see much of the powdered face last night and these are different clothes – still micro and tight but all black and no gold. Sex in the morning is supposed to be for newlyweds or those who are just hitting pots, not people who buy it. But someone is definitely spending. And so, the girls are out in their stockings and short tight dresses and while many drive and walk to work, they are already clocked in. Things are changing. Months ago, the girls and the boys had separate working hours on this corner. There is now a shared open-plan situation.

As I leave the corner the lament is now looping in my head. Matias Xavier's *Tormented Soul* plays on in my mind. There are faceless souls drifting through the city, hovering over dimly lit street corners, trying to find a way home. Faces come and go on the same streets. Some have names, some are known and then forgotten, remembered only briefly by other nameless faces. Thirty-seven years after Independence, the song mourns those who have passed, who may have been the fortunate ones, who knew where they were coming from, where they were going and what they were striving for. Unlike us, whose lives go round in circles when we're blessed and backwards every other day. Those whose souls drift in the wind died hoping for a freedom that we now only see in the past. Matias helps us weep for a future we almost had, that keeps slipping through our fingers, always out of reach. His voice echoes our daily encounters with the destinies we have already been denied.

I walk west down Chinamano Avenue towards The Ministry building. I get to the corner of Second and Chinamano. Kombis cutting and blocking traffic allow me to cross over. The girl that Profe crossed over to chat with is not here. It is probably too early. The corner is deserted. Even the guys who spend the day at the pool table, chasing the Bindura kombis up and down Second Street, haven't arrived. There are smouldering ashes at the base of the second tree from the corner. The girls at this corner probably lit and fed a fire of twigs into the early morning to keep themselves warm and ward off rising damp. I should turn left and head towards Herbert Chitepo, but a sharp breeze nudges me forward along Chinamano. Past the Travel Plaza and the newspaper vendor and the guards changing shift outside the Avenues Clinic. One of the guards is shouting across the road to another guard, from a different company, who is standing outside the row of townhouses that are not townhouses anymore. The guard is standing outside one of the units now converted into a pharmacy; there is a pharmacy inside the Avenues Clinic, another in the Travel Plaza complex and now this new one across the road. This is another chance to turn left into Mazowe Street and go up towards The Ministry but again my sleeves are tugged down the pavement along Chinamano Avenue.

With the new pharmacy behind me, I pick up a scent of dampness. A petrichor that envelopes me and with each tentative sniff I am nudged closer to a precipice. I stop. My spirit is swung upside down. I breathe in a lungful and my mind races to the freshly cut grass of the school fields, the rain steaming off the road, wet bark of the bottlebrush tree near the front door and the red muddy plash of Natsai's feet as she readied herself to step out of the rain and into our house back in Miner's Drift. I hear her voice. It swings my spirit back upright. Each breath evokes scenes from my childhood. The particular scent unlocks a cascade of memories that moments ago, I would have failed to retrieve. The scent of rain or wet earth in itself means nothing to me. I remember it outside of time or any significant occasion. And yet in this instant, whatever balance of compounds it bears, has conjured up my sister's presence around me. The scent isn't offensive, not like the dankness at the sewage dams in Chenga Ose, or of moist mildew on fabric. It is a comforting scent, something of fresh water, leaf bark, wet earth. Familiar. I feel the dampness settle under my collar and on my forearms. My nose prickles. I raise my eyes from the ground and in front of me, at the corner of Chinamano Avenue and Colquhoun Street, I see a murky pool of water flooding the road verge. A still pool of water, no sign of pipes or overflow into the storm drain. My eyes start to water and I blink a few times. I take in a few more deep breaths attempting to summon more memories but the cascade drops down to a trickle and then ceases. My overwhelmed senses calm down and gradually, the sensation passes away.

The dampness I recall without knowing how or why has settled into my mood, a deep tearfulness. The wordless wailing of the lament has darkened the streetscape of the city.

The lament filters back into my head. The musician is Mozambican, I remember hearing that a few weeks ago. I had always assumed he was Zimbabwean. The song fills me with nostalgia. I am young again, back in Miner's Drift and scrounging for leftovers in my parents' kitchen. With The Ministry controlling all the radio stations and the one TV station, the song would play on repeat for days on end. There was no escaping it.

I shall not be going back home anytime soon. These recollections are my visits. In the song, Matias Xavier doesn't "sing". I don't hear any actual words. So, there is no way of telling where he's from through the sounds used in the lyrics. It's just him and an acoustic guitar. The Ministry will be playing it on all stations for the next few days.

⁕

The Ministry entrance hall is an exercise in minimalism. There is one counter, manned by one person, with one broken pen and no paper. A TV screen mounted on the wall behind the reception desk is playing a grainy montage of portraits of deceased chefes to the sound of the 'Ye Ye' lament. The music irks me and yet I can't stop thinking about it. I follow the desk attendant into another section of the building so she can ask for a blank sheet of paper for me to leave my details. She speaks in lightly accented Shona. I have enquired about the Chefe and after two minutes of misunderstanding and my instinctive annoyance at The Ministry employees, she realises that I am in the wrong section and directs me two streets down but within the same precinct. She then asks for my I.D., tells me to fill in a pass slip, then sends me on my way. Her accent lingers on my mind after I step out. Another sense impression that takes me back to my childhood in Miner's Drift and the workers and students who came in from areas just across the border with Mozambique when there was trouble with the MNR bandits.

As I walk down to the Chefe's office the song is now firmly on repeat in my head, the lament Matias Xavier recorded and released in 1988. I remember my primary school teacher Mr. Gumbo wailing it, out of tune, whenever he had one of his episodes. A dirge: President Samora Machel of Mozambique had died in a plane crash two years earlier. Even as kids in primary school we felt the mood of unassuaged grief and suspicion at the time. And in Miner's Drift we saw the melancholy on the faces of the arrivals and sometimes on those of our parents. A lament for the fallen hero that captured the essence of grief. Collected, funnelled, distilled. One note at a time. Grief on a seven-inch single. Sorrow spinning at 78 rpm. A mournful wail, shuffling and hissing wearily between sparse notes and pleading groans. An emotion threading between guitar strings, through worn fingers, meeting its vocal doppelganger on a studio microphone, straining past the lump in Matias' throat. I imagine Matias in a recording studio, draped in ashy sack cloths, bent over, tears streaming, pleading to the ancestors of oppressed souls. The sack cloths were what I always felt my life in Miner's Drift had become, worn by that wanderer that no one wants anything to do with. A guitar-accompanied plea to the guardians of the souls of black folk. A grainy, hollow recording, running a sonic line along the Beira corridor, to the wooden cabinet Tempest and Supersonic hi-fis and black-and-white television sets in Miner's Drift living rooms.

***

The Chefe works in the section of The Ministry that I run past on my morning route. The section with the gunnaz who are always up for a spot of fun. I walk round to the front entrance. The gate is open and the main office block is in view. On the streets, the building is called chiShake Shake, after the shape of Chibuku's sorghum beer packaging. When I walk through the gates, I expect the gunnaz stationed in the guard box to stop me. Or at least the plain-clothed patrolling the grounds to give me a suspicious look. Neither happens and I stroll up on the red-and-black brick paving. It's a slight incline. Not too taxing, just enough to make you lean forward and strain a bit. I walk right up to the entrance of the building. It looks towering from the distance, when one takes it in on the city skyline, against the other tall buildings. But here, standing right at its base, it is even more imposing. There is a brass plaque next to the entrance, stating which deceased big chefe opened the all-important building on which important date. I run my eyes from the plaque, up the building, head turned up until I feel a slight crick in my neck. In that moment, I realise that The Ministry headquarters is just a massive phallus.

"Ndipe I.D." The man standing at the desk grunts at me.

I hand my I.D. card to him.

"Where are you headed?"

"To the office of Chefe."

Something about this man.

"Does he know you're coming?"

"Yes, he's the one who told me to come."

The way he walks towards me from behind the reception desk. That limp.

"What is this about?"

"There's some work that he'd like me to do."

This man has greyed. Lost a fair amount of weight. But there is no mistaking those wild eyes and that dip-and-drag.

"Do you know where it is you're going?"

"No."

This is when Mr. Gumbo and his leg now shuffle into recall. The only thing missing is his flexible cane, Bazooka. He does not recognise me at all.

He hands my I.D. back to me.

"Climb up there and go to the 7th Floor."

I look at him one last time as he trudges back to his station. I have a fleeting recall of the terror that was his classroom. I remember that we were just kids. He towered over us. Looking at him now I am consumed by sadness, not just at his diminished physical state, but at what he must have gone through. Why he had been the monster we perceived him to be. What he must have seen and done, and had done to him, during the war. How he certainly must have been struggling to deal with the effects of the war. His war cries in Miner's Drift were surely screams of pain. And now he is here, just another cog in the broken machine, shuffling back and forth. Another soul in anguish, for whom Matias weeps.

The first door on the 7th floor is closed and labelled "SECRETARY", so I knock lightly. I repeat the action but there is still no response. A voice from somewhere down the corridor shouts "Just go in, you!" I push the door open and stick my head through. A woman sitting behind a desk stares at me. She has a closely cropped popcorn-freeze wig that has seen better days, a suit jacket with padded shoulders that was certainly tailored hastily, and a wholesale bag of cheap-brand crisps behind her desk that she either sells or is munching her way through. She does not look up from the cell phone she is squinting at in her hand.

"Have you woken up well this morning? I am looking for the office of Chefe?"

"Come in and sit here, let's see. The name is who?"

"I am called Je … Gerald."

She pushes a button on a wooden speaker and says, "Chefe, I think your person is now here," and then reaches for some papers on her desk.

"Gerald from where?"

"I am from Miner's Drift."

"Who are you from?"

"Hara, I am from Hara. Gerald Hara."

"Hara … Hara from where? Because Miner's Drift is a town, where are you from properly?"

"Hara from kwaMurehwa. That is where my father is from."

"Oh okay, your father worked in The Ministry, isn't that so?"

"Yes, and my mother also."

"Hmmm okay, okay. I see it now. What is sacred to your family?"

"We're Hara, so we're from Dziva, I think. I'm not sure."

"You children of today. But yes, I see. I am Tora also from Dziva, so your father is my brother and you are my nephew."

"Oh, I'm happy to know you, Aunt."

On the wall to the left of the desk is a large cotton fabric calendar labelled "Green Maize Department of The Ministry" with the coat of arms, a bearded cob, as the background to the grid of dates.[34] On the wall behind the desk is a portrait of the top Chefe, higher than Chefe Dhivha, in a fine grey suit, dark glasses and his palms crossed, a fierce little toothbrush moustache on his upper lip.

---

34   This place has a wild obsession with farming. People were displaced from their land to establish commercial farms. The economy was ruined by taking over those commercial farms. And now command agriculture happens under the barrel of a gun.

"Good morning, comrade!" Chefe Dhivha's voice crackles from the speaker. I can also hear his voice coming in through the door to the adjoining office.

"Good morning Chefe," I respond leaning in towards the wooden speaker.

"Mrs. Nyakatawa, is the young man facing the portrait?"

Mrs. Nyakatawa gives me a stern look and points to the portrait behind her desk. I turn my face up towards it.

"Yes, of course, Chefe," she replies.

"Right, you see that young man in your office?"

"Yes, Chefe."

"He's very clever, this one. He is our new technical consultant on the smart meters and solar projects and so on and so forth."

"Yes, Chefe. Uhmm, Chefe?"

"Yes, Mrs. Nyakatawa?"

"Sorry to interrupt you, Chefe, but there is an urgent issue regarding orders. If we could please sort it out before we proceed?"

"Haa, comrade. Anyway, it's okay. Let's go, what's the issue?"

Mrs. Nyakatawa moves papers around and then selects one sheet and draws it close to her face.

"The three-inch bearings we received from Mazhet Distributors?"

"Yes?"

"They are two inches in diameter."

"All of them?"

"Yes, Chefe."

"How many did we order?"

"Six hundred, Chefe."

A low whistle comes through the wooden speaker.

"How many did the technicians say they needed?"

"They requested three, Chefe."

"Three what? Hundred?"

"No, Chefe. Three bearings."

"Hmmm, tight. Do we have any stock of the correct size?"

"Please wait while I check, Chefe."

"Hurry up, comrade. You must always have these figures at your fingertips."

"Yes, Chefe."

Mrs. Nyakatawa whispers.

"Chefe?"

"Ehe, how many?"

"Precisely two thousand, nine hundred and twenty-three, Chefe."

"You're sure they are the correct ones?"

"Yes, Chefe."

"So, how come we just didn't issue these ones one time?"

"Chefe, you said we must just place an order. I didn't ask too many questions because it's a Mazhet Distributors order."

"Hmmm, okay. Okay. No need to shout, comrade. Mrs. Nyakatawa?

"Yes, Chefe?"

"Right. Eh, what we need to do right now is to be proactive. Arrange to issue out the three bearings and then facilitate immediate payment for the six hundred."[35]

"Yes, Chefe."

"Right, anything else?"

"No, Chefe."

"Very good. So, you see this is a good thing now. Some of these inefficiencies are why we need clever young people working with us. Like this young man here. Eh, Mrs. Nyakatawa?"

"Yes, Chefe."

"Youth upliftment, comrade. Regeneration within The Ministry. Vision 2040, eh, Mrs. Nyakatawa?

"Yes, Chefe."

---

35 Second only to picking noses in public, corruption is the most consistent national programme in the forty-year-plus history of the Republic. From airplanes, currency, famine relief grain, fuel, motor vehicles, diamonds; if there is any possibility for corruption, it will happen.

"Very good. So just liaise with him and he will advise you on which meters to buy and costing on certain projects and so on and so forth. You hear me, comrade?"

"Yes, Chefe."

"Hehe, no, very good. Don't worry about his contract and payment and so forth, I'll advise you later on how to proceed. In the meantime, just update him on the status of the current projects we have with the likes of Mazhet Distributors."

"Yes, Chefe."

13

If I want to play Nhemamusasa, if there might be a spirit which doesn't want to come out, it will come out. -Mbuya Beaulah Dyoko

Jedza

A woman sits at the corner of Chinamano Avenue and Third Street. She sits on an old paint can, her back hunched, the skin on her face weathered. She could be in her fifties or maybe sixties; sometimes she is sober. She's always wrapped up, thick winter socks, striped this time, buttoned overcoat with just the slightest hint of a skirt peeking out. She sells loose cigarettes, sweets and one-dollar airtime. I ask her for five mints. She's packing up and asks me to help her. A tired voice scratches out of her. We pick up her boxes and stock, all in one go. It is midmorning, so I ask her why the rush.

"The joints of an old woman ache," she says.

But then she peers into my eyes and asks me, "What is sacred to your family?"

I tell her that I have never really known my clan name. That my parents have never really been into totems and all that.

"This area here has the happenings of the Dziva people. It is what causes your spirit unrest," she says.

"What unrest? What do you know about my spirit?"

"I am an old woman. Those who know me call me Gogo Muchadura. Listen to me when I bite your ears."

"Isn't it that we are now in the city? How can those things happen here?"

She sighs.

"A hundred years are one day to those who came before us, those underground. They never forget and they do not forgive easily."

"All this that you are saying, what does it mean?"

She adjusts her grip on a box and points with the other hand.

"Can you see that over there it is high and then when you come over here the land is going downhill, as though we are in a valley?"

I follow the direction of her outstretched arm as she gestures,

"Yes, I see this."

She continues, "This side of the city is built on the bed of a winding river, itself part of many underground streams and pools spread beneath these streets where we spend our days."

She watches my face closely as I ponder her words. "You see the water rising to the surface here and there, around here, do you not?"

I nod.

"Before these white men came and started making us build all these houses here, this area was home to vaDziva, guardians of water, the only ones who knew how to navigate the wetlands without falling into the deep pools of water. They had musasa trees here and there, where they performed rituals required to appease the water beings present in the area, who in turn protected the downstream villages from being flooded. They also allowed the surrounding villages to access water during the dry season and in times of drought."

I start to open my mouth and she cuts me off, "Do not run, my child, listen to me while I bite your ears."

I hold my tongue. A low high-pitched sound rises from within me. What she is saying would have sounded crazy to me only a few months ago. I might have brushed it off as drunken ramblings but her words resonate with the visions I have experienced since coming to this part of town. Those vivid images that cut into my field of vision and then exit just as swiftly.

"You see all these big buildings here? Those white men drained the entire area and started building their city on the land of your people. Using their labour. If you listen carefully you can hear their cries still echoing in these shadows."

A light wind rustles through the leaves on the branches around us.

"Do you know why you see all these jacaranda trees here? Do you think these are our trees? Ah, my child, these are not our trees. They cut down all the musasa trees just to show the people here that they do not care about our ways. The jacarandas are interlopers."

I shuffle my feet. She laughs to break the tension.

"Those who came before us are protective of their blood, but they are also angry; they hold that old anger in their hearts, so be careful as you walk under these trees."

We deposit her boxes in a nearby complex. We tuck them just out of sight at the back of a garage (she knows the garage owner) and then part ways.

Two younger women had been leaning into a car window, negotiating terms, while I had been talking to Gogo Muchadura. Now, as I head back towards my place and walk past them, they have time for me.

"Ko ndeipi." One of them balances on one leg, playfully tugging at the tiny skirt that's barely covering her bum.

"Ndeipi, sistaz."

"Why don't you come and we climb each other?"

She steps forward and places her hand on my forearm. "Come, come, let's do it ... wait, wait."

Her touch is delicate. Pleasantly so.

I feign restraint.

A car stops and then she giggles and walks over to the passenger side window.

***

Early on a warm Wednesday evening I leave my flat to see if
there's a working girl down at the corner. Things are over
between Loveness and me. Sex between us had been feeble
at best and the enhancers I was taking were causing me more
problems than the sex was worth. I have embarrassed myself
with a couple of girls in recent attempts and redemption
keeps drifting further away. The Land Cruiser only slips into
her parking bay a couple of times a week, but Loveness won't
even give me an opening to negotiate something. We're still
friends, though. The ancestors are not on my side today, no
girls in sight, only the rastaz are in attendance. I greet them
quickly then turn right into Chinamano and head towards
the Jacaranda Vibes Bar to kill some time.

At the corner of Second Street there are two women
packing up the plastic containers in which they serve their
dhora sadza and rice.[36] The hwindis from down the road at
the commuter rank for the long-distance kombis going out
of the city, are digging into their Styrofoam packets. Three
or four of them are shooting pool at the table across the road
and standing a few metres from them is a woman already
working. One of the guys watching the pool game leans
toward her and says something. She sighs and takes a few
steps away from the table. She reaches into her clutch bag for
something and then snaps it shut. When she looks up, our
eyes meet. I lose my window of respectability and hold the
gaze too long. Dusk is descending and I can't quite make out
her face but the outline of her figure stands its ground. For
an instant she seems to be startled and then she composes
herself and lowers her eyes. I scrape my feet on the gravel
to get her attention and when she looks up, I am standing
before her.

---

36   Eat this heavy lump of starch for lunch on a warm day and you will
be comatose at your workstation for the next two hours. You may or may
not slowly turn into a blob of starch if you make a habit of this.

"Ndeipi?"

My voice sounds like it's coming from a little box in my shirt pocket. I clear my throat and repeat the greeting.

She replies with her eyes lowered.

"Your shoes are going to get full of water." I say, realising that the spot we're standing in is wet and feeling the urge to flirt a little.

"This place is starting to become a problem." Her eyes stay down as she takes a couple of steps onto drier, compacted soil.

"Yah, saka unonzi ani?"

I realise it's stupid to ask what her name is as soon as it leaves my lips, but I also have nothing else to say. She turns sharply, raises her face up and holds my attention with her fixed gaze. I stare back. She smiles and slowly shakes her head.

"What name would you like me to have?"

The smile is fading from her lips, but the amusement is still sounding in her voice.

"Give me the one on your I.D."

"I don't have an I.D. Can't you see that I'm a small child?"

She's joking but not entirely; she does look young, maybe eighteen.

"How many years do you have?"

"I'll tell you after we're done climbing each other."

She then shifts her weight onto one leg.

"The rastaz on that corner there, do you know them?" I point down Chinamano towards the corner gang spot.

She hesitates for a moment, then says, "Do you want me or boys?" "No, no, there is just something I want to ask you." At that inappropriate moment I've remembered Profe's story about coming to this corner.

"I'm on the job, little husband. We can ask questions once we've finished the job, or if there's alcohol."

The smile returns to her face.

"Handei paJacaranda Vibes?"

The words come out of my mouth before I've had time to think. She doesn't respond immediately and I start to think of how it will look, walking down the street with her and into the bar.

"That's not happening, it's still too early. I can't leave money on the road to go and get drunk. Pass by this place on your way back."

I conceal my relief. "It's okay, but what happens if I find you're not here?"

"You will catch me tomorrow then."

She shifts her weight.

I start walking away towards the bar when she hisses after me. I look back and she says, "So, you don't recognise me?" She is looking at me and I cannot place her face. "You don't remember me, ka?"

I shake my head. The poor light doesn't help.

"I'll tell you when you come back."

She breaks into a giggle, pacing away from me.

I enter the bar and see a regular that I drink with often. I don't know his name, did not ask until it was awkward to do so: I just call him "Bhlaaz". He calls me over to his table.

"Youngaz, Youngaz, come here, come and have a round on me."

"Ah, Bhlaaz, only if you insist."

"Listen, Youngaz, we worked a long time ago and made our money before you were born. We ate this country when it was still sweet. Here, drink this."

He pulls a beer from the ice bucket on his table and slides it over to me. I take a long pull, then ask, "Why do they still play this old music, Bhlaaz? Doesn't the DJ have new records?"

Bhlaaz laughs.

"You see the problem with you young people? You don't know nice music. These were the hits, do you hear me? Old School classics, Youngaz. You know why I like this bar? I'll tell you why. This is one of the few bars left from the good days. This bar will close when I die, I tell you."

"Yah, but why are they still playing old music?"

"To please the buyers of alcohol, us, Youngaz. Now drink your beer quietly."

We laugh and I gulp down my beer and grab another one before excusing myself.

Hours roll by. I'm sitting at the bar not watching a replay of some old UEFA Champions League match and texting Never. Telling him what I'm up to and trying to get him to maybe come over for a weekend. He doesn't reply. His responses have been irregular lately. He's probably too busy having a good time. Maybe he now has fancy new friends.

The DJ has his head tilted earnestly into his headphones and the bartender is chatting to the only other people in the bar, Bhlaaz and a new companion who is on his last legs. Bhlaaz is trying to rein in his buddy but the hero is not doing a good job because he's also one sip away from kissing the floor. He throws an arm around his buddy and they start making their way out of the bar. Bhlaaz shouts to no one in particular, "We will see each other tomorrow, same time." The bartender grins and waves. As I watch them exit, a female figure brushes past them and into the bar.

The girl from the corner pulls up a bar stool next to mine and asks for a Black Label beer. She asks me if I remember inviting her to come here and I say, of course. She rubs her nose and sniffles.

"You know kuti you're not going to put your thing inside me handiti?"

I can't tell if she's asking me or making a statement, or just fucking with my mind, trying to raise her rate. She's the last girl in the bar so she's charging up. I'm also the only guy who can walk out with her so she's really just bluffing. It's now after 11pm and it's a weekday.

"Why? Do you want us to first go to your aunt for permission before we climb each other?" I ask her.

She takes three gulps from her bottle.

"If we climb each other will you tell your friend Ma'am Loveness?" She leans back in her stool. She tugs at a band on her wrist.

I feel a sharp tug in the pit of my stomach, just above the belly button. I look into her eyes and then it hits me. I don't know if she was one of the girls who came by at the Tipperary Bar but she's certainly one of the girls we drove down with to meet Chefe Dhivha kwaTry. And now I also connect the dots from another day: she is the girl I sat behind in the kombi on the day I moved here from Chenga Ose. The girl with the Huawei pamphlet.

"So, you're sleeping with my boss?" She asks.

"Your boss, which one?"

"Just because I'm not an old person doesn't mean kuti I don't see what is being played, you hear me?"

"There's nothing being played."

"Listen, I don't care about all that. I just wanted to hear your response. But you're brave."

There is a period of silence and I nod at the bartender who opens two beers and slides them to us. A Zambezi lager for me and another Black Label for her.

"So are you working right now?"

"Why? Do you want an after-hours discount?"

"No, I meant, are you working for Loveness right now?"

"My friend, yes. She's the one who brought me here."

"Coming from where?"

"Ah, but you Miner's people are so sleepy. This rural thorn, you all step on it and then it breaks off deep inside your foot eh?"

She laughs hard and chokes on her beer, then recovers.

"I know you from Miner's Drift. You didn't see me because you were just thinking that I was a kid." She leaves to go to the bathroom with her beer bottle in her hand.

She's right that I don't know her from that joint. But I know plenty of girls like her, boys too, I guess. She is one of that kiya kiya, anything goes, generation. The kids born in the emptiness which came down on Miner's Drift after the big mining companies left as abruptly as they had come. That first generation of kids who knew that if they ever wanted to become anything in life, they would have to leave town. That generation who discovered that the saying, "You don't go to a place where you have no mother," was only holding them back in life. So, in that way I can place her, somewhat.

But also, I guess she remembers me and knows me because one never leaves Miner's Drift. Those streets and familiar corners have an allure which never fades. I could go back after my time in exile and find the same faces, now weathered, walking down what's left of the streets, hanging over the fences I leapt over in my childhood, gossiping with new neighbours and reminding me that whatever I become out here, back there I'm still Jedza wemaStedza.

When she comes back, she reminds me that her name is Penny. She says that's the name she's going by now. It's her second name, Penelope. I ask her if that's her real name and she says that she can't call herself Maidei in the city.

"Rural names don't work up here," she adds.

"Let's talk, homeboy. I'll keep you company and if you want to climb me then we'll see. I might even throw in a discount for someone I know." She laughs again and coughs it off.

***

I feel a deep sympathy towards Penny. Nothing remotely sexual. I almost feel responsible for how her life has turned out. Like I should have paid more attention or should now protect her. She appears to have lived a hard life yet is indifferent to her experiences. Loveness's girls and the girls on the street corners have just been nameless faces to me. I had never imagined one of them being someone I know. I start meeting Penny at Jacaranda Vibes on her slow nights and she talks, all the time. I listen and say very little.

Penny

Now I leave...

On my first day here, I was directed to Ma'am Loveness's flat in the Avenues. She spoke kindly and assured me that Sisi

Stella would look after me. After a brief chat, I left with Sisi Stella for her flat on nearby Third Street, where I would be staying. The next morning, I cleaned the flat and then lazed around until late afternoon. At some point, Sisi Stella said, "Iwe Penny, come with me" and we left the flat and walked down Chinamano Avenue to the corner of Second Street. Along the way, she walked with her arms out to the sides and people stepped aside for her. I followed in her wake, careful to avoid an accidental strike from her gesticulations. When she spoke, she was loud enough for me to not need to be close to her.

It was late February. I remember because the rains had stopped. The sun was still out and so we stood in the shade under the old jacaranda trees. I felt watched by those trees from the first time I walked under them. As if they had eyes boring into me whenever I turned my back. I felt eyes glaring at the top of my head and the weight of branches pressing down onto my shoulders. The unease was worse when the streets were empty. The hairs on the back of my neck would rise and I would swivel round. I jumped when a falling leaf brushed past or landed on me. It was just the two of us, Sisi Stella and I, and she would stop and stare down at me. "And what are you doing now, heh?" Then she would clap her hands once and walk on while shaking her head.

We crossed Second Street and chose a spot to stand that aligned with the second tree on the Avenues Clinic side. Sisi Stella told me to stand right in front of that particular tree. A mature tree; it wasn't a jacaranda like the rest of the trees lining these streets. I recognised the new reddish-brown leaves and the green pods: a musasa. Second Street was noisy with traffic, commuters eager to vacate the city centre. There was traffic coming from both ends of Chinamano and cutting across the chain of traffic on Second Street. The cars driving past us would line up and I kept expecting one to stop and have some man hang out through the window and ask kuti "marii short time." I wasn't sure how it was all going to work. The line of cars backed up almost to the shops at the Travel Plaza

but the cars kept moving past slowly.[37] There was no one else
on our corner. People walked up and down in all directions
but none stopped. Sisi Stella told me to stand just off the road
and call her if anyone pulled over. She then sat down on a
pile of sooty bricks arranged in the form of a fireplace and
there were half-burnt logs and ash in the disused structure.
Her seat from which she steered her corners by the horns.
She was constantly on her phone shouting instructions and
at times lowering her voice but with the admonishing tone
still present. Between scoldings and threats, she sat sipping,
now and again, from a small plastic bottle of bronco. I took a
swig. It reminded me of the Woods cough syrup I used to get
from my mother. This syrup had a bit of an aftertaste. I tasted
much more alcohol in it. After a few sips I felt relaxed. The
noise of the traffic wasn't so harsh. Soon it started getting
dark and the traffic on Second Street thinned out. The cars
were now only coming down in slow waves, releasing me
from the lingering, inescapable glare of the traffic lights
coming from both ends of the street. On Chinamano, one or
two cars would weave past the potholes now and then.

***

I must go far away...

I'd first met Sisi Stella in Miner's Drift just a few months
earlier. My destiny, a means of escape. That town was
boredom in a teaspoon, I was taking it three times a day like
medicine. For a sickness I was bottling in and desperately
needed to break away from. Janet and I were killing time
hanging around town waiting for makorokoza to arrive from

---

37   Travel Plaza still retains its name for the same reason Harare is still
called a city, habit. This centre, hard to believe from the fast-fashion
boutiques and empty units there now, used to house airline and travel
agency offices, before the country was forever broken into many small
pieces.

the disused mine shafts they were sneaking into and digging up. It was hot and humid, I was sweaty and sticky, and the roads were muddy. The smell of overripe mangoes, boiled peanuts and rotting husks of boiled maize cobs was sitting in my nose. My nostrils were blocked. *I needed to breathe fresh air*. We were posing up and down between the Post Office and Gara Wega Bottle Store. No guys were approaching us, so when evening came on, we went inside the Contaz Bar. A while later Sisi Stella strode into the bar with two other young women. Janet and I were now with two makorokoza who were chatting us up and buying us beer. Janet had chosen the one with car keys dangling off his little finger and I had to deal with the other who was doing the running around. They both appeared to have emerged from a shaft and come straight to the bar. Janet's guy had a roll of USD $20 bills the size of a cheap roll of toilet paper. He pulled the whole thing out of his pocket each time he bought a round of drinks.

Sisi Stella ordered drinks at the bar and while waiting, turned round and our eyes met. She summoned me with a slight movement of the head. I left my guy dancing alone and walked over. "How many years do you have?" She asked.

"Me? I have twenty years."

"Do you think I am stupid? I said, how many years do you have?"

"I have seventeen years, but I will be eighteen years just now."

"Why are you wasting your time with these small-town boys?"

I wanted to tell her that they were not my guys. That this was

Janet's move tonight. But I just said, "Hameno."

"Tsk. Do you even have a cell phone?"

"No."

"So, you're just letting these boys climb you for nothing?" She turned around and got a pen from the barman and wrote a phone number on a receipt.

"Call me when you decide to be serious."

The two lieutenants picked up their six-packs and followed Sisi Stella out of the bar. I watched the women get into a nice car parked across the road. I would later learn that they had been parked there for a while, observing, and Ma'am Loveness, seated in the back, had selected me and sent Sisi Stella to handle my recruitment.

***

It is best that I leave for distant lands...

On that first shift in the city, as it got darker, Sisi Stella and I stood on the deserted corner with vehicle lights shooting up and down Second Street and the odd car snaking past along Chinamano. We stood in the dark but across the road there was a working street light casting a circle of orange onto the pavement. A girl in a white mini dress and heels drifted out of the shadows and stood in the circle with a clutch bag under one arm. She was slim and the dress cut off just barely covering her bum. She had a long platinum-blonde mane that dropped over her face. Her light skin accentuated in the orange glow. She did not stand still, kept shifting from one foot to the other and scratching compulsively at her arms and legs. She was constantly looking around. Not looking out for cars as I was but with nervous trepidation as though she was expecting someone or something to jump out at her from the darkness. At that moment Sisi Stella started talking loudly about how the girl across the road wouldn't listen and that she would get beaten up one day. The slim girl ignored her and just kept pacing within the circle of light and pulling up the lower part of her dress deftly each time she was caught in the headlights of a passing car.

"You see what happens when you think you can do things by yourself in these streets?" Sisi Stella said to me, then scoffed.

"Look at her now. Just scratching as if she has lice."

"What is wrong with her?"

"That one? Nothing is wrong with her. She just thinks she's too clever and that she can do things without me. You young ones think you know everything these days."

"I was feeling weird when we came here. As if there is something in these trees. I don't know."

"Ah, there's nothing here. People just talk a lot of nonsense. If you listen to me you will be fine. Just make sure not to fall into the water," she added.

I looked behind me and noticed that there was now a small pool of water two strides behind me, deepening at the roots of the musasa tree. I clearly remembered it not having been there when we arrived at the spot.

Sisi Stella took another sip of her bronco. A car was facing us from across Second Street with its headlights on full beam. It crossed over and when it went over the road the lights shone in my eyes such that I had to look away. Sisi Stella snapped at me to look up. The lights came up slowly and drove past us. I was blinded. The car stopped a few metres past us. Sisi Stella struck a cigarette lighter and waved it under a small glass pipe.

"Go and hear what he has to say then come back here quickly," she whispered.

I walked over then bent down and peered into the passenger side window. The window rolled down. The inside of the car was unlit but I made out two men in the front. The driver spoke to me. "Sei sei, chimoko?"

"Ah, nothing. What shall we do?"

"Short time marii?"

"Twenty dhoraz short time."

"Ah, that's too much money for just one round."

"Okay, how much money do you have?"

"I only have five dollars."

"Okay, make it ten dhoraz then we can do it quickly."

"Sharp. Let's go."

I went back to Sisi Stella and briefed her. She was still waving a flame under the pipe. She passed it to me and said, "Take a hit, here, like a cigarette." I had an idea what I should do. I took the pipe and sucked on it a couple of times. Hot smoke tore into my throat and deep into my lungs. The rush was instant. Waves of euphoria washed over my body over and over again. And then a peaceful silence came over me. An exhilarating absence of anything at all. Energy surged through me. Then I heard Sisi Stella's voice calling me, "Penny! Penny! Iwe, Penny, go now!" I handed the pipe back to her and got into the back of the car.

We turned into an alley farther down the road. When they were done, the men told me to get out of the car and find my way back. I still had high levels of energy pulsating through me. Flooding me. *I wanted more.* But they were finished and one of them pushed me out of the car and they drove off. I do not remember how much time I spent in that car or how long it took me to walk back to the corner. Time was a blur from the moment I had gotten into that car. When I got back Sisi Stella was not there. The slim girl wasn't standing under the circle of light across the road either. All four corners were vacant again. I could not stand still. I paced up and down repeating to myself, *This is it! Izvi ndizvo! This is it! Izvi ndizvo!* All the time anxious for another car to pull over. This is what was missing from my life in Miner's Drift, I told myself. I can never go back to burning my feet up and down those streets. After a while I began to feel discomfort between my legs. An ache arose in my feet and knees. I felt for sore places and discovered bruises on my knees and elbows. My energy levels ebbed away and I stood once again in my original spot. Sounds around me began to drift back in. Agitation arose within me. I couldn't place what exactly I was nervous about. I felt a headache coming on. I remembered both of the men taking turns. I didn't care. It was great. *I was great.* But now shame was coming over me. I felt the eyes from the trees boring into me again as they had earlier. Except now they taunted me about what I had done in the car. I could hear distant voices rise up from the darkness. *Who is out there?* I turned this way and that but couldn't locate the source. A breeze blew now and then, nudging a discarded plastic wrapping across the road. It startled me. Wetness began seeping into my shoes. I looked down and saw that the pool of water was noticeably wider and the circumference almost touching the edge of the road. A chill blew through me. My head was now thudding and banging. When a car went by, the beam would light up the intersection and send shadows leaping across in an arc. Each time I would jump. The silence and darkness would descend again. *What was happening to me?* While I stood there confused, anxiously waiting for the next car to come by, the water behind me gurgled. As I turned to look, a form emerged and crept up the roots of the musasa tree and spread out onto the pool surface. I froze. It took on the shape of a little girl, barefoot, standing in a loose linen dress that clung sodden to her skin. The child looked up at me.

Jedza

I sit bolt upright in the middle of the night, heart thumping, back sweaty. The sound of the train is still ringing in my ears. In my moment of self-pity, lyrics come to me. "The darkness is unrelenting, we need some light," Killer T sings in *Itai Ndione*. My thoughts revert to my encounter with Gogo Muchadura and her boxes, then to Mbuya Dyoko and her musings: "Nhemamusasa is for old people. They were fighting in the forest. There and then they went to the big forest and they cut a tree called musasa to make a shelter. There they start playing mbira; the song of it they say we can call it nhema-musasa because we have cut the musasa and constructed the shelter."

Penny

Your hearts are cold...

Sisi Stella rarely comes out to the streets with me now, she has better things to do. During the week I get to the corner as the evening sets and usually by 3am my work is done. There is no more traffic after that time. All the bars are closed. Chez Ntemba Night Club would produce a mid-week trickle but it closed down. On weekends and sometimes on Thursdays, if it's a payday weekend coming up, I'm at the corner a bit earlier. Things are bad in Tipperary Bar now, some of the girls leave early and hang out on the corners. Tipperary looks poised to shut its doors. Sometimes the other girls I live with in Sisi Stella's flat come and hang out before they go to their corner further down. Things are getting so bad, they tell me, that the girl who works the pavement across the street from me is braiding hair in a salon near the Fife Avenue shops during the day.

Mukoma Josh is by his improvised fireplace grilling his green maize. I have my work premises at his stall, the place where Sisi Stella told me to hang out and wait. I used to worry about him the first couple of days until Sisi Stella set him straight. I'm not sure what exactly she said to him but he walked up to me one day after I had mentioned him and said, "Ah, I didn't know you were Stella's new friend," with a sheepish grin and then we were bho from there. He doesn't say it out but he would take me behind a tree if he ever got five dhoraz to spare. I catch him out of the corner of my eye staring at my legs, his eyes glazed.

One of the kombis from the Bindura commotion further up the road stops a few metres past the intersection along Second Street. Three zvimaSpiderman are hanging off the back of the kombi. The touts, who have loaded passengers onto a kombi, get their commission from the driver and then the three of them start arguing about how to split the notes. One grabs onto the waist of the jeans of a larger guy and the scrawny hwindi is dragged fighting past me. I take a few steps clear of them while clutching my bag tight.

It is almost evening and Mukoma Josh has left. Soon, the entire corner is deserted again. *Why does my body ache? Why is my mind never at ease?* I have been anxious for this moment. Waiting for everyone to leave so I can take my first hit of the pipe. The bronco quietens my nerves but at some point

I need to get my proper fix from the white smoke from the glass pipe. The girl in the white dress from across the road is not here every night. She must be making more money at the hair salon, or whatever Sisi Stella was talking about could have gotten to her. That's not my concern. The pipe has one or two hits left. I don't want to waste them before I get a guy. **Why is my life such agony?** Let me light it anyway. Whatever happens will happen.

I'm hungry for something to happen. **Why does time move so slowly?** A guy walks up to me while the guka heat is coursing through my veins.[38] Some office worker on his way home. He is trying to make small talk. Nervous guy. Probably a first timer. The type who has a girlfriend or wife he respects too much to ask her to open her mouth or take it from the back. I know the type now. Thinks he's too good for someone like me. His woman will accuse him of wanting to fuck her as though she's a hure. He will not want to cheapen her by fucking her like a prostitute. And so, he comes here. There's some traffic and pedestrians still hanging about, so I'll take him back to the flat. He walks behind me of course, but it's easy to figure out what we're up to. Men like these I'll charge extra and if he's not clever I'll clean out his wallet. Who is he going to report to?

I'm back at the corner and already feeling agitated. **Why is my happiness so short-lived?** I have my own pipe but Sisi Stella only gives me a gram of guka per day. That used to be enough for the whole night. I would still be high on the same gram the next morning. Now it only lasts the beginning of the night. Sometimes I finish it all and lose my high before I even leave the flat and then work is tough the whole night.

---

38   Even when the economy and society were deep in the bowels of a rabid dog, Zimbabweans would still ask each other, "When do you think we shall hit rock bottom?" Despite the best efforts of the only party to ever govern, the rock that is unquestionably the mountain on which Zimbabwean society is seeing its naked face has arrived in the form of crystal methamphetamine. Dombo (rock), guka, mutoriro, as the ghetto youth refer to it.

I can't remember the last time I slept. I have been up for two or three days. I don't know what I would do to calm down if it wasn't for the bronco. At least Sisi Stella is not stingy with it. I'm about halfway through the bottle; it's a slow night, even for a Thursday. ***Why is everyone watching me?*** A breeze coaxes flickering flames from the dying embers of Mukoma Josh's fire, a glow that reflects off the surface of the water around the musasa tree. ***Why are they trying to burn me?*** A shadow emerges from the reflected flames in the water and slides up the roots and trunk of the tree, onto the wet earth.

"What do you seek here at this dark hour?" The shadow whispers.

"I'm working. What do you seek?"

"Buka tiende," she says. "You have suffered enough. Come, let us go."

The musasa girl speaks patiently and clearly. A soaked plain linen dress hangs off her small body and she tugs stiffly at the folds. I am indeed tired. ***Why can I never find rest?***

She begins to slip back towards the tree and lower into the water. I cannot let her leave. ***Why do my limbs ache so?***

"Wait. Where are we going?"

She looms closer.

The girl faces me but like the last time, I cannot see her eyes. Water continues to drip down her face and body. The weak firelight shows her cheeks and the outline of her head but the eyes are dark hollows.

Oh, won't you take me out of this misery?

Jedza

As it turns out, between my electrical rewiring hustle and the consulting work at The Ministry, I still have plenty of free time in this flat. I reach for a Thomas Mapfumo LP and find the song *Hanzvadzi*. As I look at the song title my sister's face comes into my mind. Natsai has been on my mind ever since I moved to the Avenues. I feel her presence at odd moments and right now I feel her hand guiding mine in picking out this record. A worn album cover, I blow dust off the surface. One of those with his laughing portrait and the flying dreadlocks and the red, gold and green bands. It is one of those albums that the Contaz barmen played on hot Saturday afternoons and I know all the lyrics but have chosen to make my own connections to the song. A couple of days ago, Profe gave me some tobacco snuff, which he said clears his mind. I had mentioned some of my bad dreams and he had assured me that it would raise any underlying issues to the surface. I'm willing to try anything at this stage and so I shoot it into my nostrils for the first time. It kicks me into alertness. I place the needle on the record. One mbira sounds like two and the notes seize me and slow down the time. Ashton Chiweshe plays the lead guitar and when he does it's tempting to believe that's why the barmen in The Contaz call him "Sugar". I feel the mbira reach out to my ancestors, old and new, in a deep melodic mourn and when Sugar strums his guitar, memories of Natsai flood in. I feel a tightening and constriction in my throat. The mbira plays the anthem *Nhemamusasa* and Sugar's guitar wails around the keys. Hearing this ancient melody played with band instruments, from speakers in the Avenues, makes my ancestors' voices sound familiar. Mapfumo weighs in with his baritone vocals,

What shall we do,
With the brother of your mother,
Who refuses to work his fields?

There are no svikiro in the flat. If these mbira rhythms summon my ancestors and they can discern between the keys and the strings, they will find no host. My melancholy will pull my family spirits to my aid and when they find no medium, they will drift outside and cross paths with mashavi roaming the streets, before returning beneath the soil. And yet the song drags my soul back through the years, to my childhood. Through to the beginning, that age before clocks, when my time melded with that of my people before me, measured in seasons and sleeps; before and after the rains; and the eras in events, the year of the locusts, the time of the poor harvests, the day that Natsai left.

The mbira turns and turns in its cyclical rhythm, closing in tight and when I can't breathe it turns outwards, loosening its grip. Sugar's lead guitar does what only a few others have. It doesn't mimic the mbira keys, it doesn't set the beat, ride nor follow it. The bridge of the guitar anchors the strings in the land and time of my grandmother Mbuya Maswiti on one end, and on the other end they are anchored on the neck, in the time of my living ancestors. Sugar's guitar licks ride up and down the strings, listening to the mbira keys spinning around the *Nhemamusasa* melody loop, hiding behind them one time, pleading before them the next and bursting out when the chest is full.

What shall we do,
With the brother of your mother,
Who refuses to work his fields?

A hi-hat teeters on the edges of the song. Its constant bark and splash a reminder that I am in the present, here where I have chosen to be, where I have been drawn to, where I also have no choice but to be. The percussion stands in where hosho would have been rattling and setting the tempo in their gourds. And so *Hanzvadzi* rolls on, Mapfumo pleading in his gravelly voice, the mbira diligent yet with a haunting refrain, Sugar's stubborn guitar strings echoing in the distance, percussion an unashamed third wheel, smirk on its face like a secret lover at a wedding.

The lead guitar shoulders its way back to the front and starts an earnest dialogue with the voices in my head. I take a deep breath and, in that moment, I feel Natsai's hand rubbing my head in a soothing manner. A calmness descends upon me and I stretch out and yawn. Another memory stirs.

We buried Natsai in an empty casket. Mother and Father insisted that this was all the Lord's will. That she was somewhere in His arms and this was all divine, beyond the understanding of us mortals. Dampness and her scent lingered in her room, outside her window and in my mind. I would feel the dampness under my collar and on my arms and my nose prickled whenever it picked up the scent. The same uncanny sensations I now feel walking under the dark shade of the jacarandas in the Avenues, pausing on the still corners late in the night on my way from Jacaranda Vibes and now in my waking visions.

I walk over to the turntable and lift the needle to repeat *Hanzvadzi*.

I drift off but my serenity is short-lived. I wake up in a sweat, out of breath. In addition to the oncoming steam train I now have these watery visions of a female face looking up at me from beneath a still murky surface. I need to clear my head and so I go for an early morning run. I come back from my run drenched, pumped up and ready to go to The Ministry to look over some tender specifications for a contract already allocated to Mazhet Distributors. This is good timing because my hustle is really not going anywhere here in the city and I am certainly not going back to Chenga Ose, even if it's only in-and-out to wire connections. It is a few minutes after 6am and the guards at my complex are changing shifts. There is a lively discussion about some incident which happened the previous night. Something to do with some married man and a woman with whom he is having an affair.[39] The same thing happens every week, just different flat numbers, names and faces. I lean over the railings to cool down and notice Loveness's red VW is parked up on the curb and wedged in

---

39 Together with corruption and violence, infidelity is the national pastime in the Republic. No-one belongs to anyone and everyone is fair game. More than it being one big bedroom, the city is one big bed with space for everyone. Your spouse may indeed be your spouse, however, T&Cs apply.

behind hers is Chefe's Toyota. Lately he has been spending more time here. Breakfast smells are drifting in and around. Peanut butter, porridge, sweet potatoes. I never smell bacon here. I've cooled down and the morning chill is getting to me. My joints are starting to get stiff and so I walk in and put on a dry T-shirt. A Mhuri yekwaRwizi record is spinning on the deck and Hakurotwi Mude's voice is skimming off the walls. If I keep having my nightmares, then I might have to adopt his name.

Penny

My ancestors have abandoned me...

Weeks pass and the voices whispering around me get louder. The unblinking stares from the leaves above me torch the back of my neck. The hot itchiness flows down my spine and spreads through my limbs to my toes and fingers. In daylight, the hwindis run around me all day long and I can't think straight. **I can't find peace.** They haggle over coins and sometimes punch and slam each other to the ground. A T-shirt is ripped. Someone is slapped hard down the back. Sometimes one bleeds from the mouth or has a lump on the corner of the forehead. **I rub the raw tender bruises on my own arms and legs.** They light their mbanje and smoke and drink and piss around the corner. They are in no hurry to go back to their chaotic terminal further up the road on the corner of Fife Avenue and Second Street. **I need to soothe.** After dark the corner becomes quiet again. It goes back to being a discreet spot. My corner.

Sisi Stella doesn't come out with me anymore. She's only necessary when someone tries to muscle me off the corner. She comes by once or twice during the night to check up on me and to collect her money. When I'm in luck, she brings me a gram and then the night moves fast. The whining voices in my head quieten down. The insects crawling under my skin give me a break. The eyes watching me avert their gaze.

What have I done to deserve any of this? The girl in the white dress hasn't been here for a while. On those nights when she has shown up, she has stood further down the street, closer to the shops; perhaps she couldn't stand the stench of the touts' urine from the trees on her side of the road. She got too close to the shops a few nights ago and the girls on that corner chased her back down and sent beer bottles crashing after her. Being out here in these streets without Sisi Stella is tough.

Sisi Stella has been getting stingier with the grams lately. What she gives me teases me. A gram only goes into my veins for a short while and then leaves me wanting more. She's holding back on the bronco as well so my nights drag. If I was someone else I would confront her: it's just that I don't like fighting with people. My plan is to leave her to go and work with the girls across Second Street, over on Chinamano and Third. I've heard Sisi Stella had a fight with the guys who control that corner and I'm sure they will take me in just to spite her. I hear their girls have a better deal. Sisi Stella is still docking my money and working me every day with no break. At least if she was giving me more grams all of this would make more sense. ***Why must I carry on suffering like this?*** I'm not like Sisi Stella or Ma'am Loveness, they would kiya-kiya on this corner, turning this agony into hard cash. They are tough, nothing can break them. No matter how bad it gets, they'll always find another chefe, another angle to work. They will be here long after I am gone.

A car barrels down from the direction of the Travel Plaza shops. Loud music threatening to blow off its doors. It had been a quiet night until now. Almost 11pm. The girls at the shops shout insults at the car and it screeches off towards me and then slows down. The car pulls up and I know they are going to waste my time just from the *Bad and Boujee* they are playing. Probably cruising in their parents' cars. Speaking through their noses. Driving up and down the Avenues, lights on full beam, getting their little penises hard from watching us girls flash our thighs at them. They pull down the windows on my side and start shouting, "How much to fuck? Ey, how much to suck my dick?" I turn to walk away and at that moment there is a grunt from the darkness and a rock crashes into the rear window of the boys' car. The car jerks and shoots across Second Street without pausing at the intersection. A girl stands in the patchy shadows in the middle of the road. I don't know what to say to her. I'm not afraid of her. This is now my area. The girl continues to stand there, staring at me and I start to feel a bit uneasy.

The girl says out loud, with concern, "You are too young to be here."

I do not respond.

"Here, things are not standing well," she says.

"What is here? What is it that you know?" I ask.

There is a gurgling sound from the pool of water behind me, as though something is rising to the surface from its depths. The branches of the musasa tree shudder behind me and when I turn around again to look at the girl, her light running steps are already fading towards the shops.

My kin have hearts of stone...

The following week I get to the corner and find a pool table placed next to Mukoma Josh's stack of maize stalks. It is just before 4pm on a Friday, a payday Friday, so I hope to catch a few horny chaps in the afternoon. I count about fifteen guys hanging around the pool table and leaning on the wall smoking mbanje. Mukoma Josh is at his spot but he has not lit his fire. Two women appeared a few weeks ago and started selling dhora sadza and Mukoma Josh has been having a tough time moving his green maize. A mess of disposable packaging and plastic spoons strewn all over the corner are daily confirmation of their soft coup. The women at least have the courtesy to place their buckets and dish their food across the road from Mukoma Josh. The stench of urine is strongest on that side but neither the touts nor the sadza women seemed to mind. So, the touts come up in the morning and hustle their first dhoraz, grab their meals from the women and then spend the rest of the day getting high, betting on the pool table, chasing incoming kombis and pissing on the trees across the road. Watching them smoke makes the insects under my skin crawl faster. I can't let them see me hit the pipe. They would never let me rest. Even worse, I might take them on. It's better when I don't have any guka and then I can just sip away on a bottle. The bronco is becoming a waste of time though. Nothing works for long enough these days. No customers are going to approach me in daylight with this bunch milling around. Even now they are looking me up and down and it will not be long before one of them has the courage to harass me. I greet Mukoma Josh and he just mumbles and carries on staring at the pool game. My corner is gone, the place I thought of as mine. I look at the musasa tree behind me. A few metres further down a man I haven't seen before is squatting on his heels. He has on blue overalls, has spread out sacking, an assortment of old worn shoes and has sat down to the business of mending soles. Beyond that spot is a driveway into a block of flats and then it becomes the territory of the girls on the shops' side. After a few minutes I realise that this is not going to work. This corner will only work in the evening now. I make up my mind to go back to the flat to sit out the next hour or two. With some luck, I'll score a hit of guka from someone there.

It is about 5:30pm when I step out of the flat again. My apartment block, Coventry Mews, is on the corner of Third Street and Chinamano Avenue. This is the hottest spot for work and two taxi drivers run this and the corner further down on Chinamano and Fourth Street. The duo of Taxi Drivers, like Sisi Stella, recruit girls from outside the city and manage them under the direction of Ma'am Loveness. Chefe provides the necessary political protection. They are called the Taxi Drivers because they park two cars with "Taxi" stickers on the sides but everyone knows they are not taxi drivers. Sisi Stella says in the old days when the police used to come around and harass the girls almost every night, the Taxi Drivers would rush all six or eight of them into the cars and drive them off until it was clear again. The police have stopped patrolling the Avenues thanks to Chefe's intervention, but the Taxi Drivers still park on this corner the whole day, making sure the girls are working. Gogo Muchadura sits on her paint can on the pavement a few metres from the cars. Her sweets and cigarettes neatly laid out on top of a cardboard box beside her. She is wrapped in a thick brown coat on this warm summer evening, hunched over and seems to be dozing but the three girls on the corner mill around her, taking turns to look up and down the street whenever a car turns in their direction.

"These streets are no place for you young ones," Gogo says while reaching out and tugging my arm, "Listen to an old woman like me. I have been here and seen things."

"Ah, Gogo, don't worry about me. I'm just doing this quickly and then I'll sort my life out."

"That is what we all said, my child. Now look at me. Do you think I was always an old woman seated here?"

"Ah, Gogo, okay, I hear you."

"What flies up must come down and land. Never forget that, my child."

"Sure, Gogo."

I walk towards the two cars and ignore the threats the girls are hissing at me. Two of the girls have faces that are much lighter than their limbs and folds of flesh roll down their sides. The tight tubes they are wearing show the curved profile of their stomachs even in the fading light. I recognise the third girl. Instead of the shaggy blonde mane she now has a black bob wig. She is still in the same short white dress. She has found her way here. ***Why can I never escape?***

The Taxi Drivers do not give me a hard time. I was expecting them to be cold and rough and to maybe even laugh me off. They tell me that they will not steal one of Sisi Stella's girls but that I'm free to come join them when I'm done working off my debt.

"We can fight with the police any day, my sister. Ah, but to fight with Sisi Stella, hmm, no."

"But you can talk to her, perhaps?"

"Ah, my sister, Sisi Stella is a tough nut to crack. She is a lion amongst lions that one. But when you are finished with her, ah, then you can come and we will talk."

I also pick up a hint of concern in their voices but I don't know; maybe I'm just hearing things. I'm dreading going back to my corner. Sisi Stella wasn't at the flat and none of the girls would give me a hit. I need strength for tonight. My joints are aching and the insects are itchy under my skin. I can feel the eyes watching from everywhere. *Why can't I catch a break from all this just for a day?* I make my way down Chinamano Avenue towards Second Street and I can see, in the dim amber light, that all the touts are now gone; no shoe-mender as well and no Mukoma Josh; not even the women selling sadza and rice out of three buckets and no one playing pool or by the wall smoking mbanje. The corner is mine again but for how long?

I scratch around in my clutch bag for the bottle of bronco, take two sips and then a third longer swig. I'll have to stretch the little that's left.

The traffic is constant and it feels like I'm in for a busy night.

Jedza

Something was in the air last night. The leaves were still. No voices came through my balcony. Sleep came in broken pieces. Shards stabbing me awake and then dropping out into the darkness. They would float down a water-filled tunnel, some slipping into a tangle of roots making up the tunnel walls and I would sink deeper into a labyrinthine slumber. Always some dimly lit corner of the Avenues. On some nights it is Penny's face staring up at me, unblinking, unbreathing, under the film of water. Other nights it is Natsai's face, in a calm pool, strangely comforting. In the last frame, she moves. Her face rises closer to the surface, becoming clearer. My heart starts thumping in my chest. I shut the image out, too scared to look at her face and wake up in a sweat. I stay awake until the first rays of light point in through the trees across the alley.

***

I've been walking up and down Chinamano between my flat and the Travel Plaza shops since midday. It is now early evening and I have run out of things to buy. The corner gang have run out of quips and I'm out of banter. The full complement is there on the corner of Fourth and Chinamano. Banana Cart Guy is teasing Profe for not making a move on Penny when he had a chance; Profe is claiming to have a real girlfriend whom none of them has seen; two new guys are swaying in seated positions on the concrete blocks; a third new guy has a set grin as he leans against the concrete waste bin. Profe gestures towards me and then jogs over. "Mukoma, you still have not told me if that tobacco snuff I gave you helped."

"You know what, I knew there was something I had forgotten to mention."

"It worked, right? That one is good. I got it from kwaRwizi. Those people don't play games with their fodya. It's the real stuff. What? You don't seem happy, Mukoma."

"No. It's not that I'm not happy. There was nothing wrong with it. I don't think so. Except I'm confused. I haven't stopped having those dreams but I think the fodya has changed them to something else?"

"Something good or bad, Mukoma?"

"Ah, Profe, I don't know. Now I'm seeing my sister but she's in the water. I just don't know."

"Your sister, is she still with us?"

"No, she left us long ago."

"Hmmm, Mukoma. You know what? You might need to see a sekuru or mbuya who can look into your people. Remember the fodya is just a small part of these rituals.

Maybe you need a proper bira where you can reach out to those who have gone."

"Ah Profe, there I don't know. That sounds like deep ways of the people that I am not familiar with?"

"No, Mukoma, don't worry. Don't worry, you are my mukoma. If you are free one of these weekends I can see what I can do to help you."

"Sure, Youngaz. We'll see."

I spot Penny's figure turning into Chinamano from Third Street and stride off after her. Banana Cart Guy whistles after me and I ignore the taunting behind me. She crosses Chinamano and stops by the Taxi Drivers. I slow down waiting for her to take off and eventually have to stop because she takes a while. I fiddle around on my phone and walk off again when she pushes on towards her corner. I pass the Taxi Drivers and nod at the girls there and one of them asks me if I'm not keen on a short time, which I turn down, nod at Gogo Muchadura hunched over her box of sweets and carry on down the pavement. Gogo Muchadura turns her face up towards me and widens her eyes as if she is looking at a vending license officer. She stretches her neck up towards me and I lean an ear down to her. She whispers, her voice hoarse, laden with caution, "Hold tightly what I tell you, my child. When you eat this fruit, when you chew, do not forget that it also has bitter pulp."

I nod and thank her without fully understanding and push on towards Penny. I catch up with her before she has a moment to settle down. The corner is deserted save for the two of us. I greet her hurriedly and then search for a way to enquire without sounding weird.

"Penny, I had this dream. Maybe it's nothing, I don't know." "A dream about what?" Her voice is weak.

"You. I dreamt that you were in the water. Underwater."

She is silent. Breathing slowly.

"In water, me?"

"Yes. I saw your face staring up at me out of watery depths."

I wait for her to respond.

She just stares at me blankly while scratching incessantly at her arms. Her eyes and cheeks are sunken. There is a glassy quality to her seemingly larger eyes. For a moment the image of little Shalom slams into my mind. Penny's unresponsive silence is broken by a harsh cough.

She coughs and sputters violently and then beats her hand on her chest to compose herself. I tell her about Natsai and how she just disappeared somewhere in this place and the strange sensations I feel walking around the Avenues and she asks me if I'm feeling alright, if I need a beer. She laughs me away and tells me she'll catch up with me at the bar. She clutches her chest and holds her breath to suppress another bout of coughing. Beads of sweat have formed along her brow.

"I've already told you about this thing that comes out of the water," she says eventually. "But I don't know, maybe my mind is playing with children."

"So, you haven't seen anything at all? Or felt something?" I push her.

"I don't know what I've felt. It starts to get cold out here," she says. "Time-time I get bored. Maybe I should stop taking this bronco. Maybe it is pulling things towards me." *Life is just hard for me now.* She's mumbling and I can't catch her last words.

I turn and head for Jacaranda Vibes. I leave her bent over, scratching, looking around, coughing up phlegm and spitting it out. I need a drink now. More than one. Halfway down the road I turn to look back at her. It feels like a parting and I stare at her as if to remember this moment, fix her thin, bent–over figure in my mind. I make out her form in the dusk but her face is a featureless blur. Her raspy coughs echo down the street. Once in the bar, I drink fast to numb myself, cheap gin this evening. Now and again I open the pouch in my pocket, pinch some of Profe's fodya between my fingers and fire up my brain. My heart thumps to a beat. *Chitima Nditakure* rings between my ears,

Look, the days I have left on this earth are only four,
See, I am dying as I stand,

Look, you men have now abandoned me,
Train, carry me away,
To where others have gone

Penny doesn't walk in. At some point I walk out or the bar staff urge me to go home. There are taxis and voices and girls laughing outside the bar. A breeze passes through me. It slides under my collar and wraps my chest and back in its coolness. It blows from the right and whirls around me. I stumble on through the darkness. A street lamp flickers through the shadows to the right. Beyond the swirling breeze around me, the night air is still. I walk on down Chinamano towards my flat. Past Penny's spot. It stands there taunting me in the greyness, the odd musasa and the pool ominously blacker and gurgling. Tree branches twitch and scrape against one another. I curse the place under my breath and then I curse it loudly. I stumble around the edges of the pool of water to the tree. I grip its sides for balance and rattle myself in my attempt to shake out its secret. I curse it into the darkness.

Look, this mountain that I must labour over,
To fulfil my destiny in this life,
This mountain shaped like the head of a male goat,
It is full of vicious baboons

At some point I find my way home, stumble through the dimness of my flat and flop onto my bed. The visions start flashing in before the back of my head hits the pillow. I lie on my back and all the sensation in my body drips from my face and my limbs, so that my body is impaled into the mattress. First, faces flash past like pages from a new book with a stiff spine. The crisp sound of the pages blends into the rustling of the leaves from the branches leaning towards my balcony. The voices of girls screaming at each other pierce my right ear and crashing bottles ring out in the left. The rush of air from the fluttering pages carries the scent of rotting jacaranda flowers and rain steaming off tar. Banana Cart Guy's face flits past, then Profe, then a long flurry of temporary corner gang faces and then Penny's face caked in make-up. The face masked and the hoarse choking cough like some deep warning. And then the scene hovers over the corner of Second Street and Chinamano Avenue, dim with shadow.

Penny

This realm is not for me...

I finished my bronco hours ago. Insects won't stop stinging and tormenting me, clouds of tiny winged creatures, and the itching from bites and welts is relentless. Myriad eyes in the dark trees are watching me but I must work. Maybe Sisi Stella will send one of the girls from the flat to me with a pipe or maybe even a whole gram. I position myself near the musasa and touch up my lipstick. The small girl appears, dripping wet.

"Why am I not afraid of you?"

"Why do you think you should be afraid of me?"

The sound comes from a motionless mouth.

"I don't know. Maybe because you are not a real person."

"What am I?"

"I don't know. A ghost?"

"Touch me."

I move forward and touch the girl's arm with the back of my hand. Her skin feels cool and wet. I catch the scent of fresh bark. The coolness spreads over my hand and up my arm, driving away the insects and relieving the feverish itches. The little girl stares at me out of two glistening dark hollows. I ask her something.

"Do you live in this pool of water?"

"No, this is just an opening."

"An opening to what?"

"Do you know njuzu?" She whispers.

"I have heard of them from others. But I don't think they are real."

"We," the little girl says, "are them."

They remove their hand from mine and instantly, the insects crawl back and the itchiness resumes. *Am I forever doomed to suffer in this world?*

"This world is not for us. If it is respite you seek, take off your shoes and take my hand."

I pull off one shoe and then the other, a relief to step out of tight heels. My feet squelch in mud and my itchy aching calves find cool relief. The njuzu turn back to the water and reach their hands out to me. I close my hands around their clammy fingers and follow. They lead me into the chilly water which rises up to my knees and I realise I am standing in a bottomless pool, no ground below. The njuzu pause, turn around to face me and then slide their hands down my sides. It is a tender movement and I shiver as the coolness washes over my skin. Peacefulness filters into my body. Anger, frustration, thirst, cravings, the aching and tensions in my muscles, bruises and obscure hurts, my longing and loneliness all dissolve away. They hold me suspended over depths and then rub my feet, using each of their hands, until they are one with the water, permeable and softened. They embrace me and we descend until the water is level with my waist. I try to move my feet but cannot feel them. What I sense now are the winding passages below me and the entangled roots winding down into the depths. The njuzu rub their hands further up my body until the water comes up to my neck. Their small hands slide up my throat and cover my ears and with one last shared gulping breath, we submerge.

Now I leave,
I must go far away,
It is best that I leave for distant lands,
Your hearts are cold,
My ancestors have abandoned me,
My kin have hearts of stone,
This realm is not for me,
And now I depart for distant lands.

14

BIRA

kwaRwizi, 2018

I hear drums playing, You young men have set me loose, I hear our drums playing, This is me unchained, I hear your drums playing, Now I just wander without end, I hear our spiritual drums playing, Now my eyes bulge like round nuts in the firelit darkness **-Ndanzwa Ngoma Kurira/Thomas Mapfumo.**

Jedza

Stay with me a little longer. The moment I close my eyes, A face floats up towards me. It starts as a grey circle in the depths and slowly rises up the longer I peer into the water. It almost breaks the surface and then it begins to pull away, sink back down. I feel a strong urge to call out, "Dalitso!" but nothing comes out, I can't open my mouth or cry aloud. My throat tightens. The face is just out of reach, a dim oval. I touch the surface of the water and concentric ripples obscure the face. The outline wavers and then fades away. The face slips out of sight, disappears into the watery darkness. And then my sister Natsai taps me on the shoulder.

"Who are you looking at?"

"Ah, Sisi Natsai, you remember my old friend Dalitso. We used to be friends in crèche," I reply.

"But there is no-one there."

"There he is, in there." I point at the pool of water but it is an empty greyness, widening liquid circles in a hollow spiral.

"Where's Dalitso?" Natsai asks. She stares into my eyes and my heart starts pounding.

Arise, let us go,
Come, let us be off
Summon the young men who fight war

"Gerry, where is Dalitso?" The thumping in my chest speeds up to a deafening rumble. I hear the train roaring towards me. The distant whistle pierces my ear drums and with it comes the intermittent sideways shaking. Natsai starts to walk away. The rumbling gets louder and my heart is banging around inside my chest like a headless chicken. The train is coming in from all around me. I want to run from it; even so, I stay in place because I want to recognise the face in the water. Why is Natsai here? I want to get on the train but I am afraid of where it will take me. Afraid I will miss a step, stumble or fall, that this merciless iron engine will run over me and crush me beneath its wheels. I can't hear myself think, am speechless, shattered. The train sounds as if it is almost upon me, the noise is deafening.

***

Arise, let us go,
Arise, let us be off,
Summon the young men who fight our battles

I can't go on like this. Yet again, I wake up with my head pounding as though a dozen hands have been drumming away on it the whole night. I am drenched in acrid sweat and the sheets are soaked. Trembling, I reach out for my phone and my hand falls on the empty pouch of tobacco snuff. That brings me back into wakefulness, the reality of where I am

now. I remember Profe's offer and fix myself up to go down
to the corner.

Profe has come back to the Avenues, to his corner. He
seems fit again, looking healthy.

"Ah Mukoma, it is you whom I have been waiting for," he
shouts out well before I get to them.

"Waiting for me?"

I join the gathering, nod to and greet all the rastaz. They
acknowledge my greeting in varying states of sobriety.

"So, as I was telling these rastaz here, you can see I am fit.
I am back to my usual self. But I must leave you," Profe says.

"This one speaks like a grandfather at a funeral. Just say
your story like this, 'ga ga ga,' like an axe chopping wood,
Profe." Banana Cart Guy sets the whole corner roaring.

"Who will tell us what the rate is now that our Professor
is leaving us?" another rasta mocks.

"Hey, you guys, let me speak seriously. I have received my
calling so I'm going to live with the people of kwaRwizi. You
all know them."

The banter dries up and Profe goes around patting and
mumbling pleasantries and seeing off each of his mates.
I stand aside while they brave their emotions, sorry to see
him go. The mood lightens up when Banana Cart Guy starts
singing an offkey and out of time rendition of *Itai Ndiwone*.
"Who are our real friends in these times of need?" The whole
corner erupts.

I have so many questions, for Profe, some to do with Penny
who has suddenly disappeared, but mostly for him. I ask him
how much this departure has to do with his experiences at
the foot of the musasa tree.

"I might have been ill that day," he says, "but I swear on
my grandmother's grave I felt there was something unseen
happening at that corner. You know the way you feel
sometimes when you're walking alone at night and get the
sensation of being watched or of a presence in the darkness
around you? That prickly sensation at the back of your
neck. I felt that when I walked around that girl and placed

my hands on that small musasa tree. Since then, Mukoma, I have travelled to different places in search of an answer. Mostly they wasted my time. VaPostori, the miracle pastors, the jumpy-jumpy prophets, all a waste of time. Deliverance Night, Judgement Night kudii kudii, haiwawo. In the end I just went to the council clinic near my house and they gave me some tablets which are working fine."

"So, if you fixed that problem with tablets, then why are you still leaving us?"

"Ah, Mukoma, you are speeding. Slow down so you can hear my story clearly. I then spoke to this one old guy, Sekuru Takawira. He lives in my street and worked in the Avenues as a driver for the British Embassy for many years, a long time ago. That old man has so many stories, I tell you. He said he knew what happened in that place, particularly to people for whom water is sacred, because of the history there. People falling mysteriously ill, others disappearing forever. He is the one who directed me to the vaDziva svikiro who resides in kwaRwizi, the place of the river. That is the place where all the underground streams meet."

I'm listening but my mind jumps to another concern. "Do you think what this old guy told you has any connection with the disappearance of Penny? You know, the girl who used to stand at that corner there?"

"Mukoma, these working girls just come and go. We don't know where they come from or where they go when they disappear."

He pauses and stares at the ground for a while, then looks up at me.

"But from what I saw with my own eyes that day, and given all these inexplicable things happening now, what that old man was saying might explain what is really going on. All I know is that the spirits of those who are troubled find peace on the other side."

"Can they help us understand what happened to someone who disappeared a long time ago?"

"I have only begun to work with the people at kwaRwizi but I know that time means nothing to them. They can help with things currently happening and things that go back even to the time of our ancestors. What are you thinking, Mukoma?"

"I want to consult this svikiro with you."

"Ah, that's the way to go, Mukoma. You are lucky to have found me here now, in this place. There is a bira tomorrow. Let me give you the directions and we'll meet there."

Profe grins and his happiness is infectious, I find myself laughing.

Bukai tiende, bukai tiende,
Aho-a, ho-a,
Ho-aa-aa

***

So, Saturday afternoon I walk into the city centre and catch a kombi heading out east. We stay on the highway, head over the Mupfure River bridge. The kombi bounces on the uneven bridge surface and I am nudged up and down, swung this way and that, in my seat. This is all at the back of my mind though. I am mesmerised by the sheer expanse of the river beneath me. It is as if I am seeing it anew. The hairs at the back of my neck rise as I stare into the flowing mass. I trace the river's length until it shimmers in the distance. The kombi passes over the bridge, the river cutting out of sight, and I am roused back to the present.

Soon, I drop off at the first gravel road. I then get a mshika-shika from that corner to the shops, where I ask for directions to kwaRwizi. As I set off, I hear the nearby rush of a flowing body of water, the Mupfure again, now at its confluence with the Njiri. I also feel low rumblings through the earth. At some turns in the footpath, I catch a glimpse of a large body of water and at other times, a small creek flowing into the ground. I have the uncanny sensation of a return, of nostalgia, to a place I have never been. That the Mupfure, the Njiri and all the waters converging here on the surface and below, are guiding me back to myself. As instructed, I walk down a farm road alongside fenced fields, all the while aware of the presence of fluid motion around me, of the nzizi that all flow with and beside me, and then through the last wooden gate in a line of homesteads. As Profe had mentioned, the earth here is grey, damp and soggy clay. There are tall water reeds in all directions and the scent of wetness. The ground dries on the approach up to the higher ground on which the homestead stands.

Smoke is rising. There are black and blackened pots over open fires in a cooking area. Elderly women uncovering clay pots and dipping gourds into the Seven-Days brew to taste the progress.

Women dishing up food into plates and younger women carrying the plates to groups huddled in patches of shade beside huts and under trees. Around the trees some Chibuku containers are already freshly discarded and unopened ones are waiting for the food to be dealt with. I pass from group to group and put my hands together greeting here and there looking for a familiar face. Someone raises a welcoming hand from under the large leafless tree across the yard and I stride across to Profe.

It is late afternoon and people are still strolling in as ones and twos and now and again a car pulls up and parks along the fence of the homestead. One group sitting near the fire are vana gwenyambira, master mbira players. Their mbira are laid on the ground behind them and they haven't heated their drums yet. Two boys are messing around with the drums playing a half-decent attempt at some up-tempo mbende beat, some girls are making noise with the hosho, trying to strike a rhythm and little kids are raising a fair amount of fine dust with their stomping and shuffling and chasing each other around.

"A plate for big brother is needed here. He hasn't eaten yet."

Profe's words pass across the yard and in a moment plates are placed before me and two more men who have joined our group. We take turns washing our hands and tuck in. Profe is telling me about the medicine he is taking and how good it is and how his headaches have stopped and also about his calling to be a homwe for an ancestor whose exact identity he is yet to ascertain. He strongly suspects a great-grand uncle he refers to as vaCharakupa but says there may be one or two more vying for him to be their conduit.

"The medicine works but one must always address the source of the illness," he says. "Otherwise I keep getting ill and taking medication, and getting ill again and taking more medication and how can one live like that?"

I ask him what the exchange rates are today and he jokes that on occasions like this, he only deals with spiritual indicators, not financial ones.[40]

We eat. He points out two other people who are assisting the svikiro at this bira, together with himself, and says that he will have to leave me shortly to go and prepare to enter the banya as the sun sets. He comes across as a different person. As if he has been concealed behind a couple of layers the whole time I've known him in the Avenues, and now he is free to drop or discard those protective layers when he is here, far from the city lights.

He reaches for a Super Chibuku that has been doing the rounds around the tree, says "Pamusoroyi," in courtesy, takes a long swallow, passes it on and then leans back and asks me,

"Otherwise ndeipi?"

***

---

40   The Ministry announced that goats shall now be an accepted form of school fees. I should ask Profe to explain how the exchange rate between goats, USD and mobile money would work. Where would The Ministry keep the national goats?

Shadows lengthen across the ground and a cooling breeze drifts in. We sit under our tree whose shade is no longer needed: the overhead trunk and branching canopy is merging into the descending darkness. All the pots have been cleared from the fire and the drums are being heated and tested by a boy who plays mbira softly between his trips to the fire. Profe reaches for the Chibuku and leans towards me:

"That time! That time, that time, I was surely dead, big brother."

"Profe and all you guys, death, do you really know that darkness?"

"All that was left of me was my head, my friend."

"Even the head itself was finished too."

"Ah, please don't say that, big brother."

We take turns with the Chibuku and then wipe our mouths with the backs of our hands.

***

"But Profe, now that we are here, I must tell you something. That girl Penny is not the only reason that I find myself here kwaRwizi."

"But Mukoma, you now agree that you rinsed me there, you knew I liked that girl."

"Ah but Profe, you guys surely know that there was nothing going on between me and that little girl. I saw her very much as a young sister to me."

"Yah, I first thought my own Mukoma had washed me, but then I did see that you are not the type that chases dresses. So, what is the real story, Mukoma?"

"Those visions that I have. Some of them I have had from a long time ago. But ever since I came to the Avenues, I have been seeing the face of my sister, Natsai. She disappeared in those same Avenues years ago and yet I feel she is still there, lingering somewhere on the periphery of my life. She just vanished one day, like Penny. Why? Where is she, what has become of her? She may have been taken far away, yet I see her in my visions and her presence is close."

"Ah, now that issue is a big one. What I know, Mukoma, is that the ways of our people are difficult to understand. Sometimes the ancestors want one thing but then another thing happens."

"Can you speak straight please, Profe? Not all of us understand these things, my guy."

"Maybe the important thing is that you are here at kwaRwizi, Mukoma, however that may have come about. What I know is that no-one is ever really *gone*. They may now be beyond our reach and yet still remain with us. A key reason the unseen spirits take our loved ones is to relieve them of their suffering. I have, with my own eyes, seen those who have been taken from us existing at peace serving those below the ground, appearing to their loved ones from time to time to reassure them."

I will ask it, that question,
To the heavens,
We will ask it, definitely,
We will ask it

The beer has been brewing for seven days. Two elderly women have been guarding it all week; now it has been cooling since midday and the first pot of the warm musumo is going around the yard, so each person who arrives swiftly gets into the mood. One young woman lowers the pot to the ground and the other dips a mukombe into the pot; they both kneel and present the gourd to those present. This moves from hand to hand and when receiving it back, empty, the server rubs her palms.

That, why God,
Why do you give us a hard time?
And now, our relatives who leave us,
Where are they?
You, which land do you put them, that is far?

A mshika-shika I rode in a few days ago played *Samatenga* on high volume and the song has been stuck in my head since then. In the song, Simon Chimbetu bleeds. As he pleads to vari kumatenga, those in the afterlife, he weeps for me too. We have the same questions, Simon and I. Where are our relatives? Have they gone well? Are they at peace?

There, where they sit unable to speak to us,
Because I am frantic, pleading to those who rule,
For them to show me the way,
So I go back where I came from.

***

Profe left for the banya a while ago. He went off with the other assistants and at some point, I saw their outlines drifting into the hut. In the evening glow, shapes float, shift and lose definition. There is enough moonlight to make out familiar figures and to tell the female forms wrapped in mazambia from the male figures in their fabrics knotted over their shoulders. Through the open doorway, flames throw silhouettes of seated figures onto the walls. A boy shuffles behind me and fetches the last mbira from the instruments that were stacked behind the players sitting under our tree earlier.

I look upwards at the sound of flapping wings. Birds are circling in a wide arc against the bright moon. They descend in narrowing circles and then land, one by one in turn, on the outspread branches. I count each of them as they come in to perch overhead. *One, two, three, four, five, six, seven.* Under the night sky, I cannot make out the colour of their plumage but notice the shape of their long pointed bills. Herons. I make my way across the yard. I slip off my shoes and stoop to enter the banya. Inside, the sound picks up. A steady looping rhythm with a melody bouncing on it. Sounds like some variation of *Mahororo*. The shadows thrown onto the rear wall are now leaping back and forth in time to the clapping and the rattling hosho, now shaken by more capable wrists.

Me, Grandmother, my spirit runs away from playing mbira,
I turn away from them,
Because when I play them, they are heard there, way over there,
They draw attention to me

Elders are seated along the curving wall, their heads slightly bowed as they lean over and whisper to one another. They have assistants on either side of them and Profe sits in the shadow of Mbuya Dziva, the great water ancestor's svikiro. The mbira players are seated across the banya with their legs straightened out in front of them, instruments steady on their thighs. Between Mbuya Dziva and the gwenyambira stands the musasa tree around which the banya is built, barely visible in the smoky firelight but musasa presence and the tingling scent of fresh bark fills the room. Bodies are filing in: I brush up against other dancers and sway as part of the small dancing circle in front of the mbira players. One of the young women serving musumo earlier writhes on the floor as the mbira keys draw out something ancient lodged deep within her.

She dances,
Come see,
In her watery den,
Now she glides,
She dances, There she dives!

The woman on the floor gyrates and swivels around and around the tree. The gwenyambira lean into their resonators and then strum on. The playing rises to a crescendo and the path trailing the woman becomes soaked in water seeping through from below ground. Kutsinhira, the response, on one end; kushaura, the call, on the other; the mbira notes lock in. In the smoky light, flames reflect and flicker in their glazed eyes which now appear round as glistening nuts. In the tight circle pushing in around them, feet shuffle and stomp and hands clap in time to the drums. Now and again a voice leads a song and a response picks up, again and again, until it dies out and another voice starts up a different call. The young woman on the floor writhes and glides in her watery track, the restless spirit within her not letting up, the mbira reeling in the catch from within its submerged cave.

In her watery den, the sun goes down,
She dances,
In her cave, darkness sets in,
She dances,
In her watery den, the sun sinks,
She dances

The sound of the mbira subsides. Only one player plucks on, his head to one side, feeding off the applause, the clapping hands that respond to him. The other two lean back against the banya wall and palm, pinch and shoot snuff up into their skulls. A wail pierces the dancing circle and a chorus of responses rise up. Stomping reverberates on the floor and the clapping gets sharper and louder, the lone mbira notes barely audible. A long drawn out ululation rings out and the source leaps within the tight circle. On the floor, the writhing form is relentless in motion and fevered rhythm, locked into its watery dance with the strand of melody coming from the solo mbira. Her body a vessel through which a taken spirit has been summoned and drawn up, to commune with those of kin present in the dancing and singing bodies.

Come see her,
She dances,
Come see, before the sun rises,
She dances

When Mbuya Dziva arrives into her svikiro, he lets out a
series of shrieks as his consciousness welcomes hers. The
assistant swiftly retrieves the svikiro's white arrival fabric
and drapes it over her shoulders. Mbuya Dziva has arrived.
Whispers of "Mbuya vasvika," spread around the hut, music
fades out and the dancers scramble for space to sit, avoiding
the fire and the shallow pool in which the young woman
flounders. The writhing trembles out of the form on the
floor. She slowly comes to and looks around her, wet and
disoriented. Her whites are now browns. Her expression
drained, her eyes hollow and dark. Two women help her out
of the banya. Mbuya Dziva struts back and forth with her
head bowed, her svikiro uttering her words with his voice
now shrill in high-pitched register. Her assistant follows her
around as she asks who is gathered here, who has summoned
her, and are they willing to hear what she has to say? Will
they heed her advice? Her assistant interprets her rich words
spoken in deep chiZezuru and Mbuya Dziva cackles,
    "These new days are not as they used to be. The sun rises
differently for these grandchildren of mine, but do they even
see it, these blind ones? These grandchildren whose eyes are
younger than mine, me, an old woman, I see what they do
not see. Do you see, my grandchildren?"
    "No, Mbuya, we do not see."
    "The seasons used to bring rain early but do they bring rain
now? Do the rains not come late now? Seasons change and
these grandchildren who have lost the ways of our people do
not even see. Do you even still work the earth like our people
worked the earth?"
    "We do not, Mbuya."
    "Listen to how they speak to me. They just answer like
this, ridiculing an old woman. These grandchildren who
have lost the ways of their people. Do you even respect me,
your grandmother?"
    "Yes, Mbuya, we respect you."
    "You answer my every word as if you have an age with
me, you who were born yesterday. Me, your grandmother,

who was born before the year of the locusts; Me, who walked through the land of the tall grass; Me, who put an axe to the musasa, munhondo and the muhacha; Who am I?"

There is incoherent mumbling.

"Do you not hear me? I said, *Who am I?*"

"Mbuya Dziva."

She shudders and shrugs her shoulders violently.

"You answer me, you who still have your mother's milk on your nose. Me, your grandmother, who made our home there, where men who fight wars were summoned but feared to tread; Me, who swam the depths of these caverns and marked their entrances with the musasa so that men who fight wars would know where to tread, without falling in and drowning. You, who look me in the face, do you want to see who I am?"

"No, Mbuya." All in the banya lower and bow their heads.

"Do you think you can look me, your grandmother, in the eyes?"

"No, Mbuya."

She laughs, "These grandchildren who have lost their ways.

"The words I speak, do you not hear them with your ears? Why must my homwe here put words on top of my words, for you, my grandchildren, to understand me? Are you not from my womb?"

She cackles.

She settles before the shallow pool and dips her face into the water. She raises her head and sprays water from her pursed lips in sweeping arcs across the banya. After further remonstrations and warnings, she says she is ready to receive those who want to consult her. I step forward and go down on one knee.

"Look at this one who cannot even kneel properly before a grandmother like me. Do you have no respect for Mbuya who came before you?"

"I respect you, Mbuya."

"What tongues is this one speaking?" She asks her homwe.

"Forgive these grandchildren of yours Mbuya, their ways are now those of men without knees, but they want to learn."

Mbuya Dziva grunts.

"Who is before me, tell me who you are?"

"I am Hara, bird of the water, that which perches on high branches and swoops down low, vaDziva who dwells above and below water."

"I am of the bird of the water, that which perches on high branches and swoops down low, vaDziva who dwells above and feeds below water," she repeats, then adds, "Do you know who I am?"

"No, Mbuya."

"I am Dziva herself who dwells in the water, who gives birth to Hacha who sleeps in the water but breathes the air, who in turn, herself, gives birth to Tora who lives on land but feeds in the water and above it, who gives birth to Takada who first grew wings and lived in water, on land and perched in trees, who herself, gives birth to Hara, bird of the water, who perches on high branches and swoops down low, vaDziva who dwells above and below water. Do you see that I am your grandmother and you are my grandchild?"

"I see this, Mbuya, and I seek your words."

"Do you believe in what we do here?"

"Yes, Mbuya."

"Those who do not believe in what we do here are always free to leave. Let it not be said that they are held against their will. What do you seek from this old woman, my grandchild?"

"I have a sister who is lost. We do not know where she is but we believe she may have been taken. I see my hanzvadzi, she who comes before me, in another realm of wakefulness, or sleep. She comes to me and I wish to know what became of her."

"I see. Where are the elders of your people and why are they not here? Why do they send the young ones to do the work of the elders? Do they not believe in the work of the ancestors?"

I shut my eyes.

"I ask for your forgiveness, Mbuya, they do not follow the ways of our people, but I am here."

"Those who lose their way shall find their way back. The ways of our people have been here and they shall continue to be here long after we are all gone. These are not matters of the flesh."

I hear Mbuya Dziva pinch snuff from her pouch and snort it into her nostrils. She lets out a shriek and shakes her head, rattling the beads around her neck.

"It happens, at times, that those who came before will take those who still walk, sometimes when they are in distress, at other times when those who came before have their reasons which we do not understand. I see your sister who comes before you. She is descended and she will rise again. Her spirit is strong and she reaches out to your people but her people do not see her. If you look for her in the ways of our people you will find her. Do you hear your grandmother?"

"I hear you, Mbuya."

"There are those here who will teach you the words and ways of our people, which are forgotten by many in these times, and in that way you will commune with your sister who comes before you. It is well that you believe. Her heart is heavy and that is why she reaches out to you from the depths. Do you hear me?"

"I hear you, Mbuya."

"She will guide you through this life and in turn you will guide others. These are the ways of our people. Do you hear the spirits when they bite your ears?"

"Ehoyi, Mbuya."

"These are the gatherings that we have walked here for on this day. When you have prepared, when you are ready, you will summon your ancestor and you will commune with her."

At the sound of these words from the svikiro's mouth, I open my eyes again and blink out the wetness. I had adjusted to the sting from the smoke inside the thatched roof and round walls of the banya, but hot tears had welled up when I squeezed shut my eyes. I look into the svikiro's eyes and a wave of unease passes through me. I avert my gaze.

"I hear you, Mbuya."

"Your eyes, the way they fill with tears, there is something else in your heart, which causes it to be unsettled. You may choose to keep it inside but remember that what is inside the heart is hidden, a child who does not cry dies in the cradle."

"There are things I see and hear, Mbuya. Things which I do not understand. Sometimes a train carries me, other times it runs over me, but always I hear it and it makes my heart beat. I feel as though this train took my life out of my hands and keeps it always beyond my reach."

"My grandchildren speak to me of things brought here by those that are without knees. To me, their grandmother, an old woman who walked from the land of the tall grass in the time when days were long. This is the darkness that comes down on my grandchildren when our ways are forgotten. When they cut down our trees whose roots drank from our waterways. When me, your grandmother gets angry, then you will say that I have turned my back on you."

Mbuya Dziva lets out a shriek and shakes her shoulders.

"My heart is heavy but you are my grandchildren. Lose the ways of the people and you will see me clearly. You are hiding behind your finger, my grandchild. Go to the place of your visions and confront the baboons which stand on that mountain; look beyond that finger which you hold before you. I am your grandmother and I have spoken. Do you hear me when I bite your ears?"

"I hear you, Mbuya."

"Once in each nostril. Do not rush it."

I reach out my hand. She shakes some fodya into my palm then prays over it. I take a pinch and snort it into each nostril and then strain up onto my feet with the one free arm. My knees are relieved from the hard floor but that respite is lost in light-headedness and then the rush of tobacco into the roof of my skull. Her homwe tells me that I am done and I shuffle to the side. He quickly clarifies all Mbuya Dziva's words and instructions in plain, more accessible Shona. It is as I believed. I need to purge an ill wind, a vengeful spirit, and cast it into a beast. The spirit speaking through her also says that I will gain clarity once I perform the ritual. That my eyes will open to what is weighing me down. Preventing my life from moving forward. I now watch others like me, who want to commune with their taken, summon them briefly and connect.

Now in her den as the sun rises,
She dances,
There she descends,
As she dances

***

The beer in the pots has cooled down. Mbuya Dziva has since descended and her svikiro now sits drinking, in his place, with the other men of the village. The music is now outside, people gathered around a huge fire in the centre of the yard and the dancing raises a fine dust that hangs over the scene whenever the early morning breeze stops blowing. I sway and clap and sing back responses with a hoarse exhausted voice. Shuffling my feet this way and that, resolving the tensions that have been bound up within me for days and weeks and years. I now hunt for the pot and linger where I find it. I dip the gourd and take a long sip, pass it on and dip it back in again. We are on the margins of the urban districts and the air has rural notes. There is also the chilly dampness of a swampy area mingled with the fine sprays from the surrounding rivers as they flow into one. Stars are out and an empty darkness extends beyond the edges of the circle of firelight. I'm out of tobacco and I won't need any more. When the sun rises, it will be a long day of blowing the caked remnants out of my nostrils.

I reach into my pockets, front and back, and then start looking at the ground around me. If my phone has been dropped on the ground here, then it will have been smashed to pieces already. I walk across to the tree we had been sitting under in the afternoon and fumble around the spot I sat in.

Dread washes through me as I imagine that my phone has been picked out of my pocket or picked up off the ground. I retrace my earlier movements.

The only place left to search is the banya. I peer in at the entrance and it is dark inside. The embers in the fire only cast an orange glow that does nothing to illuminate the room. The glow from the fire outlines the edges of the pool around the musasa tree in the centre. I trace my way around the hut in the darkness feeling gently with my feet, toeing across inch by inch, hoping to find my phone. After going around the room twice, I sit down in resignation. I'll have to get another one. I lean my back against the wall and shut my eyes.

A figure enters the hut. The rustling of feet on the floor awakens me before I am conscious of the drumming music coming in from outside. My eyes have adjusted to the darkness and I can make out flowing garments around bare feet but not much more than the outline of a human form. The figure hums a tune and kneels towards the embers. It pauses. Looks furtively around the banya. I pause my breathing. It turns back to the burning coals and blows into its hands. Flames flicker briefly followed by pale plumes of smoke. A pungent smell of burning herbs fills the room. The figure carries the smoking clump between its hands to the edge of the water, kneels before it and places the herbs on the ground, while chanting and humming. The glowing clump reflects in the small pool of water surrounding the tree. Music drums in from the yard outside and spurs on the dancing. As I stare in puzzlement, a gurgling sound rises from the depths of the water and a small body breaks the surface up to the level of its chest. The kneeling figure faces upwards briefly and receives something from the smaller figure. I hear words exchanged between the two figures. There is a tone of mutual recognition in the voices. At that moment I wonder if this is a form of visitation. I swallow, blink long and hard to clear the burning sensation out of my eyes and when I look again only the larger figure is in the room, dusting itself off as it leaves the hut.

15

Ndangariro

When, in my melancholy, I think of
My roots,
Oh, how I long for
My home.

Transport out of the city offers plenty of choice. You just have to navigate the touts who control the hiking spot. They will extort a fee from both you and the driver that stops to pick you up. They may rob you in the process. I am soon squeezed into a Japanese-make van, squeaking and rattling out of the city towards Miner's Drift. The driver hunches over the steering wheel and weaves and brakes and shouts through the traffic congestion. I stare out the window at the crowded pavements, office workers, vendors, hustlers, police constables with their baton sticks, all buzzing and scrabbling, arms swinging. Soon, we drive through the suburbs towards the outskirts of the city and approach the first toll gate on the Nyamapanda Highway. We exit the toll gate and the road opens out, clear of the city. The driver relaxes back into his seat and slides into travelling gear. I sink into my seat, gaze out into the changing scenery and hum the song *Ndangariro*. The landscape is now green, quieter, the light brighter and air cleaner. Familiar markers appear, the old sign posts and then neglected farms. Here and there I see some farming going on.

Ploughed fields with irrigation centre pivots spanning them, workers in blue overalls hard at work. Roadside stalls made from poles and thatch with tomatoes, onions, maize, ground nuts for sale - hopeful yet weary eyes panning as we pass. Fences being repaired. Some fields standing neglected with attempted crops wilting in the sun, goats gnawing at them. Clusters of huts on desperate sub-divisions. Stray goats, cattle and chickens wandering close to the road. A recently-opened Gochaz Joint promising roasted meat, sadza, cold beers and rooms to hire. The highway runs parallel to the railway line. It is mostly out of sight but now and again, I see the shiny rails carving out a hillside or crossing over a stream or river on a bridge. Half-an-hour into the journey, we cross the railway line on a flyover bridge. I look back and forth down both lengths of track curving away into the distance and realise that I no longer feel the anxiety of my dreams. What I feel more strongly is premonition. Destiny.

I drop off a few kilometres before we enter Miner's Drift, drop my backpack at my feet and wait for a mshika-shika going out to Dendera Growth Point. Not a long wait as it is an end-of-the-month Saturday and people are travelling in and out of town. The road here is now patchy and mostly gravel. We roll on with dust clouds billowing behind us. The landscape is now dense mupani forest with patches cleared for resettled small-scale farmers. They should be commercial producers with fields of tobacco or maize intended for the market, but tend to be subsistence farmers who also pan rivers and scratch the earth for gold to eke out an existence. Unstable mounds of earth mixed with the rubble of broken rocks from their makeshift shafts and tunnels are dotted around the hills and plains right up to the roadside. Without adequate support, farming and mining like their forebears did in an era long gone, disrupted, now back again. Grown men squeezing into narrow apertures to pass up roped buckets of soil, no safety harnesses, no defence against drowning, suffocating, being buried alive. Women in the fields with children in tow, tilling with calloused hands and sweat pouring in glistening streams down rounded backs. Now and then we slow down while some herdboys steer their cattle off the road, but this part of the journey doesn't take long.

Then I find myself walking down the once-rutted scotch cart track, like my father and his father before him in returning to a place they never really left. This broken devastated land that somehow finds a way to nourish the spirit despite its barrenness. I turn into my parents' homestead. I'm hot and thirsty, finely dusted from head to toe.

My parents are seated in the dappled shade of a guava tree in the front yard. Chickens scatter, high-stepping and pecking at the ground like bent-over yet spritely old people with their walking sticks. Father sits upright on a kitchen chair paging through some book or magazine, Mother reclining with legs stretched out on a reed mat. She leans forward and squints in my direction.

"Ah, my grandfather who rode away on a bicycle and never came back again!" she exclaims. "Baba vaNatsai, is this not your son who has now remembered us?"

Father drops his magazine onto his lap and looks up as I approach. "Ah, it is him indeed."

"The prodigal son himself, Baba vaNatsai. Now we must surely kill a chicken for him before he takes off again."

I go down on one knee.

"Let me arrive, my parents."

"Hezvo! Baba vaNatsai, is this your child coming here with all these manners? Ah, what can we say?"

"Arrive, arrive and welcome, our child."

"How have you been, Baba naMai?"

"We have been well, if you have been well?"

"No, I have been well. And you, how are you at this time?"

"Oh, we are strong. The body aches here and there but what can one do as one ages? And you, how are you?"

"I am as healthy as one can be in these trying times."

We pause in silence.

I drop my bag onto the reed mat and fetch a chair from the kitchen. Mother looks up at me.

"We would have said 'Let us relieve your hands' but we see that you have come with empty hands. Not even a single shopping bag, my son?"

"Ah, Mai, I did it this way so I could travel faster. Don't worry, I am here. I will go into town tomorrow and get one or two things."

"Heheeeede, Baba vaNatsai, you see your child? He still has that fast mouth of his."

"Let the child rest please, Mai vaNatsai."

***

As the sun goes down, we sit under the same tree having sadza, pumpkin leaves and one of Mother's tough, flavourful chickens of the people. I can feel both parents' eyes on me as I plough through my food. It has been a while since I've had a good home-cooked meal. Mother's hand has always set my stomach right. Afterwards, we laze about, feeling the stretch in our bellies and allowing the food to digest: sighing, burping, picking our teeth with dry grass stems and sucking between our teeth. At last, I break the silence.

"Ah, but now you live far from town. I had to walk and walk even after the mshika-shika dropped me off."

"But this child, though. Even when you were in Miner's Drift this homestead was exactly where it is today."

"Ah, Mai, I just mean that it's far compared to the house we lived in when we were in town."

"It would feel closer if you visited more often."

"Mai vaNatsai, he is a young man. He will tire of running around and settle down. Give him time."

"No, Baba vaNatsai, we have given him a long string. Look at him now. Did he even tell us when he left Miner's Drift to go to the city? We had to hear it from people everywhere that 'Ah, Jedza is in Harare', 'Ah, Jedza is now here, Jedza is now there', 'Your son Jedza owes so-and-so money.' And now the Jedza of it all is here eating my chickens with his mouth. Ah, Baba vaNatsai."

Mother claps once and then sighs.

"Mai, I was just sorting out some issues. Things are getting better now. I needed to leave Miner's Drift for a while."

"But you never wanted to come here and help your ageing parents, my child. What kind of child does that? The work here on the homestead is hard. It needs the hands of young men. But you were always up and down doing things we never understood."

"Mai vaNatsai, you know he was employed nicely and he had his apprenticeship until things went bad. The same thing that cost us our pensions and landed us here also happened to these young ones."

"Baba vaNatsai, you're always defending your son. Look at me now struggling around here at my age. If it's not my back, then it's my blood pressure."

"Ah, Mai vaNatsai, do you not have the girl who comes to help you and the boys who tend the goats and the cows?"

"You know those ones are no good, Baba vaNatsai. They are lazy and always stealing. My chickens disappear every day and the goats, Baba vaNatsai, don't even get me started on the goats. Every month they say 'Ah, Mother, that goat died after swallowing a plastic packet,' but we never see the carcass. Next thing, they are going to make one of your cows eat a plastic packet, if you're not clever."

"These things happen, Mai vaNatsai, but they're not as bad as you're putting it."

"The living out here would be much easier if I had some grandchildren helping me here. Others have their grandchildren living with them. This son of yours is not giving me any grandchildren and Natsai just left us without grandchildren."

This is the opening I have been waiting for. I raise my eyebrows, but Mother closes the gap.

"Do you even have a passport, my son? Other children whose mothers go to church with me get their passports and go overseas. Before long they are already sending their parents money to survive in their old age. Some mothers really gave birth, hey. But, my family…" she claps once, "only the good Lord knows what I did wrong."

"That's enough, Mai vaNatsai."

"I'll stop. What more is there to say? My daughter just disappeared there into the wind. Now my son is just everywhere like the wind itself. Who knows how many children are calling him their father out there? We leave it all in the Lord's hands. What else can we do?"

***

Father and I sit outside the kitchen door stripping off the tough outer sugarcane fibres with our teeth and chewing the stalks. The sky is full of stars. Mother is inside reading her Bible by lamplight and humming hymns at intervals. It is a warm evening, slowly cooling down. The distant grunts and grinding of haulage trucks and buses drifts in faintly on the breeze. Closer though reverberate the sounds of jubilant drumming and singing from the villages around us. Drumming rhythms that are now familiar to me. More music can be heard emanating from the sungura records playing from nearby farm bars. In the yard, I hear the flutter of wings as large birds glide overhead to land on high branches, squawking and calling as they settle in for the night.

"Baba, do you still have your records and the record player?"

"It's back there with all the other things. I was hoping you would help me connect a solar power supply so I can play it from time to time."

"Ah, Baba, I know I promised before but this time I will sort something out before I leave."

"So, my son, what is it exactly that you are now doing for a living?"

"I'm just doing this and that, Baba. But my prospects are looking good."

"Hmmm, I see. A man must have a steady income for his family. An income generated from honest hard labour."

"That doesn't cut it anymore in this country, Baba. Look at what happened when the dhora fell and you and Mai had to leave town."[41]

"That happened to everyone. We cannot dwell in the past crying about things that we cannot change. Besides, I always wanted to move back to farm our land some day. What happened just made things move faster."

"But Baba, things here are not looking good."

"There is potential in this soil, my son. Your mother and I are on the farming input schemes list this year so we are looking forward to a change in our fortunes."[42]

Listening to my father, I struggle to see the man I trailed behind in my youth. I do not understand this faith he still has in this system that has failed him so terribly and for so long.

The drumming sounds louder.

"Do you know which village is playing these drums tonight?" I ask, after a silence.

"The villagers here have a lot of energy for drumming all night but you don't see them in church on Sundays."

"Can I ask you something, Baba? What do we find sacred?"

"Gerry, you know the answer to that question."

"Yes I do. But how come we never hold any of these ceremonies?"

---

41   Do you want to know what happens when a Reserve Bank fiddles with the currency and tanks the foreign exchange rate? Good law-abiding citizens have their savings, investments and pensions wiped out. That's what. happens. If anyone had a pension in Zimbabwean Dollars, regardless of how many millions it was, between 1997 and 2008 the Reserve Bank reduced it to rolls of toilet paper.

42   Do you want to know who has never been serious about farming? The Republic. For people who fought a war and comrades for whom "Land!" was the rallying cry, we have an astonishing disdain for any serious attempts at viable farming programmes. Farm input schemes are an Eating gig. They are perennially looted and many seasons, because of the gazetted state-controlled mandatory crop prices, one easily makes more money selling off the inputs on the black market, particularly diesel, than from tilling the land.

"Your mother and I are Christians, Gerry. Can you imagine us going into huts with n'angas and then walking into church on Sunday?"

The drums roll in louder still.

"Remember when we had the funeral for Sisi Natsai, Baba?"

"You were young then."

"Yes, but I can still recall some things."

"What is bringing on all these questions from you, Gerry?"

"Oh, nothing really. I was just wondering."

"Your sister has been gone for a long time."

"Yes, she has. I was just wondering if there was a ceremony for her, perhaps here at the family village? Did we beat her grave afterwards?"

"Ah Gerry, what do you know about kurova guva?" Father raises his voice. "Mai vaNatsai, come and hear the things your son is asking me."

Mother steps outside. The drums are louder still.

"You know what, Baba vaNatsai? I was struggling to read my Bible in there because these villagers started playing their drums of the people. Now I hear your son talking as if he is one of them. What is wrong with you, Gerald?"

"It is fine to have questions about life, my son, but some of these things are unChristian. They do not add value to your life."

"Baba vaNatsai, I tried to get your children involved in the church but they both refused, now look. Your son is bringing demons into my house. Gerald, are you also smoking these drugs that are making children's heads go upside down there in the city? Are you bringing satanism to your parents, Gerald?"

***

There is no point in suggesting to these two that there is a way in which we may commune with Natsai, that she may be gone, but is with us. A way to lift the veil that shrouds this family, my life, in torment. A way that has always been with us, has been ours, if only we accepted. If Mother had a sacred bottle in the house she would douse me in holy water while I slept. Father looks like a tired man inconvenienced by my questions, not knowing how to reply. Briefly, I wish he still had the answers he had for me when I was a kid.

I remain outside after they have both retired to bed. The ngoma from the ceremony closest to me drums on with a rolling percussive rhythm. The stars are even brighter overhead. I think back to my nights in Chenga Ose and notice how this time and place feels so different. Now I am clear-minded; there isn't as much tension in my shoulders. I am not as afraid of the darkness or the shadows. I have less fear of what is to come. I have faith. My ears lean into the notes riding in on the night wind. In the branches above and around me, the occasional flapping of wings now comforts me, like sentries stretching and shifting from one foot to the other.

In the morning, my parents are both up early for Sunday service at Rugube Mission Church a few kilometres down the gravel road. I thought Mother would have been rapping at my door before the crack of dawn but it seems she thinks I am beyond redemption now. They call out to me as they depart and I get up to stand in the doorway, squinting into the morning sunlight. "I'm just going into town to pick up some things," I say. "I'll be back before you go to sleep."

They set off towards the road. Mother is wearing her pale blue coat, as all respectable married Catholic women do. She fits right in with the other Madzimai eRuwadzano, the women's prayer union. Father is wearing one of his old suits, carefully pressed, hanging from his gaunt frame in folds. As they walk, he'll practise his choral harmonies for the hymns at Mass. They still resemble the model Catholic couple of my childhood. With mixed emotions, I realise they'll never change.

***

I step out of a mshika-shika in the late afternoon and notice that Miner's Drift now has a traffic light.[43] And there are a lot more people than I remembered in the streets. Jobless youngsters hitchhiking to Harare or returnees facing the other direction, heading for the Mozambican border. MaBrasso selling fake gold in their loud viscose shirts and shiny pointed shoes, looking out for cross-border haulage trucks. Kiya-kiya hustlers hawking fuel in five-litre plastic bottles, or queueing for diesel at the service stations, crowding around vehicles stopping to pick up passengers. Makorokoza with bulging pockets strutting around their dusty cars and whistling to young women. Older women raising dishes filled with boiled eggs and groundnuts up to long-distance bus windows.

A bunch of singing kids approach me in the khakis and greens of my primary school. I wonder if this is how lively and carefree I was twenty-odd years ago, and how they too will have to face and climb the steep mountains I have had to climb. I let them pass and then walk down the road, brushing shoulders with touts and sellers, turning down offers for cell phone chargers, airtime and a haircut. The ChiPutukezi of recent arrivals mingles with the ChiShona and ChiShona-Putukezi blend of those who have been here longer or were born here. There is the bank, closed most days, and now a locally-owned Regent Commercial Bank, the ghost of the old Barclays Bank now stuck in the small faded eagle logo in a side window, missed during the rebranding. There is the Post Office in bold white, red and blue livery, no longer the quaint closet with its musty odours of dusty ledger books, spilled ink and yellowing stationery. The mail sorting room is now a busy cell phone repair and second-hand appliance shop. The phone boxes stand empty with neither coin phones nor cables hanging out. In the driveway of the municipal offices stands the colonial plinth, a brass

---

43   A big chefe came down in a long convoy of cars and security to officially open the traffic light. He came back a few weeks later to cut the ribbon on a new rubbish bin that is positioned outside the post office.

plaque commemorating the town's 'founders' long removed, election graffiti whitewashed over as are the tree trunks each year, the relic retained merely because it has been there and still is. There stands the Contaz. Not a single thing changed on its facade. Never will be sitting in there, waiting for me. I cross the road but stepping onto the pavement I change my mind about entering the bar. It occurs to me that I haven't really thought about meeting up with Never in person; I'm not sure how much he knows about my affair with Loveness. Even though we are now all adults, some cuts run deep. And I have more urgent business, shall come back here when I'm done. A sense of renewed purpose invigorates me. As I walk past the Contaz though, a figure in loose-fitting jeans and somewhat-white shirt with unbuttoned sleeves lurches towards me.

"Jedza! Kamupfanha Jedza! Aaaaaaah!"

"Never?" My heart stops.

"Ah you, little boy, you, don't be arrogant, you hear me?"

And so I give a civil grin while Never grips and shakes my shoulders, does a little dance and then says, "I'll make you shit, mupfanha Jedza, buy beer, you hear me?"

"But Never, what is it?"

"What is what, mupfanha Jedza?"

"Why are you looking like this? What's wrong? What time did you start drinking?"

"Ah you, I'm drinking my money. What troubles you about that?"

"My guy, when did you last change these clothes? Have you been going to work?"

"Ah, they retrenched me! They think I care about them. They just closed their little mine and they retrenched me! They don't know me nicely, mxm."

"You didn't tell me you had lost your job, my guy."

"Ah Jedza, what were you going to do about it? Again, you were busy there at your Harare. Heh? Busy eating money and climbing Harare girls, heh?"

I need some air.

"Listen, Never, let me go somewhere quickly and then we'll sit down and talk."

"Aah Jedza, now you're spitting me out. Me, your best friend?"

"Wait for me here, Never. I'll be back just now."

"Mupfanha Jedza, your problem is that ... do you want me to tell you what your problem is? Your problem is that you think you're clever, you hear me?"

"Never, wait for me here, serious."

"You want to play that old trick on me, heh? To make me wait for you like I'm a little child. I'll make you shit mupfanha Jedza, you hear me?"

No reasoning with this one: I buy him two quarts of Castle Lager. Meaning I give him five bucks to do it. He heads back into the Contaz. I had timed my arrival here for early evening to avoid such an encounter with some daytime drunk I hardly know, but did not imagine the guy would be Never. The moment I hand him the money he slaps me across the shoulders and assures me that I'm the best friend he has ever had.

I'm still not certain what exactly is happening. Might our old roles be reversed when I sit down with Never this evening? I really believed Never had escaped the curses of this town. His confidence and success served as a reminder of what I believed my life could have been, if I had not had these shadows hanging over me.

I need a black goat.

Swerving right, I weave through the buyers and flea market stall owners busy with last-minute evening trading. The railway line is in this direction anyway so it's alright. The stalls being closed are those selling electronic accessories, shoes and clothes and then fruit and vegetable stalls appear the closer we get to the railway track. The produce stalls are run by the older looking faces, some familiar, those who have sunk roots here and seem destined to stay. The electronics, ordered cheap and sold fast, are run by the younger looking, those newly arrived here or into adulthood, squatting here and there and raising money to get out of town, to move on to seek better fortunes. I pass the last line of stalls and the space opens up. There is the stench of chicken and goat shit and the live animals restless in cages and pens. I walk up to one of the guys selling goats, someone I've known since primary school. One of those people I wasn't really friends with, we just knew one another by sight. It's an awkward conversation. We ask each other where we've been, what we've done, if we're now married, where so-and-so is and the last time we saw this or that person.

"We are just locking-locking, to survive."

"That other person went to Texas."

"Things are dry."

"So-and-so is now in the UK."

"Things are pressed."

"This person is now there, in South Africa."

"I'm just selling this-and-that to raise money to go overseas."

No-one ever returns once they leave. Those who leave town and country with dreams of coming back one day, will sit around in their adopted homes wondering how the years have slipped by so fast and how come they still haven't made that grand return in the big car, with smooth skin, a diaspora accent and kids who only speak English.

Pleasantries end with the ever useful: "Otherwise, how is everything else?"

We do not exchange numbers and when I leave, I have a small compliant black goat slung over my shoulder. I carry on towards the railway crossing with slight unease.

The distance between the highway and the railway line feels much shorter now. When we rode out as boys it felt like an epic cycle tour. We would never have been able to ride so confidently through all these crowded bodies and vehicles. The lead-up to the crossing is mostly built up now, structures that seem undecided on their state of completion. Speakers blaring out at entrances. Passersby lingering around shop fronts. I keep walking to where the buildings end, then carry on in the descending darkness, alone now on a dirt track leading up to the railway line. The railings at the train tracks have fallen away, one or two rusted stays jut through tall grass and clumps of bushes. I step onto concrete sleepers and look down at the two rails. The quarry stones are barely visible. Looking up, I stare down the rails to the right, then to the left. There is minimal pedestrian or vehicle traffic here now, the new main crossing is a distance farther down to the right. I place the lightly bound goat on the ground, feel around in my pockets for a pinch of fodya, draw out the small ball of paper and shoot up. The rush is instant and I sneeze right away. Give myself a second to regain my balance and brush the top of my nose with my sleeve. In that moment I am the boy on the cycle racing towards the line, I'm also the train coming back into town. Elbows flared, little legs pumping and eyes teary. Leading one moment and Takunda passing me the next. The sound of the train horn drowning out my thoughts briefly and then the slow tumble. The tumble that has been locked away in some vault within me and the foghorn that sounds an alarm every time my mind wanders towards those memories. I go down on my knees and clap as instructed by Mbuya Dziva. My cupped hands boom in the recess of the approach to the tracks.

"Hear me, vaDziva who dwell in the water, who give birth to Hacha who sleep in the water but breathe the air, who give birth to Tora who live both on land but feed in the water and above it, who give birth to Takada who first grew wings and lived in water, on land and perched in trees."

I pause for my words to be received.

"Do not be startled vaDziva, it is only I, your grandchild Hara, bird of the water who perches on high branches and swoops down low, vaDziva who dwells above and below water. It is I who kneels before you and pleads that you hear my cries, for a child who does not cry dies in the cradle."

Wind rushes around me. It rustles the tall grass around me and whistles into my ears.

"Those who are young err and it is up to the elders, who have lived before us and are wise, to correct us. Your grandchild has done wrong and has carried this wrong on his back in all that he does as he walks where he walks. It is your grandchild who asks that you, his elders, who are in the ground and the air, release this load from his back, as your child who has seen the wrong in his ways and cried to those who come before him."

I take another shot of the fodya and clap again. The measured booms reverberate into the dusk. A shiver rolls through me, starting from the bridge of my nose, I sneeze thrice in quick succession. The shiver then surges through to the back of my head, squeezing time into a compressed plaything and suspending me in the darkness. My shoulders loosen and I slump over my knees. My arms hang limp by my sides. I sway this way and that, numb to all around me. Sensation starts to return up my back and into my shoulders, the load begins to lift. That now familiar release which follows from endless cycles of rhythmic dancing and singing along around many fires and being urged on by mbira players and beaters of drums.

In this brief moment of clarity I am transported through the tumble again, Takunda in the dust before me, my angry attempt to push him out of the way, Dalitso crashing into us, and I, in my fit of rage, pushing him into the path of the train. My heart beats hard against my ribs. At this place it latched onto me: yet in this moment that I acknowledge my fall, the ngozi, that spirit of vengeance which has bound me in anguish, accepts my atonement and frees me. I accept my actions, account for them fully, and at the same time liberate myself from being forever bound by them. A burning scalding lump surges from deep in my belly up through my throat and hurls itself out of my gaping mouth in a violent purge. It attaches to the black goat at my feet, who instantly breaks free and bolts off into the darkness, bleating loudly. The train sounds its horn, long and hard, then rolls past, this time never to return.

Acknowledgements

To the ancestors, in all the forms they appear to us. We give thanks.

My gratitude to Bibi Bakare-Yusuf and Layla Mohamed at Cassava Republic Press for giving this work a most fitting home. To my agent Emma Shercliff at Laxfield Literary Associates for championing my literary affairs. To my editor Mary Armour - you helped me realise my thoughts and ideas into words beyond what I believed possible - my neverending gratitude.

To Percy Zvomuya, friend and literary mentor. This work and much of my writing would simply not exist, or would at best be in a state of despair, without your presence, discussions, ideas and perspectives. May you receive as you are generous.

To my family, blood and chosen, who have stood by me and hyped all my pursuits and endured my humour. Gabriel, Tiara, Takudzwa, Chiedza Jaravani, Percy Chiweshe and Sarudzayi Njerere.

This manuscript has passed through many capable hands. My gratitude to the following people who, in various ways, have facilitated its transition from a few clumsy pages to the expression it is today: Geraldine Mukumbi, Duduzile Mabaso, Petina Gappah, Panashe Chigumadzi, Ellah Wakatama, Goretti Kyomuhendo, Racheal Kizza and Mable Amuron at AWT, Kate Wallis, Mapule Mohulatsi and Florence Madenga.

The artists whose songs have inspired this work and propelled me through countless hours of conceiving, writing and editing. Whose lyrics and sentiment permeate every line. For being generous and even enthusiastic in allowing me to quote their work in this book. Thomas Mapfumo, your entire catalogue stands before me as a spiritual expression and preservation of our culture in this dance with modernity. You are the griot whose decades of spiritually-inspired work have given me an understanding of our culture and the role of the artist and art within it. May you live long. Simon Chimbetu (*Samatenga*), Tanga wekwa Sando (*kuMbare*), Shingirayi Sabeta (*Ndamutswa*), Kelvin "Killer T" Kusikwenyu (*Itai Ndione*), Mbuya Beaulah Dyoko (*Nhemamusasa* recording and interview by Akhie Lavoie). Thank you.

I am grateful to the mbira players and vocalists who have kept the canon of tunes alive through their individual interpretations both recorded and experienced in person. The tunes, lyrics and sentiment have inspired and are expressed throughout this work. Pertinently, *Mahororo (Mbira Trip) & Gwendurugwe* as performed by Mbuya Stella Chiweshe; *Mahororo* as performed by Cosmas Magaya & Mbuya Jenny Muchumi; *Dangurangu as performed by Forward Kwenda*; *Nhemamusasa & Nyamaropa* as performed by Hakurotwi Mude and Mhuri yekwaRwizi; *Chigwaya* (whose lyrics propel the water entities), *Bukatiende* and *Taireva* as performed by Brian Nyamayaro Chikwepa.

All translations of lyrics throughout the novel by myself.

To my fellow social media malcontents on Twitter whose banter keeps me sane and whose well-timed instructions for me to get back to writing have, in no small part, pushed me to complete this book. I give you thanks.

Otherwise,
Farai.

Q&A With Author

1. **AVENUES BY TRAIN is your debut novel, what inspired you to write it?**
There were multiple influences that inspired different sections of the novel. For instance, earlier chapters were inspired by memories of mysterious events from my childhood that bordered on the supernatural. I grew up in a town that drew a thin line between fact and folklore. I guess I was trying to reconcile that way of life with the country and my people as I now understand us.

2. **How does the title, AVENUES BY TRAIN tie into the story?**
One of the myths I heard growing up was centred around the railway line. Stories of ghosts at the train tracks and the occasional death on the tracks. The train tracks as the line dividing the suburbs from the ghetto, is also a metaphor for carriage and exile, out and away. All these themes were given form in my mind by songs such as "Chitima Nditakure" by Thomas Mapfumo and "Stimela" by Hugh Masekela. With escape comes destination, and the Avenues district of Harare was the affluent destination for those seeking their fortunes and bright lights. The Avenues district of Harare, exudes something of a mystical aura; the streets are shaded and shadowy during the day and dark and dimly lit at night. It's a place in flux – colonial buildings being replaced by newer architecture and commercial developments going up on corners with street vendors and sex workers. A place of contradiction;

a place for those who seek themselves to either find themselves or forever be lost.

3. **You write about a newly independent Zimbabwe and the traumas of the colonial era. What were you trying to achieve in exploring the effects of colonialism on individuals?**
My aim was to bridge a gap between the past and the present. We are neither a people nor an era in isolation. To show that there is continuity. We are living the same lives as our ancestors; and we are also preparing the way for our descendants. Everything is connected. In current discourse, there is a compartmentalising of events of the past as being done and separate from events today. I wanted to show that on a national level, we are living the consequences of the past, and on an individual level we are living the consequences of the actions of those who came before us. However, I also want to inspire hope that we who live now, are simultaneously creating our present AND the future. And we can and should learn from the past, from those who came before us, our ancestors.

4. **The story is framed around Jedza's journey to freeing himself from the Ngozi through communal spiritual practices. What informs your decision to shed light on African spirituality and cultural practices?**
African spirituality has been misrepresented and maligned, historically. Yet we have a wealth of knowledge systems and practices that are unique to us and readily adaptable wherever we are in the world. Jedza's journey shows how we can reconcile with our true selves, reengage with our culture and align it with our modernised lives. These practices are a firm base to engage the world on our own terms, not on borrowed and assimilated colonial terms.

5. **Music is referenced throughout the book, what is its significance in both the story and your writing process?**

Music as an artform is quite possibly the main inspiration for my writing. Mbira music in particular. There is the cyclical structure to mbira music which involves the interlacing of multiple melodies emanating from the same repeated chord structures. The result is similar to a mosaic of melodies from which each person extracts and hears those melodies which speak to their disposition. In a literary sense, I try to write themes, subtext, extended metaphors and other literary devices, in a manner that allows the reader to perceive multiple narratives and themes, with varying prominence dependent on the reader themselves. Ultimately, music leaves you with emotion. You may not remember the lyrics or the chord progressions; you may recall only parts of the chorus or the melody, but what sits with you and never leaves, is how you felt. I aim to leave that effect on the reader.

6. **With references to Zimbabwe's history, Shona culture and spirituality, how did you carry out research for the book?**

Months and months spent in the National and other archives. I also have fellow writers and academics who shared researched material with me. I also read, albeit critically, the canon of anthropological writings by Terence Ranger, David Norman Beach, David Lan, Peter Fry, Michael Gelfand, Paul Berliner etc. and Zimbabwean fiction writers such as Solomon Mutswairo, Yvonne Vera, Shimmer Chinodya and others who engage with Shona spirituality. I also consumed numerous media, films, music from global cultures on how they perceive and engage the spirits, in particular the water deities.

Fortunately, Shona culture persists and even thrives to this day. In some ways it has been bruised by the colonial encounter and appears to live on the margins of society, certainly in urban areas where it is subordinated to traditional and Evangelical Christianity. As one moves out of the towns and cities into the peri-urban and rural areas, the culture returns. I was fortunate to have friends and to meet artists and cultural practitioners in urban areas who follow Shona spiritual practices, and who allowed me to engage, learn and take part in these ceremonies. I was able, in my own small way, to decipher and reconcile the anthropological archive with the practice of Shona spirituality as it lives today.

7. **Your writing is distinctive and engaging as you carry the reader along with the conversational tone of the footnotes. What do you think this style adds to the reading experience?**

The footnotes are my way of nudging the reader and whispering in their ear. As they read, I tap their shoulder with some juicy titbits; and add some "inside info". I want the reader to know that all these other wild events are happening above, below and around what is on the page. I want us both to step away from the page, only for a moment, to shake our heads at the madness informing what is on the page.

8. **How does it feel to finally have your book out in the world? And what do you want readers to take from this story?**

I feel excitement. Loads of it. I want readers to question what they believed they knew, what they took for granted. I want them to put the book aside and look up issues and events that were only on their periphery, or that they had not encountered yet. I want readers to have more and deeper questions about things, issues, places and people they would ordinarily flip past. I want readers to be entertained, shocked, angered. I want them to be hopeful and empathetic. I want them to be proud to have African heritage. I want them to view Africanness in a positive light.

Production Credits

Transforming a manuscript into the book you are now reading is a team effort. Cassava Republic Press would like to thank everyone who helped in the production of *Avenues by Train:*

Publishing Director: Bibi Bakare-Yusuf

Editorial
Editor: Mary Armour
Copy Editor: Layla Mohamed
Proofreader: Boluwatito Sanusi

Design & Production
Cover Design: Jamie Keenan
Layout: Deepak Sharma (Prepress Plus)

Marketing & Publicity
Marketing and Contents Officer: Rhoda Nuhu

Sales and Admin
Sales Team: Kofo Okunola & The Ingram Sales Team
Accounts & Admin: Adeyinka Adewole

Support Avenues by Train

We hope you enjoyed reading this book. It was brought to you by Cassava Republic Press, an award-winning independent publisher based in Abuja and London. If you think more people should read this book, here's how you can support:

Recommend it. Don't keep the enjoyment of this book to yourself; tell everyone you know. Spread the word to your friends and family.

Review, review review. Your opinion is powerful and a positive review from you can generate new sales. Spare a minute to leave a short review on Amazon, GoodReads, Wordery, our website and other book buying sites.

Join the conversation. Hearing somebody you trust talk about a book with passion and excitement is one of the most powerful ways to get people to engage with it. If you like this book, talk about it, Facebook it, Tweet it, Blog it, Instagram it. Take pictures of the book and quote or highlight from your favourite passage. You could even add a link so others know where to purchase the book from.

Buy the book as gifts for others. Buying a gift is a regular activity for most of us – birthdays, anniversaries, holidays, special days or just a nice present for a loved one for no reason... If you love this book and you think it might resonate with others, then please buy extra copies!

Get your local bookshop or library to stock it. Sometimes bookshops and libraries only order books that they have heard about. If you loved this book, why not ask your librarian or bookshop to order it in. If enough people request a title, the bookshop or library will take note and will order a few copies for their shelves.

Recommend a book to your book club. Persuade your book club to read this book and discuss what you enjoy about the book in the company of others. This is a wonderful way to share what you like and help to boost the sales and popularity of this book. You can also join our online book club on Facebook at Afri-Lit Club to discuss books by other African writers.

Attend a book reading. There are lots of opportunities to hear writers talk about their work. Support them by attending their book events. Get your friends, colleagues and families to a reading and show an author your support.

Thank you!

Stay up to date with the latest books, special offers
and exclusive content with our monthly newsletter.
Sign up on our website:
www.cassavarepublic.biz

Twitter | Tiktok: @cassavarepublic
Instagram: @cassavarepublicpress
Facebook: facebook.com/CassavaRepublic
Hashtag: #AvenuesByTrain #ReadCassava